CHARTING BY THE STARS

CHARTING
BY THE
STARS

BY LINSEY ABRAMS

H

HARMONY BOOKS / NEW YORK

c.2

For my mother and father
and
for Ingrid Sischy

Designed by Elyse Shick

Published simultaneously in Canada by General
Publishing Co., Ltd.
Printed in the U.S.A.

Library of Congress Cataloging in Publication Data

Abrams, Linsey.
Charting by the stars.

    I. Title.
PZ4.A159Ch   [PS3551.B66]   813'.5'4   79–16760
ISBN 0–517–53898–9

CONTENTS

"Things look at us as we look at them.
They seem indifferent to us only because we look
at them with indifference. But to a clear eye all things
are mirrors, and to a sincere and serious eye
everything is depth."

—GASTON BACHELARD

"Will you help me vacuum?" my mother asks one Saturday morning after breakfast.

"All right," I say, grumbling about my status as assistant housekeeper. We pull the Hoover out of the hall closet, and my mother walks first into the living room while I drag it behind.

"What's this?" she says, bending over to pick up a piece of paper from the floor. It is folded. It has her name on it. "I wonder what it is?" she says again, curious.

"It's probably a note from Daddy," I say. "Telling us where he is this morning." As she unfolds it, I plug in the cord, turning to ask. . . . Ashen, she hands me the piece of paper. And her hands to her stomach, my mother suddenly vomits in the center of the rug.

PART ONE

Chapter I

DREAMING BIRTH

MY FATHER'S A MAN YOU CAN HAVE FAITH IN. Even my mother goes to him when she needs advice, though, if possible, she likes to come to her own conclusions. In bed at night, a performer of mental gymnastics, my father seeks to outwit any problem my mother might mention. He thinks about it deeply, picks it up like a barbell, turns it around in his mind, hoping to raise it above his head with the straight arm of solution.

Today, as it happens, just when we could use his muscular shoulder to lean on, he's not here. The weightlifter is out of town. Still, he calls the hospital every half hour from phone booths. He has twenty dollars' worth of quarters and dimes in his suit jacket pocket, which makes it bulge.

Any news? he asks the floor nurse.

Your wife is still in labor, she answers. It will be at least another several hours.

All right. I'll call back, he says, and he hangs up.

My father's apprentice, I lay out the facts for myself like a set of weights. This is what I know about the birth canal: others are excavated, dug out (the Panama, the Suez . . .); this grows itself hollow from the inside out. The atmosphere here is the gray foam of clouds. This is the dark and tubular cylinder of a gun barrel, and I'm the bullet waiting for my mother's trigger finger. My head in readiness, my mother cocked for birth.

My heart beats to her contractions. I snap my fingers to her pulse. Her muscles are the straitjacket I wear; she encases me like a tunnel with light at the end. I want to see this light, and my head will lead me: cue ball of my opening shot, football helmet of my first forward rush. Bald round planet in search of a halo. But what, exactly, are all these things? I wish my father would call back and tell me how to be born.

(My father lay next to us in bed.

What if there's something wrong with it? he asked.

I kicked him through my mother's belly.

Warren, my mother told him, the doctor says everything is fine.

I mean what if it has only one arm? he said.)

If these are my arms, I have two. I have ten toes. Is this too many?

More facts: I'm going to hear jazz. I'm going to taste martinis. I'm going to make love. . . . I'm going to watch plants go dancing. I'm going to listen to a time bomb tick. When? I'm exhausted, dispirited.

Speculations: If my mother has given up hope, false alarm, she'll say. It's clear that Angela has decided against being born after all. . . . But this isn't true. I'm getting anxious. I do a flip to try to calm myself.

And what if our doctor is incompetent or a drug addict, even, hooked on his own prescriptions? Or what if he's not here yet? They'll have to send a caddy out to the ninth hole at top speed, ducking golf balls as he runs. If the doctor makes it to the hospital in time, perhaps it's we who are late, speeding through traffic in an ambulance at full siren or stopped for a red light in my grandfather's Packard.

What, if by a miracle, the birth is successful, and in a case of mistaken identity, the nurse delivers me into the arms of the wrong woman on the morning she's to leave the hospital for home? Her milk will taste like brine; I'll refuse to drink and grow weak. Neighbors will speak of her bad habits. She'll figure in her husband's nightmares. My own mother wears dresses in the latest styles; she makes them herself on the Singer. Sailors whistle at her in the street. She and my father will jitterbug until almost sunrise just five nights after our return from the hospital. But what if they've claimed someone else instead? Surely my father will recognize me first and set the nurses straight.

Into the nursery he'll stride, in search of his daughter. He'll thread his way through row upon row of babies, like a farmer in the field looking for a particular hybrid he has invented himself. Perhaps he'll tire slightly because there is something happening during this time called the baby boom and not a single crib is empty. But he'll persevere, and when he arrives at my side, This is Angela, he'll say.

(Ros, do you want a boy or a girl? my father asked.

I have no preference, said my mother. But perhaps a girl would be nice. To go with Benjie.

When they grow up, we can do all sorts of things together, he said.

We'll have a foursome for bridge, she replied. We can play mixed doubles.

A child in the arts, a child in the sciences. You can take her to the ladies' room. I'll take him to the men's. . . .

It will be so convenient, said my mother. But what if it's not a girl . . . if it's Arthur instead, after my father?

Then we'll put a wig on him, my father said.)

Arthur. In a long horse's mane. How I rode him like a jockey down the final stretch, outdistancing all the other possible contenders one by one, until just before the finish line when I rose in the saddle, leapt from his back, and hurled myself before him over the wire. How we set off for my mother's affections in two identical, gassed-up cars, just after my father's single sperm found its mark, how I altered Arthur's road map imperceptibly, gave him false directions at the genital junction of the legs and sent him off. To where? Arthur behind my ears, Arthur under my fingernails, Arthur in the tiny cracks between my toes. Still, I'm the luck of the draw, and my mother will know it's me.

Suddenly I'm jingling like the change in my father's jacket. I'm the coin seeking to escape my mother's pocket. I'm tumbling falling doing somersaults reversing my direction with a twist of the hips. I'm an expert diver, slowing my descent. I'll make her wait a second longer how she'll hold her breath how she'll wonder if ever I'm coming. Is this a child, she'll ask herself, who will never be born? Sinking. Swimming. Pirouetting. Leaping down her . . .

I'm on my way, I shout. The walls of her vagina muffle the sound. Can she hear me? My mother awaits me; she anticipates my arrival; she's received the message of my kicks and spins. I'm shooting down her, my mother like a slide, and when I reach midair, a cork shot from the popgun of her thighs, I'll find her.

I'm wearing my mother's cervix like a hat, like a pair of eyeglasses, like a belt, like an anklet. Now the anklet is the doctor's hand; his hand is the hook I dangle from, bait for my own life, target for the slap that inflates me like a tire. Breathing is like speeding. My mother's eyes are the green lights, her two arms the tender roadblock of the criminal who longs to be caught. "Angela," she whispers. Red and wet with blood, I rest my cheek on her breast.

Waking up is knowing that you have been asleep. I sleep much more than the average person, the one who wakes early to a stomach of worries. It's time to sleep again when the mother sings. All my mother's melodies sound the same, but the lyrics are varied: "Don't sit under the apple tree with anyone else but me. . . ." "Oh it's a long, long way to Tipperary. . . ." "Speed bonnie boat like a bird on the wing. . . ."

When my father joins in, I sometimes hear harmony, but after a few bars my mother always changes to his tune.

"Baby," he says. "Can't you stay on key?"

"No, I can't," says my mother, "but, after all, you didn't marry me for my singing voice."

"I sure didn't," he says, and he puts his two hands on the sides of her head and gently combs through her curly, thick hair with his fingers. This is affection. Then he kisses her on the lips. This is affection, too.

They blow me kisses from the doorway. Kisses are in the air. The light's extinguished with a quick flick of my father's finger. Kisses are lurking in the dark.

Soon sleep will cover me like a mask, and if you remember what it has been like to be asleep, this means you've been dreaming. My dreams are a saga; the mask is always changing its features, transforming itself through a lineage of faces. I've dreamt my family from the first kiss.

Today, all day, I've been dreaming about my grandmother's wedding, about the train trip she took with my grandfather to

California for their honeymoon. She can't get over how here the sun *sets* on the ocean. . . . About how they stopped off in Mexico City, to visit their friends Patrick and Llewelyn at the embassy, which is where they bought the silver brooch. I've dreamt through 1926; my mother has just been born. My grandmother says the brooch will be her daughter's marriage gift.

My grandfather is a Methodist. He doesn't smoke or drink, and while he passed out no cigars after the delivery, this is not to say that he wasn't pleased. My grandmother is weak from childbearing. She lies in bed under a flowery, hand-sewn quilt and realizes that she must have no other children. The doctor has told her so.

The dream continues and the mask's hue changes; my mother is a blue baby. When she grows up, her favorite color will be blue to remind her how narrowly she escaped an early and tragic death. The next week a pair of movers came into the bedroom and took away the big mahogany bed, replacing it with twins, light, the moving men said, as feathers. But the two beds weighed on my grandfather's mind.

During her convalescence, my mother's mother passed the time quilting an identical cover to the one she had made for her nuptial bed and a miniature copy to adorn the crib of her daughter. For a year or more, the three of them slept side by side in the close bedroom of their familial circumstance.

Once my grandfather rolled over to face his wife and daughter; his bed was on the end, nearest the door, lest a burglar might enter. He got up in his bare feet then and stood above my grandmother's bed until she opened her eyes.

Do you think? he asked.

No, said my grandmother, but she threw back the marriage quilt and moved over for his body beside hers. He kissed her on the throat and slept the whole night through with his arms about her waist. He dreams of the long, full skirts of his youth, of the parasols and hats trimmed with bright ribbon bands. He sees her in her high school bloomers, captain of the girls' marching team:

I've set my cap for you, he told her one night.

And what a nice cap it is, said my grandmother, who was shy in receiving compliments, and while he traveled to St. Louis and Cleveland, selling soap powders and pastes, she finished high school and started playing the piano for the church. She gave recitals; she taught young girls their scales; she accompanied opera singers in Boston. When later her daughter turned out to have no ear for music, she was disappointed, but by that time she had grown older and realized that there were fewer things to sing about than when she had been young.

In her twenty-seventh year, she received a letter from Chicago, return address the YMCA where her husband-to-be had taken up residence almost a year before.

> DEAR VIOLA [she read],
>
> Chicago is windy and colder than Alaska this time of year, and I think it's about to freeze me solid. I need a new overcoat to replace the one I came out here with. Would you order me one at Sweeney's? Same size. Only don't have it sent because I'll be there to pick it up on December 15th. I'm coming home for Christmas and for good. I'd be the warmest guy in town if you'll marry me in the spring.
>
> Yours,
> ART

In the return mail, she sent him a letter with a single word printed at the top of the page. Then she sat down at her piano and wrote a song. The lyric was simple:

Yes, yes, yes. [she sang]
Yes I will marry you.
I have waited.
I never dated other beaus.
Now I'm slated
To be mated to the one I chose
Long ago.
Yes, yes, yes.
Yes I will marry you.

The musical composition was intricate. She repeated the lyric over and over, using it backwards, arranging it in counterpoint, deleting every other word, interpreting it in all the different ways she could think of; she made a sort of chorus of the yeses, and every bridge was a yes, yes, yes.

That night she took from the trapdoor of the piano bench every sheet of music it held. She played each one through and all the rest she knew by heart, not skipping one movement, one verse, one repeat. She played feverishly to an empty house, and her performance was flawless. When she finished, for a single moment she made the keyboard her pillow, and anyone entering the room just then would not have heard the few quick sobs beneath the jarring chord her forehead had played. She shut the piano then, turned off all the lights, and went up to bed.

My brother has learned to burp. He has added burping to his repertoire of noises.

"Stop burping, Benjie," says my father. To my mother he says, "Not a word out of him yet, but he can make every sound in the book. He'll probably grow up to have an enormous vocabulary."

The dog is eating the chocolate cake. From my high chair I spy the dog eating the chocolate cake. From my crow's nest, the dog out in the sea of the kitchen is eating our dessert.

"Damn," says my mother as she runs to the clatter from the dining room. "Shotsy," she cries. "No." The dog scampers on her short legs back through the dining room, her dachshund snout camouflaged in chocolate frosting. But it's a poor disguise; the ruse doesn't work. Daddy chases the dog and puts her out the back door. Daddy has an eye for camouflage.

Here behind the curtains of my eyelids, my mother has imagined it a changing room, having shed her smocked dress, her wool skirt with the matching V-neck sweater, her black cap and gown for a suit. My mother has grown up.

On the lapel of her suit is pinned a small beige button. Yellow is for basic security clearance; gray is for the next level up, permitting access to more important documents and otherwise restricted areas of the building; green is for selected congressmen and policy advisers. But sporting a beige button, there's nowhere you can't go, no information you can't be privy to. Beige is for the President, the battle strategists, the Ph.D. specialists, and, of course, the generals who even in peacetime bustle in and out of the Pentagon. My mother's color is beige. My mother can be trusted with secrets.

Beige is also the color of Gwen's uniform. Gwen is my mother's roommate in Washington. Gwen is a marine.

So what's going on, Roslyn? she asks over dinner. They don't tell the enlisted man anything. . . .

Sorry, says my mother. She knows that although Gwen has a claim to beige, she is not top-secret beige. The truth is, Gwen, I'll have to go to the grave with what I know, some of it.

That's sort of romantic, isn't it?

Yes, says my mother, who in spite of her commitment to her country and the war effort is a young woman at the time, too.

Well, what if somebody got you drunk? asks Gwen. And tried to pry information out of you? A spy or someone. In the throes of love . . . They find this funny.

I'd never marry a spy though, says my mother. She sighs. Marriage is on her mind.

(Will you wait for me? the sailor asked her in the dream yesterday. He held her close with one hand; the other held his white hat. I mean, will you not say yes to anyone else until you talk to me first? He chuckled. I wish you weren't so popular, he said.

But his gray eyes reminded her of two portholes looking out on fog, and she started to cry; she buried her face in his shirt; she saw torpedoes coming through the portholes, silver invitations for the whole ocean to follow inside, to in turn swallow up the tiny ship that had swallowed it down, gulp after gulp. She looked up. His shirt was all wet. I will, she said.)

By the way, says Gwen. I met some handsome marines today. Two.

Really? says my mother.

They're at Cherry Point, says Gwen, in training. But they fly in once a month. They have our number.

Of the two marines, who do call, my mother likes best the one who is my father. He tells her what it is like to be an airplane navigator. We have a complicated instrument panel, he says. But if it fails I know how to chart by the stars. I'll tell you a secret, he says: I often fly the President himself.

He explains to her all the particulars of his work. My mother, because she is good at hers, doesn't tell him anything.

If only I could go overseas, he says. Besides, on the tests, I'm particularly good at sighting enemy positions from the sky, especially those that are heavily camouflaged. My mother is glad that he's not overseas. My mother, the keeper of secrets, tries to disguise this. But the camouflage expert, he sees right through her.

Rub-a-dub-dub, three men in a tub: Benjie and I, mum in the middle. She holds me upright. "Just like a convoy," says my mother. "Want to do the dead man's float?" she asks Benjie. He tickles her back, lowers his face into the water, and blows.

I'm an only child, my father said on his next trip.

So am I, said my mother.

I was born in Savannah and both my parents are dead, he told her. When I was twelve, my mother expressed the desire to move from the farm where we lived, so my father set her up in a house in town, and he and I stayed on at the farm. But I visited her often. It was a quick train ride.

My father owns a soap company, my mother told him. My mother was once a pianist. I graduated from Bryn Mawr last year and I'm twenty-two years old.

I'm twenty-seven years old, he said. I went to college for one year when lack of money prevented me from continuing. I was going to be an engineer.

I'm going to be a lawyer when the war is over, she said, if they start accepting women at law schools.

My mother was very well educated, he replied. When I had

to leave school she was especially disappointed. My father, on the other hand, figured I could do it the way he had. He told me I could jolly well teach myself. My father would often sit with a bottle of whiskey until sunrise, reading, when he'd get up from the chair, change his clothes (he was a very particular dresser), and head off for the railway office where he worked.

My father doesn't drink at all, she said. We're Methodists.

I'm an agnostic, he told her, and I've been in barrooms all over the world. When I was twenty, when I left school, I became foreman in a cotton mill. And there was nowhere to go from there, no possible promotion, so I packed my things and went to sea. I shipped out. When you're in port, all you do is drink. . . .

I'm fluent in French, said my mother. I was a government major, and great literature makes me weep.

I cried for the first time, he told her, when I received word of my mother's death. We were docked in New Orleans, lucky thing for me, so I just followed the rails to my father's office, and we buried her together. When he died, I packed up his personal effects, sold the rest, and withdrew the hundred dollars that was in his bank account. It was cancer that got her. And he drank himself to death. I would ask you to marry me, he said, only I'm married already and I have a son.

And I'm engaged, said my mother. To someone overseas.

This is how they fell in love, and as it was already eight o'clock in the morning, my father put on his cap and left.

When he arrived at the base to report for duty, he sent his wife, whom he hadn't seen for several months, a telegram (asking for a divorce), which my mother received later that day (the words were different but the message was the same) as notification from the war office of her fiancé's death at sea. As she lay awake that night, she reread all the sailor's letters and invented what their life together might have been like. My father, in his bunk, willfully recollected the two years of his marriage.

My grandmother and grandfather are peering over the railing of my crib. Smiles and waves like a bon voyage from a cruise ship deck. My grandfather has a package. He's unwrapping it. Is it for me?

"See how pretty she looks in it," says my grandmother. "It kept pretty well, didn't it, Arthur?"

"That it did. That it did," says my grandfather, tucking it under my chin.

"It kept pretty well. Just like us," she says and shakes her head. "Did you remember the other present?" He nods and I shut my eyes for sleep.

"I wonder if we should have waited for some appropriate occasion," I hear him say.

I'm getting married, my mother told first her father, then her mother, when she called from Washington. She has had trouble getting through; all the circuits are busy. The war is over. Today, when the news was announced (although my mother knew a few days before), a general picked her up in the street and twirled her like a top, danced her around like a crazy waltz. And she kissed him, although it's my father she plans to marry.

The bomb has been dropped on Hiroshima where the heat was so intense it caused the flowers to bloom instantaneously, like the ones on the quilt that covers me now. The war is over.

To whom? asks my grandmother, thinking of the sailor drowned in battle. She can't imagine who my mother might be marrying.

His name is Warren, he's southern, and he's a marine, says my mother. And we're not getting married right now (she hesitates) because he's in the middle of getting a divorce.

You bet you're not, says my grandmother, and she hangs up the phone with a bang. This hurts my mother, who never, herself, expected to get married under such circumstances.

My grandmother starts packing right away. My grandmother is planning a trip.

He's uneducated, she tells my grandfather after the letter arrives. He even has a child. We had such plans for Roslyn . . . and besides . . . She looks at him. We gave up everything for her.

I'm mad about you, says my father.

I dream about you, says my mother. When he's there, he spends the night on the couch because if, by mistake, he gets her pregnant and his divorce is delayed, they'll be in big trouble.

We'll be poor at first, he says. I've got to support my son.

When is your discharge? she asks.

In ninety-seven days. Will you marry me? he asks her again.

Yes, she says, as usual. They are always asking each other to get married. They propose to one another all through their engagement, waiting for the divorce. They're storing up yeses for the times ahead.

Will we always be in love? my mother asks.

Oh yes, says my father, gleaning another to store away against the future. He won't think about his first wife; he won't think about his parents' separation. He knows that being in love dictates that every proposal must be the first no matter how many times he asks her. It is the continuous present, a vacuum.

Will you marry me? he asks every day on the phone when he calls her up.

My grandmother has taken up residence in Mexico City with her friends Llewelyn and Patrick. She's been visiting for three months. She will not help with the marriage plans.

I'll come home on the day of the wedding, she tells her husband in a letter. My mother shops for her wedding dress, the invitations, alone. My grandfather sees to all the details of the reception.

Marriage. Ha, says my grandmother.

Some work and some don't, says Llewelyn. But the truth of it is, you never can tell at the beginning anyway. That's the time everything looks rosy.

At the reception, everyone is red in the face from drinking or dancing, or just because it's warm for June. My parents are having such a good time they don't leave their own wedding until three in the morning. My mother dons a new suit for their escape. Her fingers miss the beige button, searching her unadorned lapel while the rice pelts them.

I wake up in the same pose in which I left my mother in the dream, pausing on the stairs leading down from the reception hall. My hand is clutching the lapel of the flowered quilt my mother slept under as a baby. The silver brooch, which she never received, is in my fingers.

All in all, things are going smoothly, says my mother.

As smooth as my Uncle Clayton's whiskey, says my father. Home brew. Benjie is balanced in his lap. He's testing his son's reflexes: tickling his feet with a ball of cotton, holding a pocket watch to each of his ears to make sure he can hear the tick, waving different-colored swatches of material they're considering for the new couch cover in front of his eyes. He seems to like yellow best, says my father. What a kid. He picks up a textbook from the arm of the chair.

Want another? asks my mother. A second one?

Yes, he says.

I mean right now, says my mother. Right this minute.

You bet, baby, he says.

At my father's graduation from business school, he wears a cap and gown. In just a few months you'll be needing a style like this, he says, placing his hands on her slightly rounded belly.

I'll take it in any color other than black, says my mother.

Wait till my first raise, he says, and the next week he starts out as a management trainee in an electronics firm. The apartment will definitely be too small for a family of four, so the moving van is ordered and it drives out of the city to a small white house where the family of three awaits it.

Benjie learns to walk. At my father's thirtieth birthday party, the punch is so strong that two people pass out. One of them is my father. From joy, he says.

Chapter II

ANGELA EN ROUTE

THESE ARE THE DIRECTIONS TO OUR HOUSE, which my father typed up very carefully one day and had offset at the small printer's office in the center of the town where we live:

1. Do *not* go into Boston proper. Follow route 128 north, thereby circumscribing the outskirts like a hemline. Continue for approximately forty-five minutes.

2. Exit at 12A.

The police car's right behind us now like a hand poised for the imminent tap on the shoulder. But we're almost there. Will we make it?

3. Continue en route for approximately five minutes. (The speed limit is strictly enforced.)

It's the sound of a siren. My father will not pull over.

"Pull over, Warren," pleads my mother. "It's only a ticket."

"I didn't do anything," he says. My brother Benjie, next to me in the back seat, is staring out into the darkness. Two headlights, penetrating as searchlights, scan the interior of the car. Seeking what? Finding a family in transit.

"Christ," says my father. We screech to a halt on the shoulder, the gravel sparking and spinning out from under our tires into the night. The officer turns off his headlights, leaving us in darkness together. I hear my father roll down his window.

4. Continue on route 1A through the town proper (past the red brick public library, past the Bessie Buker School, past the white, steepled Methodist church).

Now my father *is* speeding. Hellbent on killing us all, my mother says. But I'm a brilliant lawyer arguing a case for survival, pleading for the manic pressure on the gas pedal to ease. I put our defense in the form of questions needing answers. Who was Bessie Buker, anyway? I ask my father. A teacher? A nun who took her own life rather than take her final vows? Did she or did she not harbor militiamen in her kitchen, melting treasured pins and necklaces into bullets over an open fire late into the night? Daddy?

5. Take your first left after Mike McCord's riding stable and proceed for one-quarter of a mile. (If you come to the John Quincy Adams Regional High School, you've missed the turn.)

Was she burned for a witch the night her own son met a paroxysmal death in his cradle? Bessie at the stake who heard no voices but her own anguished screams? Or did she die, without regret, a spinster? Did she? Did she?

"Why don't you turn around in the high school parking lot?" my mother suggests. Dividers are everywhere. Our headlights sweep like a lighthouse beam. Our car's a top, loosed from the hand. Or are we the rocking boat our headlights search for?

My father, like a man newly blinded, following, as he must, his own directions. Daddy, in the darkness, fumbling over the Braille of a bumpy lane toward home.

6. Turn right into the driveway.

The front door is pink; the siding is white and in need of paint.

The pachysandra lining the flagstone steps up to that door has never filled in. My mother, she'll tell you herself, has spent years watering it, but she never can get the right-hand side to take. Tender surgeon, digging in the sandy soil, she transplants healthy young specimens from the other side once a week, but it never does any good.

"Warren," she says to my father. "I'm at the end of my rope. I can't get that side to fill in no matter what I do."

"Doesn't bother me."

"Look, it's all dirt. It won't grow ever since you got the edge with the power mower."

"I hardly clipped any of it at all," he says in a tone quite final.

Saturday mornings at eight o'clock my father gets up to battle the lawn: khaki pants, white T-shirt, his hair cut short as that lawn ought to be. By ten, he's in for a glass of lemonade with port wine, a pink cooler, but he doesn't even sit down, just drains the glass standing up. And you can't talk to him because he hates the lawn. He hates the power mower that sputters and spits and then dies going up the hill because the manual choke is broken.

"I never heard of a front lawn that's all hill and crabgrass, anyway. Pinecones, rocks . . ." Every now and then you can hear a rock rattling around in the mower blades, then a zing, and it shoots out of the trap on the right-hand side, in resolute trajectory like a rocket. Only the constellations are beyond my father's reach. He hit the dog once, with a rock, but she was all right.

He mows the lawn back and forth and back again, uphill, downhill, uphill, the veins standing out on his forehead, pushing the goddamned mower, hoping it won't die on him this time. "Goddamned hill for a front yard. Crabgrass, toadstools, dandelions . . . Down south we've got regular lawns like you're supposed to have. Or else you just let it grow. It's Saturday, and I'm Sisyphus on a binge. . . ." He blames this on my mother. She's a Yankee all right; you can tell it a mile off.

And this is New England, with too many rocks for my father to bear. My father, who transplanted himself into a new climate and, like the pachysandra under my mother's care, never took root.

"Want to play catch, Daddy?"

"No, Angela."

Sometimes he doesn't talk for the rest of the afternoon, just sits in the room with the sliding glass doors and stares off into the woods. The lawn is cut.

In the heart of the woods, there's a tree house my father built for me. Square, hardwood cloud where dreams sit, only a ladder and a trapdoor (opened) away. Or reverse it: how I descend into waking, how I open the trapdoor like an eye and climb down the six crosspieces of the ladder to a sensual world. Do I find us here?

Certainly I find the rusty old tub in the ground, in the hole my father dug for it. A tub full of fresh water for my brother's goldfish to swim in. They died young, all of them, one day bloated, floating on the surface of the water when he went to change it. My father scooped them out and buried them, one by one, until none were left.

He buried the first dog, too, hit by a car on the Fourth of July. He was always mowing the lawn or burying things. Maybe that's why we moved to the city, and when the second dog died, we had her cremated. But by that time, Dad had hopped a freighter for Singapore with a suitcase and two crates of books. Dad, away on a dream tide.

Surely my mother is a woman of her time. The fifties and early sixties have been good to her, and she wears shorts and an all-over curly blond hairdo rather than the skirt and sometimes ponytail of her contemporaries. My mother will listen to anything, and she asks me sincerely every day when I come home from school how my day was. Dr. Spock's book and *A Guide to the Female Orgasm* are what I found in her bottom drawer when I looked.

So when the Sputnik was passing over our town for the first time, it was important for Benjie and me to see it. Five o'clock in the morning, rousted from our warm beds. *Bonjour,* said my mother. This was French, and every Christmas my brother and I learned a different carol in a foreign language. First sitting in the bathtub, the three of us; then just the two of us when three could no longer fit, my mother conducting from the john seat; then by the piano, when seeing me naked had begun to make my brother uneasy and my mother became interested in music again. This is the same mother who wrote a different well-known poem every week on the wall behind the breakfast table in big poster-paint letters, so we would know that there was life and there was art, too.

My father is in bed at the house in his sweatshirt and boxer shorts. He wouldn't get up, damn him, damn him, damn him; and it's Benjie, mum, and I in the station wagon, parked on the railroad bridge, lights out, not another car in sight.

The predawn sky is the fabric for stars, each with a different and special meaning, like the flag I pledge myself to every morning at school.

"That's it, that's it," says my brother. I see it finally.

Blinking, imposing, man-made metal shot into the sky, it traverses the navy-blue heavens like a planet gone wild from its orbit. Over my hometown, over my head, over my sleeping father, like some shooting star predicting the separate lives of the people below.

Don't you slam the door on me, he says to my mother and throws open the bedroom door, missing her nose by an inch, so hard that the handle on the other side punches through the wall plaster like a fist. The hole was there for a year and nobody filled it in. An open mouth, it reminds me of harsh words.

Warren, says my mother, but this time she is scared. What has happened to the balance? What has happened to the seesaw motion of this marital scale? He shouts; she holds her body from him. He snarls; she won't talk to him after my brother and I go to bed. He retires at ten; she plays the piano until two. "The Blue Room" over and over to a sluggish metronome. He gets up at six, sits alone in the dining room with a cup of black coffee and a Camel cigarette; she sleeps in the middle of the bed, stretched out, until it's time for us to go to school. What does he think about, trying to stare through the forest, in between the pine trees? Her. What does she listen for in the long pauses between the piano notes, in the silent gaps of scales? Him.

Love each other love each other love each other enough, I chant in my lilac-colored bedroom late into the night.

"Don't you slam the door on me," I hear him shout.

"Warren," says my mother. I'm out of the bedroom in an air-raid frenzy. What was that noise, explosive, destructive, like a bomb dropped? "Come on, kids, come on, kids," says my mother, and we're into our coats, through the door, outside, and down the front steps to the two-car garage with the little secondhand sportscar and the station wagon. Tonight I notice that our station wagon is a Ford. Naming of names. My father is a Bastard. My mother's a Runaway Wife, and my brother and I are the Kids, riding in her wake.

A moment before my mother starts the engine, I hear the back door slam in the night. Pop's a wild man again. (But, no, I never called him Pop in my life.) Daddy, Daddy raging through the woods behind our house, in the dark. Hitting his head on pine branches; throwing himself on banks of hills, shirtless, to bruise himself on the sharp rocks. Will he dig up the dog? Throw salt in the goldfish bucket?

At my grandparents' house, my mother's first home, we spend the night. We have fled three miles. But this is Timbuktu, I know it. The act's the distance, not the miles traveled. Good-bye, Dad, good-bye, Dad, good-bye. But, of course, I couldn't have known that then.

Art and Viola nod their heads as my father's wife tells our story, in brief outline. Good for you, I think, not to embellish, but still my father is acid in their mouths, behind closed lips. This I know: we have betrayed him. We have betrayed my father by being here. I am crying in the bathroom because my father is *not* a brute. Big huge sobs that rock me in the rhythms of his forest gait.

After Benjie went away to school, my mother moved into his room. On vacations, when he came home, she sometimes crept into the other of my twin beds in the middle of the night. Stealthily, but who knew stealth better than I?—slipping quietly through the woods, not snapping a twig, not sending one small rock flying, not disturbing any living thing.

Lying awake after that, I can hear the fire horn sound. Three short blasts and one long one means our neighborhood. Two short ones describe a school on fire. Two long blasts and two short ones mean a nuclear attack. I have a printed card in my wallet that says so. Down in the basement we have a shelf of canned goods, a package of plastic forks, and a transistor radio. Why do I always hear it two long and two short?

The person serving me dinner tonight is not my mother. It is a Martian who has taken over my mother's body. And where is my father? Out managing my brother's Little League baseball team. That's where he is when I need him. My mother never forgets that he was out of town for both of her deliveries. My mother? . . . I mustn't panic.

All right, I'll test this Martian out, trick it, ask it questions it couldn't possibly know the answer to:

"What's your favorite color?"

"Blue."

"When's my birthday?"

"October fourth."

"Where does Daddy have a big mole?"

"Under his right arm."

Martians are intelligent by nature. That's why they've landed on Earth before we got a spaceship to Mars. A civilization superior to ours, years in advance. They have no wars; all local travel is by thought projection. They can enter the body of a human at will, and they decided to come to the United States first because people here believe in the melting pot and would attribute their strange ways to being Polish or Czechoslovakian.

"Do you want some more milk, Angela?"

"I want a beer."

"Angela."

"I want a beer with hot fudge sauce." If it doesn't bat an eye, I've got this Martian.

I hear footsteps on the walk. Daddy? Just inside the front door I throw my arms around my father's neck. Daddy, in the nick of time. He's haggard and just like a coach in his green baseball cap with the yellow *B* on the front. Before the Martians landed, that was the kind of simple pleasure I took: gluing the *B*'s on all fifteen hats for the Braves' team.

"Who won?" asks the Martian.

"The Pirates," says my brother. "I walked ten people in a row."

"I had to pull him out," says my father gravely.

"I know," says my brother, and they hug each other.

"Ten?" my mother asks. They both nod. Benjie disappears from the room, to look at his globe I guess, as he often does in times of stress. Is he looking for the Ivory Coast, the Brazilian Basin, the Tibetan Highlands? My father is.

But sometimes waking to a Saturday morning, I find them in bed together.

"The reason waffles are better than pancakes," says my

father, "is because they have more exposed surface to absorb the syrup and butter due to their intricate pattern." My father is not like other fathers. He's not a good sport. So it's unlike him to talk about pancakes and waffles on a Saturday morning, precisely because it is a Saturday morning. Can it be he's going to cook breakfast, the way it is in books in a series, in other lives? He joins the universe in an act of will. My father is trying. Ah, there has been a truce in the war between the states, with both sides still willing to negotiate.

I'm a field marshal on vacation, lying in the middle of the bed. It's story hour on the radio, and all three of us listen attentively until my mother gets up. Lie back down, lie back down, if I had a rope I'd tie her to the bed. But it's only to the bathroom, and while she's gone, I'll ask my father about the viscosity of various brands of maple syrup.

Me, I have no memory at all, like a lady who lost it in a car crash. This morning is every morning, and like the radio story's ending, all will work out well for us. True love is as real as a Valentine in your hand, passionate as its red hot color, more durable than the cardboard it's cut from.

"Look at the picture, look at the picture," says my mother from the other side of the locked bathroom door. In the picture, a naked but shapeless woman is standing with one foot on the seat of a chair and the other on the floor, inserting a Tampax.

"I can't do it," I yell at my mother, lowering my left foot from the toilet seat to the floor, stomping around on the bathmat. "This is horrible." I throw my fifth Tampax in the wastebasket. "I can't get the right angle."

"Just feel around."

"Why do I have to?" I shout through the door. "All my friends use sanitary napkins. Even their mothers do. . . ."

"That's old-fashioned," she replies. Nothing will convince her. "Just try it again." Why can't I have a normal mother? I'm no avant-garde kid. I get one inside. It hurts, it must be in sideways. I pull it out by the string. I hear the front door opening.

"It's him, it's him," I whisper to my mother. "Send him away."

"Hi, Benjie," I hear her say. "Listen, I forgot, I also need a quart of milk." This is his third trip. Is he getting suspicious? I wait, humiliated, behind the door.

"Where's Angela?"

"In the bathroom." He bangs on the door.

"Get out, get out," I yell, warding him off.

"It's locked, you ninny."

"Go on, Benjie. That's enough," says my mother. I hear the front door slam.

"Is he gone?"

"Yes," she says. "Angela, just get one in and leave it. It takes getting used to and I can't send Benjie out for anything else. We've got three quarts of milk already." Now I'm under pressure; it's a twenty-minute bike ride to town and back. But I know I have good study habits and I read through the pamphlet that came in the box once more, carefully.

"Just go sit in the living room," I tell my mother through the keyhole. I put my left foot up on the toilet seat again, unpeel a new Tampax, cover it with my mother's KY jelly, and slide it in. I pull out the cardboard holder and jump around a little bit to test whether it will fall out or not. It won't. I put on my underwear and my bluejeans, and meet my mother in the front hall. She's smiling.

"How does it feel?" she asks me.

"None of your business," I tell her. After that, I change it every half hour, for practice.

Actually, we never ran away from my father, not even once. There was no need. Dad racing like a maniac in the dark along a bed of silent pine needles? Mum flooring the blue Ford down a lane of rock maples en route to Timbuktu? Nope.

I better stick to the facts. First of all, every car we ever bought was blue. My mother's favorite color: blue. Now my grandmother's favorite color is aqua, this is common knowledge. My mother's blue. In a family you know these things. Mine's lilac, you can tell by my room. Well, this says a lot about generations to me, continuity with a twist. Aqua minus green to blue plus red to violet, from the bloodstream of the uterus through the umbilical tube to the embryo, and there you are.

To be sure, that was the wrong story I told before. I heard it on the radio one Saturday and forgot its origin. The fact of the matter is that my mother has her blue room, a blue world. The living room is blue; the cars are always blue; sometimes she even colors the applesauce with blue food coloring.

My mother wallpapered our upright piano in a blue flowered pattern and she plays while I sing along:

We'll have a blue room
A new room, for two room
Where ev'ry day's a holiday . . .
We will thrive on, keep alive on
Just nothing but kisses
With Mister and Missus . . .

This is what my father said when he very gently opened the door of the bedroom, which my mother had not slammed in his face: "Did you chill the champagne?"

"Yes, darling," says my mother.

Afterward, we are sitting in the living room drinking champagne in the crystal glasses, which are hardly ever used, to celebrate my father's new job. My father has had a success in life, and there will be plenty of money now.

Still, my allowance has always been adequate. I have no complaints. Gentle Dad, Dad with a twinkle in his eye, and I'm telling you every Saturday he cooks us waffles on the waffle iron. From scratch, and they are superior to pancakes, anybody knows.

The next day in school I can't remember any of the words for the spelling bee. I don't win. I'm put out.

"Angela doesn't know how to lose gracefully," says my old windbag of a teacher. This is true. I'm my father's child after all.

My father is on top of me. My mother is away for the weekend. He's trying to put it inside me. Why did she go and leave me here alone? No, Daddy. No, no. I'm tearing at his back, until the blood I find below the skin paints my fingernails red for the first time. Is this how a girl grows up?

I'm poking at his eyes, and he smells sweaty and close-up. The hair on his chest scratches. He's so heavy, and I'm pinned like a prom queen and a wrestler, waiting for the last entangled dance to be finished, waiting for the endless count to be up. Stop it. My mother will be outraged. What will my mother say? I can't tell my mother. He's kissing me . . . in my mouth, on my neck. . . .

He's sitting across from me at the head of the dining room table eating the hamburgers I cooked. My mother's away, so I'm cooking for us both. He didn't. But the question is, would he?

Does he think about it? Does my mother like it? Yesterday a girl down the block was raped. That was the word, *raped*. A man picked her up in a car and took her off into the woods. First rule of thumb, my mother has said, never get into a car with a stranger. He put it inside her and she started bleeding. My brother told me that. The man in the car raped her. Why do adults do it to each other all the time?

"I like my hamburgers well done," I tell my father. "So do you."

"That's right, Angela," he says. "And I like them with ketchup, while you prefer mustard."

Secretly I'm thinking about dessert, the chocolate cake I baked for my father from a mix. I'll serve it from the dining room, cutting it on a plate with a silver cake knife, the way my mother does. At the table, a woman presides.

——————— Chapter III ———————

DISCUSSIONS AT DINNER

I N THE BIBLE, IT SAYS SOMETHING ABOUT GIVING things up and then getting them back a hundredfold. This idea is mysterious and thrilling, quite out of the ordinary. Like the day that I found the gold and silver beads on the dusty floor of the hall closet, way in back, unstrung, tiny as single caviar eggs, so shockingly beautiful that I ate them. I like to lie on my bed, legs erect, the soles of my feet pressed to the wall, grappling with the unexplainable, wrestling with the miraculous. . . . An example of this would be if, perhaps, outstretched in this way, parallel to the floor, I might suddenly, like a balloon released from the hand, defy gravity and walk up the wall. My mother says there's no such thing as miracles.

"In other words," says my mother, "it's not in the act, the occurrence, but in a person's point of view, instead."

"To the contrary," says my father. "Certainly there are unexplainable events, but perhaps there's no such thing as illumination." Religion is confusing.

Outside it's sunny, but I've drawn the drapes of my bedroom against any distraction. I know that if you are concentrating on keeping to the beat of the fox-trot in the luminous ballroom of the gym at dancing school; if you are conscientiously seeking to capture the flag, edging silently around boulders, climbing to treetops for an aerial view, scouring the floor of the pine forest behind the house; or if you are bobby-pinning your hair to large pink rollers, wondering if nevertheless it will lie flat for an entire evening—you will not be illuminated then. Because illumination avoids the worldly.

People riding in cars, having cookouts: what do they think of? Yellow divider lines and hamburger smells. Because illumination seeks solitary places to hatch itself, just as birds carry wisps of hair, single straws to secluded places. And if illumination is like an egg, then this is why spiritualists have wandered in sandals into deserts, searching for an oasis of trees where, slipping easily from the two thongs, they begin the ascent through the branches to their goal. And this is why others have shaved their heads bare and traveled as beggars, their shorn locks cleverly arranged to disguise the extended bowl as a nest. Still others make retreats into a wilderness where they sit on the ground, cross-legged, and fast until their hunger is so strong that, like a magnet, it draws the egg to them. But what will my method be? Nowadays beggars are vagrants, and the wilderness has been divided into lots and sold.

"Angela, you're too young to leave home," my mother says, sitting beside me on the couch in the living room.

"Would you like me to grow up to be like those two robots next door?" I ask her. "The only thing they think about is being girls."

"They are happy as they are," she tells me. Pleat-skirted high school sisters, alternate sitters from down the block who, when I propose a dazzling argument as to why I should be allowed to stay up an hour later, will not be swayed.

It's past your bedtime, they say. There's been a change in plans, I tell them. Ten o'clock, they singsong me. Didn't you know that daylight savings begins at midnight? I ask, amazed. Spring ahead, fall back? It's October, they tell me. They will not be confused. No imagination . . .

"What if I come home for Christmas?" My mother, on the other hand, has imagination, is persuadable. "Think of Jane Eyre, Joan of Arc, Anne Morrow Lindbergh. . . ."

"They weren't twelve years old," replies my dogmatic mother. "You would be shanghaied in a shot."

"And I would escape," I tell her. But I know she's right; I've seen it in the movies. "Tell me this though," I ask her, "if I don't go in search of it, will illumination come to Massachusetts?"

"Things are where you find them," says my mother, but, still, she gets out the Atlas and we look at the Fertile Crescent and the Nile Basin. We plan a trip, which I shall take at a later date. My initial explorations will be aquatic: I'll hire a barge for the Nile, sighting pyramids through binoculars, glowing red in the sunset like oxalis leaves closed up for the evening. Red as the Red Sea, where I'll learn to float, where I'll dive deep, certain always to surface. And where Africa and Asia meet, I'll float, in a boat again, through the Suez Canal, landlocked briefly, only to wade at the junction of the Tigris and the Euphrates. Refreshed, moistened, I'm ready for the desert, with its flat silence, its cool sand of evening which could cover you like an envelope flap, sealing up your story forever with the breath of a desert wind. But, undaunted, I'll follow invisible tracks along the wide beach of the Nile, over dunes, past oases, to an invisible line that my feet will detect and clear of themselves, like a jump rope. Back and forth and back again (left foot, right foot, both feet), crossing, recrossing, and again the Tropic of Cancer.

"I'll wear a white scarf and a trench coat," I tell my mother.

"You'll take dark glasses and an umbrella," she says.

"I'll hire a camel with two breast-humps to ride between."

"They're not breasts, Angela," my mother says.

"I know. And I'll watch pyramids cast their shadows, breastlike. Pyramids aren't breasts, either," I tell her.

"The umbrella," she says, "will shield you from the desert sun."

"I'll take calamine lotion, Six-Twelve, and a canteen."

"You will have a guide," says my mother.

"You always wreck everything," I tell her.

At dinner my father agrees I'll have to have a guide.

"There aren't any street signs, Angela," he says. "Why there aren't even any streets. The desert is a vast expanse where sometimes even compasses point in the wrong direction. Believe me," he says, "I've tried to navigate the desert from an airplane. There are few landmarks."

"But, of course, there are the stars."

"Of course."

So if temporarily I give up my trip, it will be a hundred times better when I finally take it, because if you're willing to give something up, it will be returned to you many times over. Surely I'll find what I'm searching for, sitting in the saddle-back of a miraculous camel, riding through the eye of a needle, the compass needle that points (always) the camel and me in the right direction of sandy progress. . . .

If you lose something, then you'll get something back in its place. If you're willing to let a thing slip away, then the principle of return takes over. These seem to be variations on the Bible dictum, though it is hard to understand just where miracles leave off and luck takes over.

For instance, is it a coincidence that just six months after Benjie went away to prep school Uncle Freddie arrived in his place? Or is this a small miracle? A minor, personal miracle of sorts? We gave up Benjie and got back Uncle Freddie, who happens to be a hundredfold more fun. But this idea needs further thinking, discussion with my mother or Uncle Freddie himself, and don't forget the "Uncle." He insists upon it, although he and my mother are only first cousins.

"Freddie," I shout from my bedroom, feet propped up against the flowered wallpaper.

"*Uncle* Freddie," he says upon opening the door, "to remind me how like a sister your mother was to me in our youth, how we were close as siblings, how now we talk to each other every day about nothing in particular while uncovering at the same time things that are true and important. . . ."

"Like in giving up something you will eventually get it back a hundredfold," I tell him. "Right?"

"I try to look at things that way," he says. But Uncle Freddie's tender face is a different portrait of giving things up. Right now he's in the middle of giving up his home and his whole family in a divorce.

And every time I leave, Ros, he told my mother in the kitchen, the dog wags his tail and whines; he rolls over. He doesn't understand. I could tell the kids; that wasn't so hard. But the dog . . . the dog just doesn't understand because you can't tell a dog. I was the one who fed him; no one else would ever do it. If I wasn't home, the dog went hungry. The way the dog looks at me when I leave . . . Even though Uncle Freddie got us in return, I guess it isn't the same.

Freddie, said my mother, forget the dog. You've got bigger worries than the dog.

"Angela, put your feet down."

"I'm allowed," I tell him. "I'm strolling through lilacs."

"You are?"

"Uh huh. Want to try it?"

"Oh yes." He lies down beside me on the bed, his stockinged feet propped against the lilac-flowered wall, his glass on the rug beside him. "It feels so good," he says, sighing. We wiggle our toes up and down the wallpaper print.

"Did you and Mummy go down to the sea together every summer?" I ask to cheer him up.

"We swam hand in hand through the sea of our youth," he says. "A school of two fish."

"Were you the best man at their wedding?" I ask.

"Three days before the ceremony," he replies, "the rings were entrusted to me. So they wouldn't be lost. You see, during this time your father was leaving his keys on department store counter tops, forgetting to put the telephone receiver back on the hook after he finished a conversation, putting the iron away in the refrigerator. . . . So the rings were entrusted to me. I slept with them under my pillow. I wore them in the shower. I taped them to the inside of my underwear, pardon me, Angela, whenever I left the house. With Freddie the rings were safe."

"And . . ."

"Oh," he says, "so I stayed up the whole night before the wedding, composing toasts, writing them down, revising them, committing them to memory. Humorous ones, profound ones. Some that were very clever. I'd had practice before, you see, making up limericks."

"For a swell time," I prompt. He looks to the wall, as if there's something written there, like the changing poems in my mother's kitchen. But his eyelids descend like clouds, and it's clear he's not looking out, but in.

"A toast for a swell time to Warren and Ros
Now promised forever so give your applause
To a couple that's happy and young and carefree
I hope they've enjoyed it
That's the way marriage ought to be."

"Bravo, bravo," I applaud. And the clouds of his brows seeded, he bends over to pick up his glass from the floor and raises it, drinking off the rest of the clear liquid in a long swallow. "Bravo," I say again, but I wish I hadn't asked for this particular toast.

"I've remembered that for thirteen years," says Uncle Freddie. "Quite a mind, eh Angela?"

"Like a steel trap," I tell him, but my father says he's getting a little fuzzy these days, that the gin is pickling his brain. Regardless of this, Uncle Freddie does look awfully run-down for a man of forty, with a big belly and a slow, rambling gait. My father says that when the three of them were young and used to run together, Freddie was the most handsome man around. It was incredible, said my father. Women used to swoon at his feet with regularity.

At dinner, my father is in a bleak mood. The little red sportscar, his pride, his hobby, the one he tunes himself, broke down on the way home from work. My mother had to go and pick him up on the highway in Uncle Freddie's car (since the station wagon's engine blew up and we had to pay to get it carted to the dump). He was waiting by the side of the road, alone, the little car having been engaged by a tow truck and carried off to some garage.

"It must be the carburetor," he says, crumpling his napkin.

"Could be," says my mother.

"It wasn't the spark plugs," he says. "I checked the points."

"How will you get to work in the morning?" she asks.

"I'll walk," he says.

"Warren."

"Well, maybe Freddie can drive me. If I can get him up early enough."

"I don't know. He's out with Allen Ryan. That's who picked him up tonight since I had to borrow the car."

"In that case, he'll never sober up in time."

"Warren."

"Don't worry on my account," I tell them. "I'm aware of the situation. Though it makes me sad."

"It makes all of us sad," says my mother.

"Car trouble," continues my father, "is the basis of our cultural malaise. Everyone courts it, from a clerk at Woolworth's to the captain of a polo team. Cadillac owners, drivers of '54 Chevys, families with boatlike station wagons: no one is exempt. It's like death," he says. "It's unavoidable no matter how conscientious you are."

When I come home from school around four the next afternoon, I find Uncle Freddie and my mother in the den still eating lunch. Irises adorn the tea table, though my mother scolds him for buying flowers for her when his only income is his unemployment check. A big bottle of wine accompanies the flowers.

Don't encourage him, my father has said.

I've talked myself blue in the face, my mother tells him. I've talked until my teeth vibrate.

Very anatomical, says my father, but so's the effect on his liver.

I know, I know, says my mother, but no one else can make him stop unless he wants to, and he doesn't want to. So I join him, to try and make him less lonely while he's here. At least he doesn't drink martinis at lunchtime anymore.

"I have made a dish," my Uncle Freddie tells me, "which you will not believe the exquisite flavor of until you taste it. 'Oysters Caribbe,' taught to me by a very inventive chef in New York." He pours me a glass of wine, spears an oyster with his fork and puts it in my mouth. Thanks to Uncle Freddie, I am the only person in my class who has successfully eaten sweetbreads, tripe, *and* shad roe. This has gained me a kind of respect.

"Delicious."

"Colossal," he says.

"Hello, sweetheart," says my mother, oyster-kissing me. "Freddie, tell Angela the one about the midget from Ireland," she says. In New York, where my uncle goes to look for work every few weeks, there are never any jobs, but he comes back with plenty of new jokes and recipes. Things, my father said, you are most likely to pick up in a bar. I'm sure he had at least two interviews the last time he was there, my mother said.

If only Freddie could become a maître d' or a raconteur, but he, like the rest of us, grew up in a family where you're supposed to be a salesman or an engineer, instead. Even so, he reminds me of Johnny Carson.

"*Ring-a-ding-ding*," he says. "*Zowee*. It seems, Angela, there was this midget from Ireland," he begins. "About your height."

"Just tell the joke, just tell the joke," I warn him, and he putts around the den, punctuating his story with short arrested swings. The three of us howl with laughter.

"So how was your day?" my mother asks me.

"Let's see," I say, thinking, sliding up close to her on the couch. "First, I had a fight with Jennifer Small at recess. . . ."

"You hit her?" my mother asks.

"No, no. A verbal fight. I massacred her."

"That's not very nice," says my uncle.

"Would you rather I'd lost?" I ask him.

"Certainly not," he says.

"Sometimes, though," says my mother, "discretion is the better part of valor."

"Does this have something to do with turning the other cheek?"

"Yes," she says. "In a way."

"Plus, I got a ninety-five on my history paper," I continue. "I'm an expert on the Phoenicians," I tell my uncle.

"*Scoo-be-doo*," he says.

"But Martin and Billy, as usual, did better," I tell my mother. "Both have photographic memories," I explain to my uncle, "so you can see what I'm up against."

"Who told you that?" my mother asks.

"I made it up," I confess, "but it's probably true."

"Angela hates losing," my mother tells Uncle Freddie.

"Who doesn't?" he says.

"And the field hockey game?"

"We lost again," I tell her. "But as you know the other team

is composed of far better players, and what can you do as captain
of a team with no talent? I do my best; I scored two goals, but
then I had to sit out with a stitch. . . ." I'd do anything for the
team, but ever since the game I passed out, my mother made
me promise to lie down on the bench for a while whenever I feel
funny.

"Maybe we should go back to the doctor," my mother says.

"But he says I'm in A-One health," I remind her. "Do you
think I have a mental illness?"

"No, darling, you don't have a mental illness."

"Well, I was just checking. Daddy says he had a mental
illness once."

"Your father?" asks Uncle Freddie.

"Yes, he said it was his youth."

"Daddy was just joking," my mother says. "How long did
you sit out?" she asks.

"About ten minutes. That's when they scored the three
goals."

"Give me a kiss, captain," says my uncle. I sit on his lap
against his big belly, and his breath is boozy. Already it seems as
if Uncle Freddie has always been here in the house with us, as if
he never had any other family but us.

But Daddy doesn't think so. Uncle Freddie is Daddy's best
friend, but if you didn't know it, it would be hard to tell. They
don't agree on anything. Sometimes Uncle Freddie will change
his mind; he'll look at things from another point of view, but this
only disgusts my father. "Stick to your guns. Stick to your guns,"
he cries. He often glares through dinner, livid with the way my
uncle thinks. "Thinking is morality," my father says. "Opinion is
an issue of conscience." My father isn't resigned to anything he
doesn't agree with.

These dinner arguments, course after course of disagree-
ments, desserts of misunderstandings, are what my mother calls
"taking everything personally" on my father's part. My mother
is what she calls "put in the middle." Me, I like to keep the
conversation moving in the right direction, and if anyone
oversteps the safe boundaries of discourse, treading on marshy

ground, I quickly steer them to a more solid territory. My mother says that this is the role of women in our family, to smooth things over. Sometimes I wish everyone would do his own smoothing.

"May I be excused?" my father asks. Then he goes into their bedroom to read from his *Complete Greek Drama*. Heroism leads to destruction and slaughter, he says. Honor to death. This isn't Sparta, my mother has said. Good God, Warren, it's the twentieth century.

If he gets in a better mood, we'll act out a scene or two. Sometimes we choose *Oedipus at Colonus,* and I lead him around the living room as if he were blinded. My mother occasionally reads the part of the chorus. Best, though, I like to mourn as Electra, and Daddy plays Aegisthus with great flourish.

Uncle Freddie returns to the den, shuts the door, and you can hear the TV voices. I help my mother load the dishwasher.

"Sometimes," she says, "my life seems like all silverware."

"Or all dinners," I add.

Recently, the house appears to shrink when night falls and everyone stays inside. And the forest behind the house grows to being endless, shadow behind shadow cast by the trees in the glare of the floodlights anchored to the hill of the backyard. Stacking the dessert dishes in the dining room, I wonder if the others are looking out into the woods now as I am. For what? My father in his bedroom, my uncle in the den, my mother in the kitchen. What is it that human beings want that they can't find anywhere? Well we're not dead yet, any of us, and I guess that's the only point at which you stop wanting.

I've heard my father grinding his teeth at night, through the walls, through the foam rubber of my pillow. If I could read the sound like Morse code perhaps I'd find out what it is he wants. And if the noise keeps me awake, I might get up and find my mother reading a novel in the living room. Or I might find my uncle in the den, his mouth agape in a snore, a bottle on the tea table (his Prohibition bar), and the TV humming the static of early morning hours. I might ask them, silently, what they want, too. But if I stay in my bedroom, they're in their appointed places anyway, imagined sentries, sleeping through their duties or wide-eyed, posted, to see us through the night.

Saturday is my favorite day, especially in the fall. The weather is particularly crisp; perhaps the sun will be shining. You can sit and think about things; you can go out and ride your bike fifty times around the block to test your endurance and will; you can read a book. You can call up friends and make plans. But today Daddy and I are down in the cellar, in his workshop, making a rocket ship control board.

"Would you like a video screen?" Daddy asks.

"No. What for?"

"So that you can see the planets as you travel through space," he says.

"In that case, I'd like one," I tell him. "And I'd like a knob to control the focus of the picture." We look through the drawers of his workbench for a knob. We find one that fell off an old bureau. "Do you think this one will work?"

"Yes," he says. "You nail it on."

"But then it won't turn," I tell him.

"You can pretend," he says.

"I can pretend to see the stars. I can pretend that I'm weightless. I can pretend that Benjie's football helmet is a space helmet," I tell him. "But I can't pretend that a knob turns when it doesn't. It's not in me."

"All right," says Daddy. "I understand. We'll have to figure something out." We do, and when we emerge from the basement late that afternoon to show our project to my mother, she's impressed.

"Where's the dog?" she asks.

"I don't know," says my father.

"Wasn't she down there with you?"

"No. What's the matter? Where's the dog?" I ask her. I can feel the dog missing in my stomach, the dog like an undigested meal. The dog in my stomach missing from the plate of her own meal. Because the dog is always hungry at dinnertime. The dog always comes home for dinner, for the solitary and nourishing dog dinner. Where is our dog?

"I saw her around eleven this morning," says Uncle Freddie, coming out of his room and joining us in the hallway. It turns out that he is the last one to have seen the dog, chasing a rabbit into the woods, barking and scooting around trees, her tail wagging in a wave of good-bye.

"Are you worried?" I ask my mother. "Tell me the truth."

"Yes," she says.

We call her name into the woods. "Good dog," we call so she'll want to come home. We whistle her special whistle. We ring the cowbell. No dog. "Blondie," we call, for the dog is a golden retriever. My mother dials a few numbers, asking if anyone in his travels has seen the dog.

"Are you worried, Daddy?"

"Not yet," he says. Your father is dependable, my mother once told me. He's good in a crisis. When it is time to worry, he worries. But not until then. Not me, I imagine dog deaths in the woods, on the highway. The dog run over by a car on a dogleg curve; the dog kidnapped by another family because she is so beautiful, escaping, trying to find her way home, pursuing us with no sense of her own direction in a dogged fashion. The dog poisoned by a neighbor; the dog being fed a hotdog injected with rat poison. The dog hunted through the center of town by the dogmatic driver of an ASPCA truck.

The doggerel of the dog's perceptions in her puppyhood. The dog dead and buried beneath the roots of the dogwood tree, which rarely flowers in the backyard. A dog's life ended.

My uncle's car lurches into ignition, and he and my mother back swiftly out of the driveway to search the neighborhood. My father follows them, driving farther afield to the police station where he will leave a description. Alone, I take the flashlight from his bureau drawer, and putting a bowl of water on the back stoop, I close the door behind me.

I start out by following the tote roads someone cleared years ago, familiar paths, traveled paths, circular and intersecting, like orbits through the space of the woods. "Blondie," I call over and over, leaving the roads now, penetrating into the heart of the woods, ducking branches, stumbling over pinecones, flashing my light on unfamiliar shapes. Squirrel noises (the beam identifies them) scare me. An owl hoots. Where can the dog be?, following the brook through the circle of woods that's defined by the street of houses circumscribing it. I cross the small bridge over the street, my feet echoing left right, left right, Blondie, Blondie. I continue along the brook on the other side. The flashlight flickers and goes out. I return to the street and follow the pavement this time, semicircular, to our house.

"Angela," my mother says, poking her head out the front door. "Where have you been?"

"Looking for the dog."

"Next time, leave a note," she says. "We thought you'd disappeared, too."

"You need new batteries," I tell my father, and I wake up twice during the night, hearing the dog at the back door, but it's only the raccoons in the garbage. The floodlights are on, and both times I find Uncle Freddie sitting in the den, looking out into the woods. A vigil for the dog. On Sunday I refuse to go to church. "I'm needed at home," I say.

We are a gloomy crew. Daddy and Uncle Freddie play cards. Mummy reads a magazine. Occasionally, I go out into the backyard to look for dog footprints, to find some clue. I start *The Adventures of Sherlock Holmes* to learn something of his method, but I can't concentrate. Every hour or so, one of us gets up and calls the dog. I love the dog and the dog is gone. I'll never have another dog. Did I always play with her enough? Does she forgive me for tying a bonnet around her head and wheeling her up and down the street in the baby carriage? The day we played cannibals and fastened her legs to a broomstick, carrying her toward the imaginary pot, chanting? Is she disappointed that she didn't win the blue ribbon at the amateur dog show Benjie showed her in? She was born with a broken tail and we never had it fixed. . . . Sometimes I've pushed the dog down off my bed when she took up too much room. Have I always searched her vigilantly enough for ticks? The dog has the longest eyelashes anyone has ever seen. Are they closed, somewhere, over her eyes?

At ten everybody goes to bed. No one wants to be awake anymore, to be reminded of the dog's absence. Counting down 3, 2, 1, in the dream, for takeoff in search of the dog on the video screen. The button turns perfectly, focusing the picture in on the Great Bear, Pegasus the winged horse, Draco the dragon, Cetus the whale, Taurus the bull, Lepus the hare, Columba the dove which flew from Noah's Ark. The sky is bright with animals, a zoo of constellations. Flying past Corvus the crow, Cygnus the swan, Tucana the toucan, out of the aviary of my journey, now. Traveling through light-years, longer even than dog years, listening to the barks of Canis Major and Minor, Orion's hounds, with sadness. Speeding on to the Dog Stars, first Sirius then Procyon, searching their misty orbs for a mortal, missing dog. Back to Earth, empty-handed.

"Angela, you have to go to school," my mother says at breakfast, reading my mind. It's no use arguing.

"All right. But I'm not hungry." And I push the bowl of cornflakes away. The dog eats cornflakes.

By recess, I can't bear it any longer. I call up my mother from the switchboard office, where Mrs. Purdy plugs in a red rubber wire and dials our number, swiftly, professionally, with a pencil.

"No answer," she says.

"Well, could you try my grandmother then, please?"

"Hello?"

"Hello, Gran."

"Angela," she says. Her voice makes me cry; she reminds me of the dog. When the bids got too high at the fair, we called up my grandmother and asked her if she would pay the extra money. It may be as much as forty dollars, we said. Do you love the dog? she asked. Already, we said. Then go ahead and keep bidding till you get her, said my grandmother. Eighty-five dollars later she was ours, but by the skin of our teeth. Stop the bidding, the owner cried, because the dog had wriggled through two slats of the pen and was peeing on my foot. That's unfair,

said the man with glasses who'd been matching us offer for offer.
The dog has chosen her family, the owner said, and she lifted
the squirming puppy into my arms. That's that, said the former
owner.

"Gran, I have to come home," I tell her. "I can't concentrate and I keep going to the bathroom to cry. What if the dog
has come home wounded and there's no one there to help her?
Mum and Uncle Freddie are out. Will you pick me up?"

"Of course," she says, and we drive out of the school
parking lot, too glum even to turn on the radio, arriving at the
house only to realize that neither of us has a key. "Well then,
we'll go out to the back," says my grandmother, Viola.

"Yoo-hoo," she calls to the dog.

"Blondie," I shout into the woods. If the dog were
illumination, how would I summon her? There's a question here
of investing the powerless, myself, with power. How to attract
the dog/egg when you're not even out of the nest yet yourself. I
decide to pray.

"If she doesn't come now, I'll give her up for dead," I tell
my grandmother. "Blondie," I bellow, shrill as an angel's
trumpet (because my prayer was sincere, you see).

"Yoo-hoo," yodels my grandmother, and a black dog streaks
out of the woods, up the small hill; he's sent the wrong dog, but
oh no, in my arms, wet and slimy, all covered with mud, it's the
dog, squirming like the first time I held her as a puppy, covering
my dress with dirt, I don't care, moving so fast shaking the mud
from her coat, overjoyed to be home, multiplying herself in my
arms, like a hundred golden dogs in the sun (the dog returned a
hundredfold), rolling onto her back so I can tickle her greasy
stomach, panting, the retriever who retrieved herself from
death.

"It's clear," says my father at dinner, "that she was caught
in a swamp."

"Quicksand," I reply.

"Something like that," he says.

"Cheers," says my uncle, toasting with the champagne he
bought to celebrate the dog's homecoming.

"Cheers," says everyone else.

"And," says my mother, "when the veterinarian told me that her hind legs were sprained, it was clear to me that she must have been struggling to free herself for a number of hours."

"Having her home is the cat's meow," says my uncle.

"In the kitchen, the dog is having her second dog dinner of the evening. Menu: cornflakes, dogfood, milk; (dessert) vanilla ice cream (in a separate dish).

". . . so, you see, it really is a miracle," I finish telling them. And, in bed, I don't forget my promise: God bless my mother, my father, Gran and Grand, Benjie, Uncle Freddie, and the dog (in random order). Yours truly, Angela.

Marie Firenze is the only Catholic girl in the neighborhood, and for this reason it is important for me to get to know her better. Because God's role is more palpable in Catholicism; you can even get the gist of it in Latin. Still, I wish I were at home now; I can't think of anything to say; if only my mother hadn't arranged over the phone to drop me off here on the way to her garden club meeting, though I'm the one who asked her to.

Marie's younger brother Paul is staring at my chest; Marie is playing with her earrings (Rachel's mother says that girls who have pierced ears are cheap); and the grandmother, amply filling a black satin dress, gray hair pinned up into a tight bun knot, bustles back and forth from the stove to the kitchen table.

"May I help?" I ask. She doesn't answer. Marie shouts something at her in Italian. The screen door with the metal coil slams behind Marie's father, the contractor, coming in from the back where the cement mixer is. Don't get yourself pushed into that, Benjie told me once. The Italian grandmother will push you in.

"The nuns," Marie tells me after lunch out in the driveway, "beat you with rulers, and they pull your hair if you make a mistake in the catechism. They say I will surely go to hell if I'm not good at home."

"There's no such thing as hell," I tell her.

"Oh yes there is," she says.

"Well, there may be hell for Catholics, but not for Protestants. It's a concept, my father says, invented by mankind to keep those who don't know any better in line."

"Oh yeah?" she says, putting her hands on her hips.

"Yeah. And, besides, the pope is a phony."

"The pope . . ." she splutters. I have made her mad as a yellow jacket. "My family doesn't want you here. Get off our property."

"I wouldn't stay if you paid me," I tell her, walking out into the street. "Your grandmother throws people in the cement mixer."

I institute a prayer at dinner that night.

"What's that?" my father asks.

"Latin."

"I know," he says, "but it sounded like 'Religion is divided into three parts.'"

"It was," I tell him. "At school we're reading Caesar. I just changed the opening line slightly to try to explain the concept of the Trinity."

"That's very smart, Angela," says my father. "Freddie, do you have to smoke during dessert?"

"I want to become a Catholic," I tell my mother over the sinkful of pots.

"Why?"

"Because they don't argue at meals. They disagree silently, and, besides, if they are Italian, it's a foreign language that the grandmother speaks and that's A-OK with me because I don't understand it."

"Angela, none of this has anything to do with being Italian or Catholic," my mother says. "We're a very expressive family, and if we feel like arguing, we do."

"Why do we feel like it so much?" I ask her.

"I don't know, Angela." My mother is dedicated to trying to answer all my questions truthfully. She's up to her elbows in soapy water. When she gesticulates, the suds implode, then disappear into thin air. Like money and years, my mother once remarked of their vanishing.

"Perhaps Daddy is part Catholic," I suggest. This would facilitate my conversion. "Because half the time he doesn't say anything either; he just sits and stares at the buffet."

"Angela," says my mother, "You've lost all perspective." There is no defense against this kind of accusation.

"Those with missions," I tell her, "have no peripheral vision."

In my room, I read passages from the black King James Bible handed down through the generations of my father's family. Mine is the last of the eleven-name genealogy written on the inside cover.

Nuns read the Bible every day; Marie assured me of this. Sometimes they don't speak one word during an entire week on their retreats. They are talking silently to God. All the nuns get along; they help out the poor. The nuns are a sort of team. They have sacrificed everything for God. The nuns have no time for argument (there are strict rules to follow, like in the army), but the nuns are human, too, and understandably they sometimes lose their tempers and beat the children in their care. With rulers, they beat other women's children; they have no children of their own. But like mothers, nuns sometimes give birth, too: to strange happenings, to miracles, to ecstasy.

Occasionally a sister becomes a saint. Like Saint Theresa (God spoke to her), who searched for him in her soul (the Interior Castle, she called it, like a diamond or the heart of a star). A saint must perform three documented miracles; Marie told me that, too. There is no one greater than a saint: not the leaders of empires, the discoverers of continents. If a nun has ambition, a calling, it's to become a saint.

I'll have to take my vows secretly. My mother will never let me convert. What about a family? she'll ask. That is not the route for all, I'll tell her.

When I appear for dinner one night in black garb, my head shaved, they'll recognize me as a novitiate. I'll have many skills; I'll be regarded as a capable nun. Sister Angela? the mother superior will say. Oh yes, a versatile helpmate . . . I'll see to the plumbing problems, which my father has taught me about. I'll

string rosaries. I'll tune up the convent truck. I'll cook Oysters Caribbe on holidays, without the wine sauce because nuns do not imbibe.

My mother picks me up right after lunch at school on Friday afternoon to go to the dentist.

"This is no way to start off the weekend," I tell her.

"No one likes to go to the dentist, Angela," says my mother. We have a double appointment, in adjoining offices: my mother for a root canal, me for the orthodontist. The green blinker light on the dashboard winks. We turn onto the highway, headed for Boston, where we sometimes attend plays or go to enjoy the paintings at the Museum of Fine Arts, but more often than not we exit off Storrow Drive in search of a parking place as near as possible to the dentist's office. My mother smoked seven cigarettes on the way to town; I count them, pink-tipped, in the ashtray. I squeeze her hand in reassurance as we part company in the shared reception room. The dentist is going to drill her nerve. The dentist, my mother has said, is one of the unfortunate realities of life. But at least, she says, the pain is to a positive end.

"Are you keeping the hardware clean?" the bespectacled monster asks me. With a little wrench, he tightens my braces. "Spit," he says. The steady jet of water washes the blood down the drain. "That should just about do it," he says, taking another quarter turn.

The dental assistant, Miss Brell, comes out of the back office. She smiles; she has good teeth. You can hear the drill whirring in my mother's mouth.

"Your mother will be at least another hour," she says.

"I think I'll go out for a walk then."

"Do you think you ought to? By yourself, I mean?"

"Oh yes," I tell her, grabbing my camel's hair coat off the rack, and I run down the stairs, not waiting for the elevator, so I'll be outside before she can check with my mother. Angela, Angela, she'll call into the waiting room. No answer.

It is windy in your hair and quite exciting by yourself in the fall city. The afternoon is gray and soon it will darken into the evening of rush hour. Already some cars have their headlights on and the streetlights glow dimly; traffic is starting to build up at red lights. My time is short before my mother and I will unlock the car doors and slide into our respective places, her at the wheel and me at the radio, to join the steady exodus of commuters bound for a suburban weekend. But the Catholic church is just around the corner.

I buy a hotdog from the vendor at the foot of the church steps, and luckily the doors at the top are unlocked. I slip inside.

The church is candle-lit and cavernous. It is the interior of Noah's Ark or the inside of the belly of the whale. No one is about, just me (Angela/Jonah or Angela/animal). Where are the priests in their womanly black cassocks? You never see their feet; they shuffle quietly behind the curtain of the long robes. Centipedal priests? Priests in perpetual motion toward God.

Following the right-hand corridor that leads up to the altar, past the aisles of pews, I notice way over on the right a sort of box with a chair in it. Inspecting it more closely, sitting down, I notice a little door in the wood, near my mouth. I open it and give my first confession:

"Today I was selfish, . . ." I begin. "I thought only of my own dental pain while my mother right now is undergoing root canal work. As you know, this is very painful. She's already been in for it twice and will have to pay one more visit. But it's I, not my mother, who complains every time we set out for Boston.

"I am competitive with two boys in my class. I hate losing; I am a bad sport. I feel superior to many of my classmates. I enjoy the praise of my teachers too much." I take another bite of the hotdog and chew for a moment. "When my father is angry, I get angry back. Once I told him I hated him, and it made his mouth quiver, though it wasn't true. This is no help to my mother, who 'smooths things over' better than I do. I sometimes avoid Uncle Freddie, who lives with us, when he's drunk, and that's the time he needs someone to talk with most. I masturbate. I don't write Benjie letters often enough. Benjie, my brother, has started to shave, and when he came home for the weekend, I laughed at the nicks in his cheeks. But in all fairness to myself it didn't seem to bother him that much.

"I'm here right now because I ran away from the dentist's office. My mother will worry about me, sitting in the chair. I have strong religious beliefs, but I often skip church. I would like to become a nun, but I know nothing of humility; I would rather be a saint. What is ecstasy? Where is the door to the interior castle?

"Further, I'm a Protestant." Here I stop; perhaps I've gone too far. But honesty, my mother repeats this over and over, can only be the best policy.

"Another thing I want to talk about is the fact that I don't think I understand the concept of happiness," I continue. "Is this a shortcoming? My mother says you can only be happy for moments, for little scraps of time. It's these, she says, that make life worthwhile. Though this may sound ungrateful, I had expected more. And when I think about it, I wonder, under such a circumstance, is there really any such thing as sin? People do slip, it's true; they make insignificant and even serious mistakes in their lives, daily. But isn't this because of their unhappiness, their despair? My Uncle Freddie is a perfect example of this. He lives with himself as if with a toothache when the dentist is away on vacation. The gin eases him, somehow. Between the moments of happiness, each of us has a method in waiting for the next. My father reads the Greeks. My mother copies poems onto the kitchen wall. . . ." I finish the last bite of the hotdog. "Is anyone there?" I ask through the dark hole of the opened door. I shut it and run down the aisle to the big church doors and, shutting them, descend to the busy street below, mingling with the current of people on their way home.

In the reception room, Miss Brell signs me up for another appointment, one month away. "Your mother should be out in about ten minutes," she says.

"Thanks," I say. I wink at her. She hasn't told.

"Angela, I hope you haven't been bored out here all this time," says my mother as she comes out of the room with the big reclining chair and the drill arm that's attached to the wall.

"Oh no," I tell her, my sweet mother, who even as they attack the nerves of her teeth with gleaming speeding drill bits, thinks of me. I kiss her on the lips.

"Ouch," she says. She makes her new appointment for the same day as mine as I press the elevator button. And in a tiny box, suspended by a thick metal cord, we descend through a shaft in the center of an old brownstone, to the street, to the world, having done our dental duty, the two of us, arm in arm, utterly, for the moment, happy.

I manage to avoid dinner by making a date with a friend for the early show at the movies.

"But you haven't eaten yet," my mother says.

"I had a hotdog," I tell her. And a discussion, too. Besides, the movie stars Elvis Presley.

When I get dropped off from the movies, my mother greets me at the door.

"I have some bad news," she says.

"What? What is it?" My eyes involuntarily scan the living room, trying to see through the walls into the other rooms of the house for imagined disasters. "Did something . . ."

"Uncle Freddie's in the hospital," she says. My father joins us in the front hall and shuts the door behind me.

"Liver malfunction," he says. My father is crying.

Saturday an ambulance moves him to the VA hospital because his Blue Cross from work expired several months ago and he has no money. The doctor won't allow any visitors until Sunday. I say prayers for Uncle Freddie in my bed. I'll pray the whole night long, but when I look at the luminous alarm clock face and it's two o'clock, I realize I've been asleep. I walk out into the darkened hall.

In the living room my mother and father are sitting on the couch together, talking. "It will be a miracle if he lives," he says. "Do you want another drink?"

"Yes," says my mother. "Another gin for Freddie," and she raises the glass to her lips, swallowing off what's left.

The VA hospital goes on forever, its corridors twisting and turning like the tubes that grow out of Uncle Freddie's arms. Wild Medusa hair. Red rubber switchboard wires, sending out messages of illness and human frailty.

"*Ring-a-ding*, Angela," Uncle Freddie whispers. "I want

you to have the car, Ros," he says. "Nobody should be without wheels. . . ."

"I'll use it until you need it again," my mother says, her eyes wrinkling.

"Hey, you SOB of a copilot," Uncle Freddie says to my father.

"None of you fly-boys would have lived to tell the tale if it hadn't been for your navigating angels," says my father. The hospital has turned back time, and the veterans, each remembering his own war, lie in a long row of beds against the bunker of the ward wall.

"Fly-boys," my uncle repeats, shutting his eyes. My father goes out to meet the doctor in the hall.

The man in the next bed is gaining altitude beneath the white sheet of his sky, until the air is too rarefied to breathe. Choking, sputtering, wheezing until the attendant wheels over the oxygen tank. My father comes back in through the swinging double doors.

"He's dying," he whispers. My uncle, my mother's cousin, my father's best man, World War Two pilot, flying toward his own death. Freddie in a nose dive.

When we get home I take down the Bible from the shelf, open it, and write Freddie's name beneath mine. Then I close it and put it in the bottom drawer of the bureau where I keep things I don't want anymore.

———————— Chapter IV ————————

SAYING WHAT YOU MEAN

THOUGH I DON'T LIVE WITH MY MOTHER ANY-more (and the boarding school bureaus in every room are identical; the same pine, four-tiered receptacles for cigarettes and Teddy bears, knee socks and love letters: our uneven growing up), still the bottom drawer of my bureau at home seems to grow fuller every month. This time capsule whose seal I'm always breaking prematurely, then carefully resealing (the handle grasped and the rectangle of its contents diminished into darkness) on an occasional weekend afternoon or on holidays.

"Angela, what on earth are you doing in there?" my mother calls from the hall.

"I'm sorting through some things."

"Again?" she says.

It's crammed with discarded hopes and ways in the form of datebooks, a six-shooter cap gun, swimming ribbons, postcards and letters, pink erasers in the shapes of animals, the outgrown wooden shoes that my grandparents brought me from Holland and, of course, the Bible I buried there in the strata of changes when I found out Uncle Freddie was dying. Memories persist.

For instance (the Bible): As things turned out (the way they often do, in a way we never seem to predict), Uncle Freddie recovered. But his progress was slow, and he remained in the hospital for several months, where my mother and I visited him twice a week, once on the weekend when my father could join us. We were his only regular visitors.

However, said the doctor to Uncle Freddie, to Great-aunt Vera and Uncle Jack, his mother and brother who'd flown in from New York, and to my mother and father, all gathered around the bedside . . . you must never drink again. If he does, he could go in a minute.

Everyone was glum; absolutes make people uneasy. And

Uncle Freddie swallowed daily the tablets that make you violently ill if you mix them with liquor.

Would this be a chemical reaction? I asked my father.

Yes, he said. Upon contact, the structures of the two substances break down, recombining to form a deadly poison. . . . Not deadly enough to kill you, he added as an afterthought, though you feel so sick that you might wish to be dead instead.

So then the cure is almost worse than the disease, I deduced. Like rabies . . . or gonorrhea.

Angela, said my mother, you've been reading too many books. But this was just a moment of exasperation; nothing was censored in our house. You could read *Fanny Hill* if you wanted to; all of us did. If you wanted to eat a whole chocolate cake by yourself and grow fat, you could. You could even choose to vote Republican in our family ballots at election time; during any given four-year period we often had a different President from the rest of the country. In short, every decision was your own. This is what my mother instituted, borrowed chiefly from Dr. Spock and the Bill of Rights, as her "hands-off policy." So when Uncle Freddie started drinking again, my mother and father remonstrated, cajoled, engaged in dialogues of logic, but they never physically tried to stop him.

It's *his* life, my mother said, in tears.

It's his *life*, said my grandmother, who'd watched her own mother pour rum down the kitchen sink at night when her father was asleep.

But that kind of technique never helps, said my mother.

Does drinking too much run in the family? I asked.

If he deliberately stops taking the pills, my mother looked at me, and continued, so that he can take a drink four days later when all the traces of the drug are gone, then, believe me, he wants a drink.

And after an all-family conference, a series of sequential local and long-distance phone calls, it seemed advisable to follow AA's advice and push him out of the nest to see if he could fly solo, no navigators this time. Still, no one felt good about the plan except Uncle Freddie, who didn't seem to care. He left us and, on a strict stipend from Great-aunt Vera, moved into a roominghouse in a little sea-town nearby so that my mother could visit him often. The money certainly wasn't enough to pay for both his board and liquor bills, but soon he stopped going to the AA meetings altogether.

I got tired, Uncle Freddie finally told my father, of standing up every day in front of a hundred people and saying "I am an alcoholic."

I can understand that, said my father.

How can he afford booze on such a budget? my mother asked.

You find a way, my father answered. I imagine Uncle Freddie breaking open children's piggy banks, searching the crevices of restaurant booths for change slipped from pockets. . . . He's got buddies who'll stand him a few, my father said. The rest of the time he probably drinks rotgut.

When we were young, my mother said, he wouldn't even ride second-class on the train. And not that anybody had any money either. He never let his mother iron his shirts; he always sent them out. . . .

I wish we had some extra money to give him, said Daddy, so he could burn out on Chivas Regal. . . .

One morning when the landlady missed hearing his footsteps in the small bedroom over her apartment on the first floor, she went upstairs to knock. She received no answer and the door was locked. So she called a neighbor who came over and followed her up the stairs in her second winded ascent, his footsteps echoing like Freddie's should have hours before, who took the door off its hinges to find my uncle facedown on the floor. A face which, when the body was turned over, appeared horribly red from a hemorrhage in the brain.

I didn't find any of that out on the day he died, but later—when the facts and circumstances seemed more important than they had initially, when we tried to make sense, finally, even of death. But by that afternoon everything was over anyway, and the mourning had (officially) begun:

"Shall the casket be open or closed?" asks Mr. McCloskey.

We are seated in the back parlor of the funeral home, which is decorated as if people actually lived here. Some of the living have shacks and tents for homes. They do in India; I've seen it on the news. This is a three-story house for the dead.

"Open," says my Great-aunt Vera. "Closed," says my mother at the same moment. Opposed, is what their joint answer sounds like.

"Excuse us a moment," says my mother, and the two of them confer in whispers while Mr. McCloskey writes on a pad on the desk, his face averted:

"Auntie . . ."

Open or closed? he writes.

"It's customary."

Suit and tie?

"Well I don't know."

The front or the green room?

"When his father died. . . ."

I lean back against the couch next to my mother. Her perfume, for the moment, permeates the peculiarly odorless atmosphere.

"That was twenty years ago," she says.

I picture the coffin ajar, like the door to Uncle Freddie's room at night across the hall from mine. For the cross breeze, he said. Or its beveled lid propped open with a slender mahogany rod, like my grandmother's grand piano wing. For the resonance, she said. Only the strings inside are the lines of Uncle Freddie's forehead, the stripes on his regimental tie, the threads of his suit jacket. How will I hear him, now that he's dead? Will he play his own strings, strum his emptied veins in a tune that reminds us of Freddie alive? This is the song whose melody the organist will pick up at the service, as if out of thin air.

"It will be too much to bear," says my mother, holding Aunt Vera's hand. "Let's remember him as he was," she says, "talking, telling jokes. . . ."

This must be the key then. The key that opens the imaginary coffin from the inside and lets life out. Clearly it's the talking, words themselves, that reminds people of their lives, that they are alive. When people meet one another, they say,

How do you do? What they mean is, I am here. Fine thank you, another replies. What he means is, I am here too. Everyone is busy letting it be known that he or she exists. Chanters, for instance, remind themselves continuously in verse of their own living.

A man in an olive suit comes into the room and puts a folder on Mr. McCloskey's desk.

"Angela, this is Mr. Stephens," my mother says. "Mr. McCloskey's associate. Mr. Stephens, my daughter Angela."

"Well, hello there, young lady," he says.

"I am here," I tell him.

"Why don't you go buy a Coke, Angela?" says my mother, reaching into her purse and pressing a dime into my open palm with a little too much force to be coincidental.

"All right."

"The strain has been a bit too much for all of us," I hear my mother say on my way to the door.

From today I'll start a new language, the language of saying exactly what you mean. Perhaps if Uncle Freddie had said what he meant rather than "I am an alcoholic" over and over, I wouldn't be across the street now. At the gas station, releasing the sweaty dime from my thumb and forefinger, careful to steer it perpendicular into the slot, listening for the plummet and clink, feeling along the ledge of the coin return for the possible coin returned, hearing the glass door behind which the caps of Cokes and root beers and orangeades shine unlock itself, pulling at every bottle neck one after the other, each one that will not be parted like a tongue from the metal jaws which lock it in its refrigerated place.

My one dime is gone. I start to get thirsty. I kick the big red machine with my toes. I try to pull the door off. I beat the three-cent deposit sign with my fists.

"Hey, kid, cut it out," shouts the attendant, running out of the little office attached to the garage where they keep the maps, the credit card machine, and the oil on shelves.

"It ate my dime."

"Tell it to the Senate," he says. He has pimples on his face.

"Go suck a greasy rag." And fleeing from him, I cross the

street to McCloskey's, heedless of traffic. Look both ways. Look both ways. I don't care if they hit me. Whichever way you look at it, my Uncle Freddie is lying in a coffin.

The funeral is being planned for three days from today; the body is being laid out.

When I ask my father what this means, he explains: "It means that the body is drained of all blood, Angela. Certain preservatives are then injected into the veins; if parts of the body are disfigured or misaligned due to some accident or as the result of a disease, the undertakers reconstruct them. Usually using wire or thread," he says. "Then they apply makeup to the face; they trim the hair or set it; they dress the deceased in his best clothes and make him look just as the people he left behind would have liked to see him look while he was alive."

"That last comment was not necessary, Warren," says my mother.

"But it's true," he says. Daddy has learned the language of saying what you mean. Daddy, however, gets in trouble for it, both at work and at home. This is something to consider. And he must be lonely sometimes, too, because Daddy says nobody speaks his language.

"Are nipples erect in death?" I ask him. "When rigor mortis sets in?"

"I give up," says my mother, throwing up her hands as if she's tossing both of us away or wishes she could. "You two talk like a couple of perverted undertakers. Angela, it's not just somebody who is dead. It's Freddie. . . ."

For the first time this seems true. He'll never tell another joke he heard in New York when he was supposed to be looking for a job; the imaginary golf club will stay resting in its bag. My father won't argue with him ever again. No more lunches à deux for Mummy. He won't tickle me anymore, which I hated at the time. Because my Uncle Freddie is dead.

The funeral will be two days from today. In the morning my mother and Aunt Vera drive to Freddie's cramped quarters to sort through a few of his things, but after an hour or two neither of them can stand it anymore and they come back to our house, which reminds them of him less.

But everything here reminds me of Freddie. The TV makes me cry. I empty his favorite ashtray of all butts. I have hidden the shot glasses in a bottom cabinet of the kitchen.

"After you're dead," says my brother, who's home for the funeral, "your fingernails and hair continue to grow in the grave. . . ."

"Make him shut up," I yell at my mother, covering my ears and shouting random words to block out whatever he might say next.

"Ben," she says. That's what they call him at school now. "If this is the kind of information they teach you at prep school, then you can start at the local high school next week and save us some money. Have I really been such a bad mother?" she asks him. My brother is chagrined.

"I'm sorry," he says.

The dog sniffs around the house with a half-smile on her face, the result of the stroke she suffered after being caught in the swamp. She is sniffing for a trace of Uncle Freddie, who always used to stroke her stomach in quite the most pleasurable way; you could tell because her crooked smile widened and her long lashes closed over her eyes, ecstatically, when he did it.

Before the private service, people come to the funeral home "to pay their respects." My father says people are very good at this after someone is dead. Who came to pay their respects after the divorce when Uncle Freddie was launched on a new life, set quite adrift? Who came to pay their respects, the sound of their marching feet playing through the long military ward where Freddie lay for months listening instead to the tinny transistor radio, while I smuggled him in chocolates and my mother brought him novels to read to escape his solitariness? Who came to pay their respects, knocking rhythmically on the boardinghouse door in a drum roll of greeting? Daddy is right.

The respectful walk up to the imposing coffin and look at it, this palpable object of death (symbol of a heartbeat suddenly ceased/the eyelids fallen/ two arms in repose/ love, memory and sadness extinguished at the brink of a synapse, like a pulled fuse). Some of them reach out and touch the shiny mahogany surface. Are they feeling for their own deaths? Leaning over the coffin, they're hushed; perhaps they see their own reflections along with those of the banks of flowers, the garden above and beside it. Can they distinguish themselves from the floral pyramid, bending Narcissi, who in the reflected pool fall in love (again) with their own lives?

Uncle Freddie's is the last name written in the Bible. Beside it is the changed date April 4, 1963. That was over two years ago; Uncle Freddie is gone. . . . And who gives a shit what my father said at the funeral anyway.

For instance (the note):

"Will you help me vacuum?" my mother asks one Saturday morning after breakfast.

"All right," I say, grumbling about my status as assistant housekeeper. We pull the Hoover out of the hall closet, and my mother walks first into the living room while I drag it behind.

"What's this?" she says, bending over to pick up a piece of paper from the floor. It is folded. It has her name on it. "I wonder what it is?" she says again, curious.

"It's probably a note from Daddy," I say. "Telling us where he is this morning." As she unfolds it, I plug in the cord, turning to ask. . . . Ashen, she hands me the piece of paper. And her hands to her stomach, my mother suddenly vomits in the center of the rug.

Last year my father left us, with a note, for another life. EN ROUTE TO SINGAPORE, we read. FROM THERE, WHO KNOWS WHAT? I'M SORRY. WARREN

Sorry? my mother said, and her arm swept around the living room. It's time to make a clean break with all this, she said later that same day.

But if you imagined the blue walls collapsing, crumbled like my mother's spirit might otherwise have been if she hadn't been *my* mother, then you would have seen that she was referring to not only the living room, the house itself, but to the then visible woods around it, to the roads that drew neighborhoods in our suburban habitat, to all the territory within what had suddenly become the circumference of our old lives. Was she really pointing, then, to the blue walls of the familiar sky that circumscribed our family years? Revolving, my mother, her arm outstretched, like the radar of the early warning system situated on a hill two miles away.

Only for us the alarm had sounded already, the tiny speck of my father (not approaching but receding on the global screen) had warned us of impending danger. And though we knew we had to be leaving, it seemed there was nowhere safe to go, no new plot of earth that the sky didn't dome. Nowhere free from the idea of danger, its metaphor of carriers loaded with troops or explosives, sailing resolutely toward us (or, in the case of my father, away).

Even so, life promotes itself. If our arms had grown too tired to climb up the precarious rope ladder of the future, searching for some space beyond the sky, a safe haven, then we hung on with our teeth.

Let's start packing, said my mother through clenched jaws.

All right, I said. And the moving men carried my bureau out the front door of our ex-home and down the steps of the spotty pachysandra embankment to the truck waiting empty in the driveway. Its drawers were taped shut so when we arrived in Boston and everything was unloaded at the other end, their contents entered my new room intact. Clean break?

Everything makes up the geography of my memory drawer. Every inch of forest. Every yard of living room carpeting my father tacked wall to wall. The miles I measured and recorded on my bicycle's odometer. An endless historical landscape, it exhibits archaeological relics, landmarks, road signs: reminders of the different directions each of us took.

For instance (the postcards): In my drawer are eleven postcards sent from all over the world in the little more than a year that my father's been at sea. I am placing the cards on my bedroom rug in the shape of a man: two cards each for the arms and legs, two cards for the torso, one for the head. I am dismembering the man now, this splendid pictorial truant, beheading him, pulling his chest in two the way he does mine. Stretching a rubber band around the pack of my father, I toss it, with the Bible, back into the drawer.

"Angela," my mother calls. "If we don't leave soon, you won't be back at school in time for Vespers."

"I'm coming," I tell her.

After my father left, we would find the dog (her particular way of missing) sniffing around his closet and the place where he used to keep his slippers behind the drapes next to the bed. Daddy, who became quite fluent in the language of saying what you mean: the masterpiece of his good-bye note.

─────────── Chapter V ───────────

RUNNING AWAY

SOMETIMES I IMAGINE US, THE FOUR OF US, AS separated from each other in the logic of compass points. Each confined to his or her westerly, southerly, northerly, easterly quadrant, never to surmount the boundaries of our common angles but to continue extending outward—each in a single, arcless leave-taking. This is silly. People are not the imagined, unimaginable distances that directions point to, the opposite, resolute NSEW from a point which I'll choose as my mother's pink front door. Because I know that my brother lives in Connecticut, being "prepped" for an Ivy League college. I know that my father is somewhere, God-knows-where, afloat; that every morning my mother walks four blocks along a Boston street now to her new job at the publishing house. And I know I can call her from the pay phone in the cafeteria for a quarter, which situates me quite nearby.

But what I know is not the way I see it; my compass needle does a dance choreographed by the rapid pulse in my right wrist, and this is the quadrant it describes:

My boarding school abuts Main Street with five white colonial houses. These are the dormitories, where we study in the evenings about Galileo, Mozart, and Proust, later going to sleep to study ourselves. In these buildings the housemothers slip from room to room at night, spectral, quiet enough to enter naturally into our dreams. They mumble numbers, like the counting of sheep. This is called a bedcheck.

Once the count didn't tally. Someone had cleared the fence.

She was hiding, probably, in one of the bushes that grow thick and hedgelike around the waists of the houses. Or she had insomnia and decided to put it to better use, tracing the footworn paths across the backyard from dormitory to dormitory, counting the number of steps between each, in case at the archery range she were blinded in some freak accident. Maybe, for a change, she simply wanted to be alone, checking for a building left carelessly unlocked elsewhere on the campus: the cafeteria with the second-floor infirmary? (Maybe she's hungry . . . maybe she's got the curse; the cramps are killing her; she needs a painkiller locked inside the medicine cabinet. . . .) Locked. The little hatbox of Plexiglas and concrete that can accommodate five seniors on its circular bench for a cigarette? Locked and, besides, she doesn't smoke yet.

Is she traversing the first of the playing fields? Testing her wind? But she's already passed the out-of-bounds line, probably trying the doors of the classroom building, the gym. Locked, locked. And I bet she's too timid to try to climb through a window of the little cabin where the teachers take coffee and post notices for one another, though she wonders what the notices say. She can jump over the tennis nets, one, two, three, but the double doors of the chapel would resist her firm pull on the iron handles if she walked the few yards to its granite steps. Last, there is a padlock on the canoe shed directly behind the chapel at the riverbank. There is nowhere to go.

Where has she been? Making a nighttime foray into her quadrant. And she didn't get caught after all. I walked right in through the front door at 7 A.M., as if I were the housekeeper arriving for work. Nobody noticed.

Saturday afternoon, after a nap in the morning to catch up, all the possible routes are the same. Only now everything is unlocked and there's easy access to any place you want to go. Even the rusty padlock on the canoe shed can be opened with difficulty, if you go to the gym teacher's office and ask for the key, promising not to lose it.

"You ask her," I tell Esther in the driveway outside the gym.

"No, you ask her," Esther says. "She gives me the creeps. She looks at you as though she could read your mind."

"I have nothing to hide," I say. Esther gets a kick out of this. In the office the kilted gym teacher is sitting on the edge of her desk. Her legs are muscular and hairless.

"Hello, Angela," she says. I run the gamut of accusations this might mean.

"Hello, Miss Flynn." I try to keep my mind a blank as she hands me the canoe key from its nail on the wall.

"Don't lose it," she says.

"Good God," I tell Esther in the driveway. "She can read minds. She gave me the key without my even asking for it."

"Oh wow," says Esther. "Emily's not going to believe this."

We lift one of the canoes down off the wall rack. Now we can forget everything, leave everything behind, except for a couple of the aqua cushions that float and the paddles. We drag the canoe to the water's edge, jump in, and push off. . . . In the spring the river floods the fields for hundreds of yards. It smells of green wood, and the different birdcalls are particularly distinct. We leave behind the reasons for the War of the Roses, the Latin declensions, a logarithm. You can travel almost anywhere by canoe, branching out from the natural path of the river in other seasons. I post an eye to avoiding trees, to gliding over the submerged stone walls of the lakelike fields without scraping bottom. We peer into someone's dining room window, surprising the people at lunch paddling over their flooded garden.

"Egg salad," says Esther.

"Food. Food. Do we have to talk about food even out here?" I ask her.

"Relax, Angela," she says. "I just mentioned it in passing."

All the girls at school talk about is food. Brownies, trifle, fudge cake, meringues, strawberry shortcake, shortbread, ladyfingers with whipped cream, butterscotch sundaes, peach Melba, baked Alaska, babas au rhum . . . Or lettuce with vinegar, yogurt, melba toast, cottage cheese, skinless chicken, grapefruit, Tab, tuna packed in water . . . In our world food has transcended its role of sustenance, taking on, chameleonlike, aspects of kindness, security, destruction, and guilt. At meals or in between, we ingest a variety of emotions in different flavors.

We beach the canoe and follow the side path around the Presbyterian church, climbing up through the grave markers of the cemetery that covers an entire hillside. We lie down in the shadow of a small mausoleum. Esther lights up a cigarette while I pull a half-empty bottle of rum from behind a fallen block of granite.

"What'll we do when that runs out?" she asks, eyeing the level of the bottle.

"We'll get Janet to make another deal with the guy in the record store," I tell her. Inmates after a fashion, we have our own ways of securing contraband. I like to imagine myself as George Raft, pacing, waiting for "the boys" to show up with the goods.

"How are we going to get the canoe home?" Esther asks. How would Raft do it?

"Well, we'll just have to return it after Flynn leaves. We'll think up some story. . . . However, they wouldn't know if we returned it today or tomorrow if we lost the key somewhere."

"We couldn't do *that*," she says, smiling conspiratorially. "And, next time, get vodka. They can't smell it on your breath." She yawns. "I'm absolutely devoid of guilt."

"Good," I tell her. "That means you're getting nice and drunk."

The gravestone shadows lengthen; the sun is losing itself behind the buildings of the town below. I take another long pull at the bottle. I'm getting sleepy, like this town that dreams itself static through assassinations, rock 'n' roll, riots in the cities. Rip Van Winkletown. We woke up and got back in time for lights out.

My mother and I are modern women; the phone is our medium. So since the weekly letter home is still obligatory, I don't send her news, just whatever comes to mind. Once I sent her a tract from the Christian Science reading room in town, with the good parts underlined. I sent her a page of my French/English dictionary from the Z's. My favorite word was *zazou* = "zoot suiter" or "cool cat." Another time I sent her an envelope of cut-out words from the newspaper so she could create any number of messages. She picked one, pasted it on a sheet, and sent it back to me. I sent her a chain letter, which had been to California and back seven times, which she broke. Can you afford two years of bad luck? I asked her. I do not intend to have any more bad luck, she said.

Here's an example of a letter I might send:

DEAR MUMMY,
These are my notes for an article I intend to write for the school newspaper, *Voice of the Academy:*

POSITIVE ASPECTS OF SCHOOL LIFE

1. We have freedom of choice in clothing; there are no uniforms. Everything about our life here caters to being "expressive"—to a point. (Example: no pants during class hours.)

2. Last year they abolished the Maypole ritual. (If they want me to dance around that pole again, said one girl, then they're going to have to tie me to one of the ribbons.)

3. You are free to go into town every afternoon. The deli has delicious toasted bagels; cream cheese isn't extra.

4. Our art history teacher cries at the beauty of the paintings she shows us on slides. Once everyone else started crying, too, so she turned off the projector and we wept in the dark.

(Think up more positive aspects as they come to you.)

NEGATIVE ASPECTS

1. Many of us live in triples. The person on the bottom of the double-decker bunk, as I am, gets awakened every time the person on top rolls over. Either there should be a system of rotation or the infirmary should dispense sleeping pills.

2. About going to bed: (a) Everybody brushes her teeth in front of the long row of sinks at the same time, 9:50. This is like being in the army, where they *pay* you to put up with such inconveniences. (b) If you are wide awake, you have to try to sleep anyway. If you can't you are likely to get anxious thinking about things. You should be allowed to read a book instead.

3. Vespers on Sunday night can ruin even the best weekend. There is often a long sermon by a visiting minister who thinks that everyone still believes in God.

4. One of the girls across the hall comes in to weigh herself on our scale every morning at seven. Someone said she has anorexia. Even so, this is no way to be awakened. People ought to show each other a little more consideration since we're in such close quarters.

5. You are expected to be cheery at all times.

6. If you break a rule, you have to saw logs for the fireplaces in winter. This is not the unreasonable part. What is is the fact that the saws are always dull.

7. Only six people signed up to visit the nursing home on Sunday afternoons. If you go away for the weekend, they miss you. And no one will take your place. Think about what it would be like if you were old and no one came to see you.

INCIDENTALS

1. We have two black students and seven Jews.

2. Girls here have names like Bunkie, Brownie, Kitty, and Muffin.

3. A number of them are daughters of famous people: senators, writers, tycoons, a movie star, a ballerina, a king. . . .

4. Some of the seniors have had sexual intercourse. Others prefer to go camping on weekends.

5. Almost everyone wants to go to Radcliffe.

6. Fourteen people belong to the debating society. Ten people have pledged their spare hours to the yearbook and the literary review. Thirty-seven are in the choir. Two make up the science club. Before it was abolished and they took away the office, forty-six people belonged to the "I refuse to participate" club.

7. Mr. Drew is a drug addict.

I think this ought to sell a few papers.

Love,
ANGELA

Angela, I heard my mother's voice through the receiver. You can't print that article.

What about "freedom of the press"?

Darling, you'll get kicked out, she said. And, besides, it's too personal.

What isn't, in life? I asked her.

But she was right, and it makes no sense to put our world into print anyway. Life here, for the most part, is ambiguous. Vicarious. Is the dandified, second-year Spanish teacher having an affair with our American history teacher, a recent Wellesley graduate? Often at lunch you can overhear them heatedly discussing the Spanish Civil War. Are the gym teachers lesbians? Is anybody else? Why did Annette take a leave of absence? Who finked on the Ecuadorian girl and got her thrown out for stealing? We have many questions. For which we supply many different answers. Ours is a world of rumor. What's true and what isn't is not of primary importance. It's the guesswork that keeps us ticking.

Almost all the students here are smart. People like to assign adjectives to each other like "smarter" or "smartest." It is socially important to excel at most subjects, but it is also desirable to have an Achilles' heel so you can join in the grousing from time to time. Mine is art class.

The drawing teacher patiently resketches my drawings, week after week, erasing lines which defy the laws of three-dimensional perspective, redesigning ellipses into fat, satisfying circles.

"Do you think this is an intellectual or a technical problem?" I ask him.

"Write me from college," he says. He is looking through my portfolio for the semester review, and he pulls out a single sketch. "I like that," he says.

"You ought to," I tell him. "You drew it."

When it comes time for the sculpture show, everyone has to exhibit at least one work. He chooses my bust of Oscar Wilde to stand in the back row. It doesn't even look human, let alone like Oscar Wilde.

"If you had a heart, you'd put it in untitled," I tell him. The next semester they let me take chemistry instead.

"Everything is made up of atoms," says my chemistry

teacher. "They are about a hundredth of a millionth of an inch across, and there are many millions of them in a single breath of air. . . ."

"Imagine that," says somebody from the back row. No one can.

"They were once thought to be," the chemistry teacher continues, "hard, indivisible, spherical balls, but it is now known that they are made up of even smaller particles. Each atom has as its center a *nucleus,* consisting of *protons* and *neutrons.* Orbiting the nucleus are *electrons.*"

Soon we are discussing neutrons changing into protons and vice versa. This has something to do with nuclear deterioration.

The teacher turns her back to us and writes on the board in bright yellow chalk: $_1H^3 \rightarrow \beta^- + _2He^3$ or $H^3 {}^{\beta-} \rightarrow He^3$

This was the beginning of the "blank-stare syndrome." I ended up with a forty-five average which, when computed on a sliding scale, turned out to be a B+. It is not necessary for girls to be proficient at science.

Sometimes my mother drives out from Boston to take me to lunch at the nearby Howard Johnson's.

"How's everything?" my mother will ask.

"A little constricting," I tell her.

"Darling, are you happy?" she asks.

"I guess I am." Happiness is a peculiar word; it takes on different meanings at different times. Here we experience a kind of happiness of opposition, like defeated Senate candidates, spent athletes who have lost the race by a stride, tragedians who cannot elude the fate of the text.

"I got a terrific manuscript this morning," my mother will say. Perhaps: "A novel about a woman who goes mad in the Bahamas. A pleasure to read."

"The Bahamas . . ." I might say, or sometimes I just lean back against the orange plastic booth and listen to her plot synopsis. It is reassuring when my mother takes me to lunch. My mother, the touchstone by which I measure my changing sensibility.

"Why is Edna St. Vincent Millay so sad?" I ask her.

"Poets are often sad," says my mother.

"Why?"

"Because it's their job to see clearly," she says.

I never want the lunches to end. Or if they must, I always want to go back to the city with my mother. But you have to persevere; it's important to branch out into places where you're not completely understood already. That way, you find things out about yourself. My mother told me this, and my mother is usually right.

On the way back to school we pass the reformatory.

"Last week," I tell her, "one of my classmates and her mother were stopped at gunpoint on this very road, at that YIELD sign, and forced by two escaped convicts into the back seat."

"How awful," says my mother. "Lock your door, Angela." I click down the button.

"One took the wheel," I describe. "And the other sat beside him, occasionally glancing over his shoulder at the two hostages. Then at a red light, at a hand signal from the mother, the two women threw open their doors and jumped out just as the light turned green and the car began to accelerate.

"The mother rolled along the white center line. The daughter pitched the gravel of the roadbed in all directions."

"How do you know that?" my mother asks.

"Because that's how it must have happened," I tell her. "It's logical isn't it? Look at all that gravel by the side of the road. Besides, I'm trying to tell a story, to make it interesting. . . ."

"Go on, go on," she says.

"Anyway, they ran directly into the woods for safety. That's what I would have done, too . . . slowly making their way back to town. When they got there, they gave the police a very accurate description of the two escapees, who were caught in New Hampshire and returned to their cells within forty-eight hours."

"My word," she says.

I like to imagine my mother and myself involved in similar heroics. But we rarely get the chance. My mother says she's glad enough, that daily life takes more heroics than I might guess.

But I know. And, besides, beyond the realm of my fantasies I am a coward, a girl:

"Angela," my mother says, "get the broom." I race past the living room, down the long hall to the kitchen, dodging back and forth as if I sensed land mines, my head bobbing up and down, to confuse the bat as to my whereabouts. I grab the broom, wielding it like a torch thrower, dashing back to the safety of my mother's bedroom. I can hear it squeaking.

"Here you are." And my mother walks out to do battle with the furry, ratlike bat.

"Angela," she calls. "Come out and help."

"I don't want to," I yell from the bedroom. She pushes open the door, furious.

"Do you think *I* want to fight the bat?" she asks me. My mother is being sarcastic. Her medium-length blond hair is sticking out in all directions, as if the result of this fright. The bat will surely get in it.

"But you're my mother," I protest.

"That's no excuse," she says. "Oh, if only your father were here . . ." But this shames us both and we rush back out into the foyer to where the bat has flown, aroused by our frenzied attack. My mother tries to sweep the bat in the desired direction (toward the open front door of the apartment) with the broom, as if it were a dust pile. Which it isn't. We must view the broom from a radical perspective. We must consider it a weapon. This is hard for us to do.

"Call the little city hall," says my exasperated mother. "Have them send out a rescue unit of some sort. . . ."

"It's two o'clock in the morning," I tell her.

"Thank you, Big Ben," she says.

The bat flutters. Its wingspan is enormous. We retreat to the bedroom.

"Let's think," says my mother, sitting down on the bed.

I do. I imagine the bat biting me, or worse, my mother. Hanging onto her shoulders with its claws, digging in. I'll have to pull it off her with my hands; I'll feel its heart pulsing wildly beneath the fur of its chest; it will be repulsive. The membranous wings will beat at my face. I'll have to throw it to the floor

and crush it, writhing, slender bones snapping, with my bare
foot. But could I?

"Oh hell," says my mother finally, and in her pink bathrobe
she charges out once more in pursuit of the bat. I follow behind
the barrier of her outrage. She is wielding the broom like a
charwoman gone mad, at last fed up with a life that has
presented her with only dust and dirt. Crazy with the repetitive-
ness, the futility of cleaning, tonight she will rid her domain, the
world for that matter, of all its dirt, all its troubles. She drives
the bat through the apartment doorway into the outside hall, but
she continues swinging, waving the broom like a flag of victory
or an SOS (has she forgotten?) until I shut the door with a slam
and bolt it against anything that might harm us. My heart is
aglow with the melody of a torch song for my mother, for her
laced armor, for her bravery.

"I guess women," she says, wearily resting the broom
against the wall, "must learn to fend for themselves."

INCIDENTALS 7. Mr. Drew, our theater teacher, not
only conducts the rehearsals for the school plays, but he builds
the sets, prompts, paints the scenery, and hangs the lights
himself. He has an unusual amount of energy; if you meet him at
the water fountain unexpectedly, you are likely to catch sight of
a red pill or two in his hand, on the way from the pocket to the
mouth. This is speed; everyone says so.

One night around midnight I climbed down the fire escape
for a walk. At the theater, light glowed from the doorjamb, so I
opened it, sneaking inside to the back of the auditorium. He was
by himself, hanging lights for the upcoming talent show. I was
the audience. I sat in the dark in the last row of seats, and this is
what I saw:

He leaned out from the top rung of the ladder, a wrench in
his hand. He wasn't tall enough to reach, but nevertheless he
lunged for the ceiling pipe, held on for a second with one hand,
with the other made a few quick turns to tighten the bolt on the
spotlight, and fell to the floor. Its beam cast his descending
shadow onto the back wall; it projected the steplike angles of the
piled mattresses on which he landed. He picked himself up,

climbed the ladder, and did it again. I watched him in his up-and-down progress for a while.

I'm not going to do this on talent night, he called unexpectedly to the back where I was sitting.

No, I don't suppose you are, I said. He began to smoke a cigarette and I let myself out into the night. Neither of us mentioned it afterward.

My theater teacher wishes he could fly; he is hoping for gravity to suspend itself just once as he releases the pipe from his hand. He'll ascend, then, to the skylight at the top of the sloped ceiling, open it, and continue to rise.

This isn't realistic. Speed should make running away a lot easier, but you have to choose to proceed in the right direction.

POSITIVE ASPECTS 3. Two brothers, Irving and Joey, own the delicatessen where we go every afternoon for bagels. The school keeps them in business. Every afternoon Irv stands behind the counter in his apron with the school emblem sewn on the chest. So does Estelle, Joey's wife.

Where's Joey? I asked one afternoon.

Who knows? said Irv. Afterward, Irv is standoffish. He wishes he hadn't told me. For weeks, Joey isn't at his usual spot beside the grill, then he's regular for a month or two. Then he's sporadic again.

One day, no one was there. The sign on the locked door read:

> *MOVING TO THE CATSKILLS. HAVE*
> *BOUGHT A STEAK HOUSE. GOOD-BYE*
> *AND BEST WISHES TO EVERYBODY,*
> *ESPECIALLY MONA, DIANE, ESTHER,*
> *JOANNIE, ANGELA AND SANDY.*

Below that they wrote the address of the new restaurant. I took it down.

NEGATIVE ASPECTS 7. When you open the front door to the nursing home, a bell rings. The chairs in the vestibule don't match, and an attendant out of uniform (it's the weekend) nods as we walk through the gray door with the window that is a mirror on the other side into the long corridor that smells of urine and disinfectant.

We enter the rooms in teams of two. All of the rooms are doubles. Sometimes one of the beds is empty. It is hard to remember who it might be that has died.

I like best reading *Tom Sawyer* to the blind woman with the long white braid. It reaches halfway down the expanse of her nightgown when she stands up. She's a tall woman and she's been growing it since she was sixteen. About your age, she said, and look at me now in a boarding school for the oldsters.

"Come in," she says, on hearing my footsteps to the door of her room. The doors at the nursing home must always be left open. "I missed you," she says, if I've been away the weekend before. The first time I met her she asked me to come closer, and reaching out with her hands she drew her fingers across my face, playing over my cheekbones, across the lips, under the chin. Her fingers defined my forehead; she lingered on my closed eyes. I could feel them twitch. You're pretty, she said.

Her roommate, the Swedish woman, sits in an easy chair on her own side of the room. I stand holding her hands; I smile at her; I offer her cookies. I try to make her take several, but she never takes more than two. She doesn't speak English.

Often, we run into her walking up and down the corridor; she always in a great hurry, muttering to herself in Swedish (we think). Every week or so she makes a break for the front door, and if the attendant is sleeping, she lets herself outside and heads off in any direction along the tree-lined street. She is trying to find Sweden, but they always find her first and take her back to the home. The nurses say she is crazy. But who can tell? No one understands her. No one speaks her language.

NEGATIVE ASPECTS 4. Judy is anorectic. She has stopped eating altogether, except for an occasional nibble of lettuce, a bite of someone else's hamburger. Judy weighs eighty-five pounds. I ought to know; I've read it on the scale. When Judy looks into the mirror, she sees a fat girl who could stand to lose weight, in the interests of health and aesthetics. She weighs eighty-five pounds. Twice I have seen Judy fall to the ground as she walks because the shrinking muscles of her calves can no longer sustain the weight of even this meager body.

Judy is running away from herself. Everything is made up of atoms, said my chemistry teacher. Judy is sending away little atoms of herself every day. Her flesh is fleeing her bones. She hopes to disappear from herself bit by bit; she is imploding. This is not a conventional manner of running away, but it works. Eventually, Judy was sent home, and a psychiatrist convinced her to cohere.

There are many different kinds of running away. In some cases it is desirable. In others, it is an act of cowardice, neglect. In still others, it is not entirely clear if the individual is culpable: Scared at the entropy of existence, a person is often tempted to run away from his daily life before it runs away from him.

──────── Chapter VI ────────

CRAZY EIGHTS

S OMETIMES I THINK THAT GROWING UP IS SIMPLY the process of unlearning most of the ideas that you understood as describing the world quite accurately when you were young. And just as the face of the physical world is always changing, these concepts (of permanence, goodness, patriotism, happiness, valor . .·. the list goes on) are gradually eroded and transformed, as surely as a tidal beach. Waves of circumstances, and not unusual ones, see to it.

"Fairy tales, fairy tales. Everything is fairy tales," I tell my mother, pointing to the television set. "Look at that," I continue. "People don't live like that. The son obeys the father. Nobody fights at dinner. The dog never gets run over. No one is ever depressed. Bullshit."

"Angela," says my mother. "Why not change the channel if it upsets you so much?"

"That's the American panacea," I tell her. "Changing the channel. Only you can't change the channel on your life."

"Well have a beer or something," she says.

"Beer and TV. We're just a regular American family, aren't we?" After a month of summer vacation, we're getting on each other's nerves. My mother's glasses rest on the tip of her nose. She puts down her *Publishers Weekly*.

"Angela," she says, "don't give up on the world altogether. You're only sixteen and you've got quite a bit of time left to spend in it."

"I know," I tell her, "but I can't seem to adjust. Things haven't turned out as I expected."

"You're just at a low point," says my mother.

"It's boring," I tell her. "I'm going stir crazy." She thinks for a moment, chewing on the frame of her glasses.

"Would you like to play crazy eights?" she suggests. This turns out to be just what I would like to do, another of my mother's perpetual good ideas, with which she adjusts my moods as easily as she does the temperature of the oven with a slight turn of the dial on the top of the stove. My mother wins seven games in a row. I never mind losing to my mother.

"Lucky at cards, unlucky at love," she jokes. But a look, like a blush or a ripple suggestive of some below-the-surface tumult, a seaquake, crosses her face. As she talks about my father, it is without bitterness. "People are who they are," she says. "Wishing them otherwise will never change them. He was"— she corrects herself with an effort to the present tense—"is the most exciting man I ever met. However, he was never cut out for family life. This was something I didn't even recognize as a possibility when he asked me to marry him or long afterward, for that matter. . . ." My mother and I are students in the same school, with its daily curriculum of unlearning the old world and redefining the new.

Other times she curses him. That bastard, she calls him. The most selfish man in the universe. Juvenile. Irresponsible, she says. I hope he falls off the goddamned deck and drowns. But we know she doesn't mean this.

Recently, I can't remember what Daddy looks like. Lying in bed at night, I used to conjure him, Daddy who one day hid himself behind a curtain and when we drew it back had disappeared. The sorceress who would find him again, pulling her father out of the black silk top hat of night. At these times, everything I knew came to me in the form of my father, everything I remembered was his face.

Now his image escapes me; the world is a fuzzy ball viewed from too far out in space. Sometimes it almost makes me physically ill. I can't remember what my father looks like.

If I run to the bookshelf in the living room and reach for the photo albums marked "1947–1958" and "1959–1964," it calms me. I look at the wedding pictures, his Marine Corps portrait, Daddy in his tennis whites, Daddy in a suit. He had changed remarkably little in the seventeen years of his marriage: same crew cut, intense brown eyes, thin lips. Sometimes he is smiling.

Besides the photographs, nothing here reminds us of Daddy. We threw out everything he left behind when we moved. It wasn't much; Daddy didn't care about *things*. Benjie wanted to tear out all the snapshots that he was in, but my mother told him this wasn't mature.

Sometimes I write questions to my father in a notebook during class. When are you coming back? I ask him. Will I like you when you do? Are you happier in your transient's life? Do you get seasick? Are you ever heartsick? Do you sleep with prostitutes in port? Do you miss us?

In spite of myself, I am in awe of my father's leaving. He grows in my mind to the proportions of a giant, a Paul Bunyan, a Charles Atlas of the soul. The vast freedom of an aquatic globe inside him, the immense strength of his single word *enough* takes my breath away. I imagine him gathering himself up, like a boy his favorite belongings, tying himself into knots, nevertheless, like the boy his bandana after all the possessions are placed inside. I see him set out, not turning once to look back (how could he?), on a road. To where? And in search of what? Something. At least, something. Whatever it may turn out to be or even if he never finds it.

On summer evenings I wish I were my father, wending his way through the crowded stalls of a foreign bazaar, noisy with other languages; sitting for hours in barrooms counting the number of times a fly lands on a glass, placing bets on the frequency; contemplating, from a ship's bridge, how a stray cloud disappears quite suddenly over the horizon. But no, flip the coin of my father's departure to land on the other side, and he's everything wrong with the world: a millionaire's conscience, the chemical aftertaste of poisoned water, a bad dream. He's the wrong direction on the map, the ciphered message which when decoded warns of disaster too late to be averted, a baby suckling a pistol barrel. He left my mother holding the bag.

Maybe this is unusual. Maybe it isn't. Men invented work so they could go off to it. But Daddy was different, Daddy did it with style. Daddy took off. . . . And what's the answer? How much do we owe ourselves and how much do we owe everybody else? Like in algebra class, it's one of the equations I never can prove.

My mother pauses in her solitaire game on the couch beside me.

"Hello?" she calls into the hall. It's the sound of the front door opening. Ben and Ace come into the living room, exploding the atmosphere with their particularly male tread. Next to my brother, my mother thinks that Ace is the most charming young man she knows. I would not qualify this judgment with my brother. "Did you have a good time?" she asks.

"Yes," they say. "We had a very good time."

"Is there any apple pie?" my brother asks.

"Apple pie?" says Ace.

"Frozen," says my brother.

"I like frozen better," says Ace. This is one of the reasons my mother is so fond of him.

"It's on the stove, Ace," says my mother. To my brother she says: "I am a working woman. My free time is precious and limited. Sometimes I make pies from scratch; other times I prefer to go to a movie or walk along the Common to reassure myself that the American concept of 'leisure time' is not just a figment of the cultural imagination."

"Is there any ice cream to go on it?" my brother asks.

When I discuss with my mother whether or not my brother is a lost cause, she says that he is just going through a phase. What phase is that? I ask her. Coming into manhood, she says. He feels it necessary to be entirely courageous, and this kind of courage usually dictates ignoring what makes you uncomfortable (into which category mothers and sisters often fit). We'll work on him when he has things back in perspective, she says. Until then, bear with him; he's your brother.

I think I see her point. Clearly the only interest that my brother and Ace have in life is in getting laid.

How far did you get? Third. Maybe you didn't get her drunk enough. She said she was starting to feel queasy. That was because of you, you faggot, not the liquor. . . .

You two make me sick, I tell them.

"Martha wasn't at home," Ben says, returning from the kitchen. "She went to the Cape, after all." He sits down cross-legged on the floor, and Ace sits between the two of us on the couch. He pinches me.

"Cut it out," I tell him, and I pinch him back.

"So we went to Stephanie's," continues Ben. "Wow, is her older sister a knockout. . . ."

"If you don't stop talking about how girls look instead of what they're like, I'm going to knock *you* out," I tell my brother.

"Here we go again," he says.

"Angela," says my mother, "if you can't think of anything nice to say, then don't say anything."

"That is the most stupid aphorism I've ever heard," I tell her. "Who thought it up, Shirley Temple? Besides, if everyone paid attention to it, life would be just like the goddamned television."

"Oh brother," says Ben.

"Nothing would ever happen either. What about Aaron Burr and Alexander Hamilton? What about Laurel and Hardy? Nothing would be serious and nothing would be funny. Life is based on conflict. Why do you think we have a two-party system? Ben, it is true that Stephanie's sister has the largest breasts I've ever seen. And if that's what you mean, you can say it in front of us, you know. This is the 1960s."

"Well, I don't know," says my mother.

"Come on, Mummy. You always say we can talk about anything. Don't you?" Sometimes my mother has to be reminded of the ramifications and varied applications of her own theories.

"I guess you're right," she says. She lights a cigarette. "They're that big, are they?" she says, puffing at quite a rate.

"Like watermelons," says Ace.

"When Angela gets her license, they'll have to add an extra lane to Storrow Drive just for her," says my brother at breakfast.

"Do you have plenty of insurance on the car?" Ace asks my mother.

"I'm sure Angela will be a very competent driver," she says.

"If you want to be on the wrong verb of a hit-and-run

accident," I tell Ben and Ace, "keep it up."

"Is that anyway to speak to a guest?" Ace asks me. But he's no guest. He spends most of his time at our house; sometimes he stays for weeks. He calls my mother "Momma Ros." She calls him "number two," meaning second son, the way Charlie Chan does. Though the cast of characters is constantly changing, it seems we always have a family of four.

It is now ten o'clock. Our family is scattered: my mother at her office, Ben and Ace at the soda factory where they drive the forklifts, and me in a classroom of the elementary school around the corner from our apartment.

The instructor pulls handfuls of blue booklets from a large carton on the floor and piles them in stacks on his desk at the front of the room. He counts the number of booklets in each stack twice. Then he takes off his jacket, rolls up his shirt sleeves, and sits on the edge of the desk, facing us. Already he has our full attention, but he pauses, preparing himself, and then he begins:

"I am your driver education instructor," he says "My name is John Manzonianini. I won't bother to write that on the board because no one will be able to pronounce it anyway. Just call me Dr. M.

"I hold a master's degree in education," he continues. "I've been a driving instructor for thirteen years.

"I know how much all of you want to pass the state test for your driver's license. And I'm going to see that every one of you does. But what I pride myself on is not just the training of drivers; it is the training of good drivers. You'll start out being safe in my hands and then graduate into being safe in your own hands. . . ."

Everyone is rapt. Dr. M. is making us think about driving in a different way than we ever imagined. Good driving is a responsibility, a duty. Driving is like voting.

"Let's not devote any more time," he says finally, "to the philosophy of driving. Let's get our teeth into the text."

Page one shows a large diagram of a car. Everything is labeled.

"Look at the picture and find the part of the car marked *a*," he says. "You'll see in the glossary on the right that this is the steering wheel." We identify all the parts of the car: the headlights, the indicators, the trunk, the cigarette lighter. . . . Then we move on to the diagram of the engine, a less familiar landscape.

"This is the radiator cap," says Dr. M. "These are the spark plugs. Note that the battery must be filled with water at all times. It isn't necessary to go to a garage to have it checked; it's a simple procedure to maintain the proper water level yourself. The generator . . . The crankshaft . . . The flybelt . . ." The thigh bone's connected to the knee bone. The knee bone's connected to the . . . Our first day is very confusing and prompts a lot of questions:

"Why does the air mix with the gas at all?"

"What causes a backfire?"

"Why don't cars have six wheels?"

"If you get stopped for speeding, is it better to wait inside the car for the policeman to approach or to get out before he comes?"

"That is not an appropriate question," says Dr. M. "Class dismissed."

"I am thinking of a word," says Dr. M. one morning, "and I am thinking about its etymology. This word has no linguistic history; you might say that it came about as the result of a sort of spontaneous generation." He savors this phrase. "Spontaneous generation. Because, you see, it was coined one day by a man who bet a friend that he could invent a word that would eventually be accepted into common usage. Do any of you know what the word is?" Dr. M. knows all sorts of interesting facts.

"*Piston?*" guesses a boy in the back row.

"*Rocker arm,*" says someone else.

"No," says Dr. M. "*Quiz.*" He hands out a mimeographed sheet of questions. "These are taken from the actual state written exam. All except for the essay, which I made up," he says. "You have fifteen minutes."

QUIZ

1. You want to back out of your driveway. You see children playing nearby. Before you start to move your car, you should:
    a. race your motor to warn the children that you are moving
    (b.) walk to the back of your car to be sure the way is clear
    c. sound your horn so the children will hear you
    d. tell the children to stay away from the driveway

2. What should you do when you are going to enter a highway from a private road?
    a. stop completely even if there is no traffic
    b. drive out fast to keep up with the other cars
    (c.) yield the right-of-way to highway traffic or pedestrians
    d. stop with part of the car on the highway to warn other drivers

3. What does a "slow-moving vehicle" emblem look like?
    a. a round green sign
    (b.) a diamond-shaped yellow sign
    c. a triangular orange sign
    d. a square red sign

4. What is the best thing to do if your car becomes disabled on an expressway?
    (a.) get your car off the road
    b. leave your car where it is and call a tow truck
    c. get out of your car and walk a safe distance away
    d. wait for the police to give you a push

5. When does a blind person legally have the right-of-way?
    a. when wearing light-colored clothing
    b. when being accompanied by another person
    (c.) when using a white cane or being led by a seeing-eye dog
    d. when wearing completely black glasses

Essay: Describe the execution of a hill start:

*(This I can do.) Make sure the emergency
break is on; start the engine; depress the clutch, shift
to first gear; press lightly on the gas pedal until the
engine races slightly; look over your shoulder for
cars; release the emergency brake while easing out the
clutch.*

"Don't pop the clutch," Dr. M. tells me for the third time.

"That's easy enough for you to say," I tell him. "I'm not trying to pop the clutch, you know." There are no hills in Boston steeper than the lanes of Beacon Hill. "You need an airplane for this kind of incline."

Ronald and Mrs. Bloom are laughing in the back seat. They can laugh now; when it's my turn to "observe," I will laugh too, at one of them. I will discuss the urban crisis; I will sing along with the radio. Dr. M. fiddles with the dial of the small transistor that is propped on the dashboard of the car.

"Couldn't we have something with a beat this time?" asks Ronald.

"You know, a rock 'n' roll or a soul station," I tell Dr. M. "Like WMEX."

"OK," he says, "but then Mrs. Bloom gets her station for half an hour and then I get mine."

"Thank you," says Mrs. Bloom. "I don't know how they can listen to all that screaming. I'm sure I don't know if it might even cause deafness."

"I doubt it," says Ronald.

"Try again, Angela," the Doctor prompts. And this time I am successful.

"Bravo," they call from the back seat. "Hooray." I head out to Charles Street and the traffic.

"I think it's unfair," I venture, "that I always seem to get the height of rush hour."

"That's because you've made the most progress," says Dr. M.

"In that case, I withdraw my complaint," I tell him. Ronald, whose face I see in the rear-view mirror, is clearly irritated at being considered second-best. Mrs. Bloom isn't even in the running.

"Did you know," Dr. M. asks him, "that the meadowlark has a range of three hundred notes?" But Ronald doesn't appreciate this kind of information. "Let's go to Cambridge," says Dr. M. "The temperature must be over ninety degrees. I know a good place to stop for ice cream. Take your next right," he says. I do. "You forgot your hand signal." He enjoys telling me this.

"If you put on the blinker and down-shift and turn the steering wheel, what arm do you use for the hand signal?" I ask him. "Besides," I gesture at the cars whooshing by us in all directions, "no one else uses hand signals."

"They are not graduates," he replies, "of the Harvard Annex Driving School. You'll thank me later. Don't resist the technique."

"All right. How many different songs does a nightingale sing?" I ask to appease him.

"Twenty-four," he says. It is hard to stump Dr. M.

"What flavor are you going to have?" Mrs. Bloom asks Ronald.

I've gotten used to being passed on a four-lane road, but I still find it unnerving when the cars flash by in the opposite direction. What if as the result of a slight error in judgment one of them sideswiped us? What if the driver of an oncoming vehicle had cardiac arrest at the wheel and swerved to our side of the pavement? Be alert to all possibilities, Dr. M. says. You can never predict what the other driver will do next; the good driver is the defensive driver; personality should never enter into driving procedure.

"Goddamned road hog." The red convertible on the left is inching over into our lane.

"Look out," says Ronald.

"Shut up, Ronald," I tell him.

"Never let the other driver get a rise out of you," says Dr. M. "Merely compensate for his errors."

"Did you want me to compensate us right into a telephone pole?" I ask him.

"You are a very competent driver, Angela," he says. "But your temper isn't compatible with a good driving attitude. There

is no need for aggression," he says. "And never so much of a
rush as we think. We drive cars beyond the speed limit; we
break the sound barrier in airplanes; we launch missiles from
submarines that part the water at incredible speeds. Everything
goes too far, too fast. We should pattern our lives along the
rotation of the celestial bodies, the planets that spin out a
reasonable time in their accustomed orbits. There's an example
for you. Listen to all this honking," he says. "Can that match the
music of the spheres?" Dr. M., our philosopher of motion,
writes something in his notebook.

"Angela," he continues, "I'm giving you a B— for today.
When we stop for ice cream, Mrs. Bloom can take the
wheel. . . ." The Doctor is right.

"Is it safe to drive while eating a cone?" asks Mrs. Bloom.
Ronald laughs. It is never safe to drive with Mrs. Bloom. Am I
going too fast? she asks. Is my arm at the proper angle?, when
she hand-signals. Is this an intersection? If it is, she recites out
loud all the right-of-way regulations.

"You can eat it in the parking lot," says Dr. M. "Take a
left," he says. I miss it.

"You didn't warn me in time."

I take the next left. Our car screeches to a halt, though my
foot is still on the accelerator. What has happened? Is this a
breakdown? But I realize that Dr. M. has just used the extra set
of brakes on his side of the car for the first time. This shakes me
up.

"Never take a turn without my explicit instructions," he
says. "It isn't just your own life you're responsible for, but
everyone else's, too. Angela, always be alert to the rules of the
road. They're there for a reason. Look," he says, pointing to the
sign. "This street is one-way."

"Think of it this way," says my brother. "It will keep you
from getting sunburned."

"I would prefer just to sit under the umbrella, if you don't
mind," I tell him.

"Think of it as a happening," says Ace. "You are a
performer."

I am buried in the sand; the only part of my body aboveground is my head. They refuse to dig me out.

I try to use this experience creatively. I try to imagine myself as a mummy: King Tut, for instance. . . . I am not lonely, buried with all my servants, a supply of money, and food enough to last me all along the journey of the dead.

This is what consciousness after death is like. The feeling is of insularity, if you shut your eyes all the world is selfhood, you experience a peculiar detachment from human concerns. Perhaps it would not be so bad to be dead; there is no guilt (dread of the past), no anxiety (dread of the future).

I am cocooned, wound round in white bandages to assuage the wounds of living. I am on my way to the hospital for spent souls. Some people don't die of disease or accident; they merely tire out. It takes an eternity to make them well again. They sip fruit nectars; they are cared for by kindly middle-aged attendants (we know them as angels); there is a constant, harmonious humming piped in over the intercoms, as if the planets sung through closed lips, what Dr. M. calls the music of the spheres. The dice sets with which the patients judge their progress, a kind of self-diagnosis according to how their luck runs, are of ivory. . . . The bed gowns are mauve. . . .

The tide is coming in. A white tongue suddenly laps where my feet should be. Now the beach is a straitjacket. It's solitary confinement, a torture chamber. It's an oven big enough for people. A womb in need of Caesarean section.

"Let me out," I scream for Ace and Ben. Let me out, loud enough for an entire mile of sunbathers to hear. I try to move but can't; this is the cement suit I wear through the imagined death by drowning, gangster-style. Where are they? The sand registers pounding feet.

"All right. All right. Calm down, Angela," says my brother.

No, the thought of an actual death is not comforting; dread is far preferable. It reflects no violet shades. It's black like a monochromatic rainbow at the bottom of the sea where no light permeates.

"You certainly are excitable," says Ace, digging around my

shoulders. I look at him. If I were six feet tall, I wouldn't be excitable either. I would have successfully defended myself against the two of them in the first place. This is what Khrushchev said to the American people: we will bury you. Much of the dynamic of the world, both internationally and on a very personal level, has to do with the use of force. This isn't right.

"If you ever do that again," I tell my brother, "I will have no choice but to take unpleasant and extreme action."

"Which is what?" he asks.

"Use your imagination," I tell him. This is cold war strategy. Nothing real is as horrifying to humankind as the things it imagines. Take Ben for example: he drops the subject.

"Actually," he says, "as a brother I've been very good to you. I know of older brothers and sisters who have locked their siblings in closets, shaved off all their hair, baked them Ex-Lax brownies. I never did anything like that to you," he says. " . . . I never thought of it.

"I used to take you with me when I went places in the neighborhood on my bike. I let you play with my electric train; you had your own engineer's cap. I always included you in baseball games. I often chose you to be on my side. . . . You came to all my birthday parties even when you were the only girl. In kindergarten when it was my turn to invite a friend from the nursery school for afternoon break, I always invited you."

"You didn't know anyone else," I tell him, but I am touched by the list of kindnesses.

He and Ace unpack lunch from the cooler while I brush off the sand.

"You just play lady," says Ace. This is an expression he has picked up from my mother. What she means is that she will no longer continue with her duties as homemaker and mother; what this could be called more accurately is "going on strike." I recline on the blanket and don't lift a finger until everything is spread out. They eat four sandwiches each. I have a Fresca and cheese from a plastic bag.

"Tell me," says Ace, "are you on a diet?"

"None of your business."

"I bet you're on the lookout for a boyfriend, Angela," he says.

"Hardly . . ."

"A short one, with glasses and kinky hair . . ."

". . . who wears his pants belted up above his waist," finishes my brother.

"Looks are irrelevant."

"A poet perhaps," says my brother. " 'Tyger! Tyger! burning bright . . .' "

"Well, what do you want in a girl?" I ask them. I regret asking.

"This," says Ace, flipping through a magazine to a page where a sultry and elegant woman is advertising a kind of Scotch. Her dress is cut very low. Her glass bears a red lipstick stain. She doesn't appear to be thinking about liquor.

"Don't you care about brains and sensitivity?" I ask them. "Is this woman well read? Could she survive shipwrecked on a desert island with just one pack of matches and a razor blade? Does it touch her that the doves return to Capistrano every year? Does it matter to her whether or not the world is finite?"

"With her it could be infinite," says my brother.

"And how," says Ace.

On the way home I drive, for practice. Ace is in the middle.

"Don't pinch me while I'm driving," I tell him.

"Don't worry," he says. "The odds are against us already. How long have you had your learner's permit?"

"Three days," says Ben. "Put on your seat belt."

They laugh at my hand signals. They laugh when I come to a complete stop at Stop signs. I'm fed up.

"The signs are there for a reason," I tell them. "If you're lucky enough to get a little help in life, a few hints, you may as well pay attention to them."

"There *is* some validity in that," Ace tells my brother.

"Angela's not so dumb," he says.

When it is time to parallel park, my brother says he will take over.

"No thank you," I tell him. On the fourth try I swing into

the curb perfectly. "We never learn to do things we don't attempt. One of Mummy's friends from the suburbs," I tell Ace, "will not drive into the city because she is afraid of the traffic. This kind of thing is not going to happen to me."

"Thank you, Susan B. Anthony," says my brother. Sometimes he surprises me. I didn't think he even knew who Susan B. Anthony was. I'll tell this to my mother when we get inside; it will make her happy to know that all the energy she puts into what she calls my brother's "awareness" is not in vain.

"Hello?" she calls from the living room. She is drinking a glass of rosé and reading the paper. "Put your suits in the tub," she says.

"All right," we say, and after showering it's time for dinner.

"Where's the party tonight?" asks my mother.

"At Martha's," says Ace.

"If you two get too drunk," says my mother, "then I want Angela to drive."

"What if I get too drunk?" I ask her. She frowns.

"Then you should just leave the car there and take a cab."

"You're very practical, Moma Ros," says Ace.

"I haven't been a mother all these years for nothing," she says.

This is true. My mother is particularly good at giving advice. When I tell her I am not popular at these parties, she tells me that although this can be very painful it's not the end of the world. Usually, when I come home afterward and talk it over with her, this seems correct. But at the time I have trouble seeing her point.

The girls, I tell her, all remark to each other what "cute outfits" they're wearing. The boys drink a lot of beer and punch each other in the shoulder. Is this what it's going to be like from now on? I ask her.

Did you dance? my mother asks.

With Ben and Ace.

They were probably the two nicest boys there, she says.

Then we play crazy eights or gin rummy and discuss how next year when Ben and Ace go to college they will certainly bring home more interesting friends for me to meet.

What will they be like? I ask her.

Oh quite sensitive, she says. And probably good-looking, too.

That would be nice, I say. Do you think Ace is sensitive and good-looking? I ask her.

Why, of course, she says.

So do I, but I keep it to myself.

Tonight will be like all the rest. I wish I hadn't come, standing here on the steps, but like parallel parking, partygoing is something you have to keep trying at.

"Hi, Angela," says Martha, opening the door. "And hi there, you two. A beer, boys?" My mother calls Martha the Perle Mesta of Cambridge.

Someone named Ralph tells me about the courses he plans to take in college. If he gets A's, he will surely get into medical school. If he gets B's he still might get in, but then his "boards" will have to be "really strong."

"Do you know why Christ didn't get into college?" I ask him.

"You mean Jesus," he says, " . . . no." He looks around the room. "You want another beer?"

"Because he got nailed on his boards," I tell him.

"That's pretty good," he says.

"My dentist told me that. If you don't become a doctor," I say, "maybe you could be a dentist. Only then you'd have to improve your sense of humor."

When it is time to leave, we are all rather drunk.

"I'll drive," I suggest.

"No, no. I'll drive," says my brother.

"And I'll fly," says Ace. "Oh, am I going to have a headache tomorrow."

"Think of it this way," I tell them. "I'm the one who has most recently been familiarized with all the rules and regulations of the road. Whereas one of you might forget to signal for a turn or drive too fast through a congested area or even get us into an accident, God forbid, I probably won't."

"Your sister is making a great deal of sense," says Ace.

I drive home, following every practice the Doctor taught me, making turns as smooth as Saturn on its axis, carrying the three of us along in the front seat of the car as snugly as water droplets in the bowl of the Little Dipper. The streetlights sparkle in the fog—a Milky Way to illuminate our path homeward.

"You're our guardian angel," says Ace as we park at the front door to the apartment building, lucky tonight. He kisses me on the lips.

The two of them go to the kitchen for something to eat. I put a stack of classical records on the stereo; I imagine the black discs spinning in space, revolving at 33⅓, being played by the needle-like ray of a star. I turn it up so loud that it covers all earthly sounds: their two voices, the conversations I remember from the party, the traffic below. I waltz with myself.

My mother pokes her head into the den.

"Angela, could you please turn that down?" she asks.

"I'm in a mood," I tell her.

"Well, just turn it down a little bit then," she says, "and I'll shut the double doors."

When they come back, I take turns waltzing with my brother and Ace. They waltz with each other. We dance a ballet which I choreograph for the three of us. I am the bird. They are the hunters. I make flying leaps, unexpected spectacular pirouettes to elude them. We are sweaty and drunk. Finally Ace catches me and we fall to the floor, entwined. He gets a kick out of this. So does my brother. So do I.

When Ace leaves at the end of August to go home and get ready for his first year at college, we are all desolate. My mother cooks twice as much as we can eat for dinner; she calls hello into the hall, thinking it's Ace, when the three of us are alone together in the den. My brother calls up girls infrequently, like one of a separated pair of terriers who doesn't understand how to stalk rabbits by himself, used to the duet of chase. I rarely ask either of them to accompany me in the car so I can practice for the road test in October. When the phone rings Thursday night, we are sitting in silence, lacking our familiar quorum of four.

"I'll get it," says my mother. She takes the call in her bedroom.

Hello? she must have said. Only once again there was no answer. Nor would there be an answer ever again because when she returns to the den she is crying, the tears pouring down her face like an avalanche of grief.

"Benjie, Angela," she says.

"What's wrong?" I ask. My mother's tears gather in the sea of her green eyes, rising along the curl of her lashes like a tidal wave of dread that will consume me. Avalanches, tidal waves . . . her crying mirrors all disasters, the natural and otherwise. Disaster . . .

There are certain moments in life that people never forget, the details of which rise and remain on the surface of memory like a scar on flesh. My father remembers that he was on a three-day leave, in a small bar in New Orleans called the Parrot's Perch, drinking gin and sodas when it was announced over the radio that the Japanese had bombed Pearl Harbor. My mother recalls that on the day her father was rushed to the hospital for emergency surgery one of the nurses in attendance received a dozen long-stemmed red roses from a cab driver she'd met the night before at an American Legion dance. Even my Uncle Jack in New York tells about the time he was talking to a client in Minneapolis, was about to cut the sale price by a penny a share when the building next door to him on Forty-fifth Street blew up.

When my brother got his hand caught in the anchor winch on a boat in Rhode Island, his eyes rolled back into his head, blinding him to his own blood pouring onto the deck, to expose their dark sides like moons. As I look at his face now, I can visualize perfectly the two white unmarked orbs, not wanting to see what is happening tonight either. We will remember tonight.

"Ace is dead," my mother says.

"No," screams my brother.

"Mummy," I tell her, "it can't be true." I run from the

room as if I could run away from it, but my brother follows me
and leads me back to the den where my mother takes us both in
her arms.

"How did it happen?" asks my brother. "What happened?"

"He was driving home from the movies with three of his
friends," she says, "on a divided highway. A car going sixty-five
miles an hour, going the wrong way, hit them head-on. . . ."

Always be alert to the rules of the road, Dr. M. said.
They're there for a reason. But what if as the result of a slight
error in judgment . . . What if . . .

"This is disgusting," says my brother.

"At the hospital they said that none of the boys regained
consciousness in the ambulance," my mother tells us. "They
were pronounced dead-on-arrival. We can be happy about this.
They never knew what happened to them."

"Mummy, is this really true?" I ask her. "Are you sure he's
dead?"

We will bury you. My brother is sobbing.

"Angela, his mother just called me," she says.

"There's a jinx on our family," I yell at my mother, but it's
not her fault.

"No, there isn't," she says. "But it just doesn't make any
sense. I mean . . . he was eighteen years old," my mother says.

"Was," says my brother. "What happened to the guy
driving the other car?"

"Nothing," says my mother.

"Nothing?" I ask. "How old was he?"

"Old. In his late sixties," she says. "And he just sprained his
shoulders, I think. His car stayed on the road."

Tonight I would like to change the channel. I would like to
flip the dial to the program of my choice. It would be a situation
comedy so successful that it would never really end but go into
reruns instead, in which no one would ever leave and no one
would die and nothing would change.

"He ought to be in the fucking geriatrics ward," says my
brother.

"I'm sure he feels bad enough as it is," says my mother.

"Goddamned moron," he says. It is easier, for the time being, for the three of us to rest all the world's senselessness on the shoulders, the bruised shoulders, of the old man.

I will remember that my brother was wearing, at the time, one of Ace's shirts. I will remember the exact position of my mother's calendar, open to Friday with all the appointments she didn't keep, laid down beside her on the couch and never picked up again that night. I will remember that I was thinking, when the phone rang, about how the blue veins in my wrist appeared dangerously close to the surface.

I am thinking of the card game crazy eights in which each player follows another's lead, placing queen upon queen, diamond upon diamond, deuce upon deuce, heart upon heart. This is called correspondence—one of the few concepts that endures, carried as a relic of childhood like a talisman into the future.

When an eight is placed on the deck, what we call a crazy eight, the rule of correspondence is superseded and any suit can be called. An eight can be played at will. This is a game of luck: full of twists and turns, a gamble. Trends will reverse themselves; the cards will seem to run in a person's favor when unexpectedly a situation becomes its opposite.

The object here is to discard your entire hand, thereby ending the game and winning. Sometimes a player is left holding an unusually high number of cards when the game is declared over. He never has a chance to play them out.

Eights turn up when we least expect them, to save us or to dash all our hopes. If, as it occasionally happens, one person holds as his last card a crazy eight, he may play it on any of the fifty-one others of the deck, automatically ending the game. The rest of the players bow out.

——————— Chapter VII ———————
TAKING TRIPS

ROM THEIR EARLIEST CONSCIOUS YEARS, WHITE
African children are taught never to pick up the radiant
colored pencils they find discarded in the vegetation
outside. Black children see them, too, though they identify
them otherwise: thin as twigs, smooth as bark, bright-hued as
tribal beads. These also to be let lie, to be circumnavigated in
the dust of the yard.

But in the face of beauty, in the sunlit rainbowed sticks of
color, perspectives meld, memory forgets itself, and the children of all races bend in homage an extended hand. Only then
do the snakes reveal themselves as child bait. Scribbling
furiously, inspired by instinct, on thin white forearms as smooth
as parchment with their two miniature stylus-fangs, writing out
an epitaph in blood-red ink. More often being lifted on small
fingers to adorn the throats of native babies, coiling into
shimmering necklaces of death.

We learned this in biology class. What we did not learn is
why thousands of black children burn with fever from the tiny
flame of a match-head-sized mouth every year while only a
handful of white children pale further to the color of their
starched hospital sheets and succumb, limp as worn linen.

"It is because," says Willa, whose father was assigned to
diplomatic service in Rhodesia for six years, "all of *us* had
nannies. We weren't expected to take care of ourselves. It was
like having your own bodyguard, the same as Frank Sinatra or
Jackie Kennedy. Our growing up was not left to chance.

"While my nanny was shooing snakes out of the back door
of the kitchen (they used to hide in the runners of the sliding
glass), who was at home looking after her own children?
Nobody."

"Perhaps this is a question for Mr. Gimbal, our sociologist,"
suggests the biology teacher.

These snakes are one of the many dangers to African

101

children, continental and predictable. In our own country where we have pasteurized almost everything and invented vaccines against the rest, we are less susceptible to natural causes of death and harm in our youth, but it is the technological and cultural demons that track us like radar.

One of the most common rules for survival is to look both ways before crossing the street. To avoid drunken drivers, born-to-drive teen-agers in their low-slung, souped-up hot rods, preoccupied housewives grappling with their lives on the fly:

I am standing at the bus stop. I wear a white harness like a sash and belt to hold me back from any onrushing vehicle, and my fellow students, too. I have a badge. I am the safety patrol.

Line up, I say when I see the yellow nose turn the corner.

Betcha can't make me, somebody chants from the rear of the line. But I am in full control; I can beat up anybody on the block. They remain in formation, like a squadron of planes. I watch carefully as they take off for the daily mission of school, up the tall steps that you have to jump, gaining altitude, one, two, three. All aloft. I swing up after them, my hand along the metal railing like a runway.

The front seat on the opposite side from the driver is reserved for me. He doesn't take his eyes from the road for an instant as he accelerates; neither do I. I am the safety patrol.

Other modes for survival? Never swallow an entire bottle of pills from the medicine cabinet and never sip anything out of the cleaning closet. It is equally important not to contract polio from swimming pools or diseases from a public toilet (girls must squat over the seat or cover it with two long strips of toilet paper, which it is hard not to drop into the bowl). When playing bows and arrows, remember to stand behind the person who is shooting so as not to be accidentally blinded.

And such rules are not restricted merely to the realm of the physical. For example, one must understand the necessity of putting the round pegs in the round holes and the square ones in their similarly shaped counterparts. Preschool children, armed for this intellectual skirmish with wooden mallets, are expected to find this out for themselves (trial and error), but if they don't catch on at first, it will be hammered into them nevertheless.

Later it will be "comprehension" and "extraction" that count: gists of paragraphs, listings in descending order of essential steps in scientific experiments, germane elements of mathematical problems.

"An airplane is flying at a speed of three hundred fifty miles per hour into a headwind of sixty miles per hour. If it arrives at its appointed destination four hours and forty-five minutes . . ." etc. It's a cinch "the distance traveled" is what you're after. It doesn't matter who's along for the ride, where they're going, or why. Multiple-choice tests illuminate the training further; your only freedom is in circling d ("None of the above") and letting your imagination run, like bare toes through wild flowers, ice-cold spring torrents along a widening stream bed.

You must shave down your perceptions, whittle away your perspective until you've shaped yourself like a golf tee, from the broad, circular base on which the ball (the universe) sits, down the shaft to its pointed tip (your eye).

But what if somebody, with a full swing, drives the universe off into the distance? And what are we doing with our eye to the ground (head in the sand trap) anyway? These are some of the questions I ask myself, sitting in classrooms through the endless fall of my last year of boarding school. Or, in other words, when can you count on a pencil being a pencil? And when is a snake really a snake? These are questions of perspective, and the most important question of all is how in a world of rampant myopia to see clearly. P.O.V., they call it in senior English. Point of view.

We are eighteen. We have successfully avoided the more obvious pitfalls of childhood. The others are so expertly camouflaged and exquisitely cushioned that we sometimes drop into them unawares. I told my mother about this.

Don't worry so much, she said. I doubt they'll have much luck in capturing you. There's a bit of your father in you, you know.

Angela in her jeans, Daddy in her genes, trying to escape the jungle snares of the big white hunters who want to catch her mind and put it in a zoo.

I dream of the tiny snakes. I dream I'm on a trip through Africa, searching for the most miserable person in all the world, the lowliest, the most unfortunate. Every time I think I've found him, every time I think I must have found her, the snakes curl themselves like horseshoes in the dust, pointing to the continuation of my journey.

Is this original sin, then, being born always better off than someone else? By coincidence of birth alone, the lucky clink of the real horseshoe against the iron rod in the ground, having more to eat, less to worry about, afforded the immense luxury to wrestle with the facts as they present themselves? But this luxury cuts with a two-edged blade: one hacking passageways through the overgrown foliage of information roundabout; the other, painfully, honing down the retina to a more perfect shape.

"Ladies, ladies," says Mr. Riley, the headmaster. "The meeting will come to order." Everyone filters in from the aisles of the auditorium, climbing over legs, lifting up piles of books, to settle in her assigned seat for the emergency all-school meeting. It is eleven o'clock in the morning and all classes that usually meet at this time have been cancelled. Everyone is seated, but the room still hums, a peculiar humming that started last night as if in a beehive that has been disturbed.

"How do you think he's going to put it?" Margaret asks me.

"I don't know," I whisper back. "Is there any euphemism for rape?"

Last night Eleanor was raped. In the laundry room. This morning Eleanor went home. If rape were a subject that could be exhausted in a community of women, we would surely be done with it by now. We exposed it to bright lights in every room of the house, we locked it inside, checking all the windows and the front and back doors, twice. We multiplied it, repeating the details a hundred times, gleaning new bits of information from girls in other houses, overheard phrases of the house mother's telephone calls. In the two senior houses there is no bedtime; in our house we stayed up talking about it until four in the morning. Somehow, in spite of all our precautions, it escaped us. No one understands rape.

Some of the details we traded with one another last night

weren't true, like baseball cards with false batting averages, incorrect World Series information. But it doesn't matter. What isn't true this time has been true in other cases. Rape is the nightmare imagination concretized: underwear slit up the crotch with a knife, penetration by rake handles, unspeakable acts which have nonetheless been realized.

"Last night," begins Mr. Riley when the room subdues itself, "one of our sophomore girls was sexually assaulted in the basement of Woolsey House." You can hear legs being crossed and uncrossed; someone coughs. "This was a very unfortunate occurrence," he continues, "and we would like to make sure that it doesn't happen again." He clears his throat and looks down at the podium.

"Margaret," I whisper, "can you believe he's reading from notes?"

"Sex makes him nervous," she says.

"Margaret," I remind her, "rape is not sex."

"Four extra security men have been hired," says Mr. Riley, looking out above the heads of this audience of females, which, even under usual circumstances, makes him uneasy. He adjusts the knot on his tie, tighter, protecting the throat in case one of us goes for his jugular vein. "From now on," he says, "laundry privileges will be restricted to the daylight hours." Heads in the tiers of seats begin to turn from side to side, lips to ears. I poke Anna sitting on my other side.

"Can you believe this?"

"What do you mean?" she says.

"Never mind," I tell her. "Christ on the cross," I whisper to Margaret.

"Will the meeting come back to order?" says Mr. Riley. "This kind of thing is upsetting," he continues, "but it's important to keep in mind when you walk between houses in the evenings. You may wish to go with a friend. In fact, I think the buddy system is a very good idea under the circumstances, especially for the next couple of weeks. . . ."

"You mean they didn't catch the bastard?" I ask Margaret. My stomach clenches.

"I guess not," she says. Sometimes I wish Margaret's blood

pressure were a little higher. She is what people are beginning to call mellow, a personality trait highly regarded in California. Margaret, I've told her, this is New England. Be true to your climate; remember the four seasons. What of Hurricane Doris, which, coming through, felled every other tree on the shoreline? "That pig," she says, as if to comfort me.

"Yes, Miss March?" from the podium. Our European history teacher, almost six feet tall, lean and fortyish, stands up. She looks like a respectable evergreen in her A-shaped wool dress.

"Your last statement," she says, "would lead me to believe, Mr. Riley, that the rapist has not yet been apprehended?"

"She's going to be on the shit list, now," says Margaret.

"As of this moment," he replies, "that's true, Miss March. But the police chief has assured me that he has a very probable lead and expects the whole matter to be cleared up shortly."

"Well, I just think that's the kind of information that everyone should know about," she finishes. Miss March, a student of history, is a stickler for facts.

"I think our best approach to this whole affair," says Mr. Riley, "is to conduct business as usual outside of the few changes I mentioned previously. It won't help to dwell on it." Eleanor, in that case, can dwell on it by herself, a particular fact that happened, unfortunately, to her. She can look for the rapist's face on crowded streets, in her dreams, on moviehouse screens; it didn't happen to the rest of us. Just thank your lucky stars. But this is no way to live, and we dwell on it anyway.

The humming begins to rise again. Do we imagine ourselves, now, a race of cuntless women? (Once when a construction worker whistled at me, Fuck off, I told him. Sew it up, honey, he said.) Or do we imagine ourselves armed? Roaming bands, buddy after buddy after buddy, carrying softball bats and lacrosse sticks? Whatever we imagine is the result of the sudden awareness of our vulnerability. Eleanor kept repeating she was sorry when they took her to the infirmary to wait for the doctor who would examine her. Eleanor was ashamed of being raped, as if the very fact of her femaleness permitting it was her fault.

Another hand.

"Yes, Becky?" says Mr. Riley.

"Well, I'm pretty upset about this," she begins, "and I don't think I'm the only one. . . ." Her speech tumbles all over itself, a leapfrog of words. "So, I think, I mean I think it would be a good idea if we could have some sort of a discussion about it . . . for anyone who wants to talk about it. To participate. We could have a symposium, some afternoon or something, about . . . being raped." She sits down abruptly. There is scattered applause.

"A symposium on rape," Margaret says to me. "The last one we had was on wildlife preservation at Walden Pond."

"Don't be such a smart ass," I tell her. "But nobody will show for it anyway." No one will want to be reminded.

"Thank you, Becky, for your suggestion," Mr. Riley responds. "It's a very good idea." You can hear in his voice that he actually thinks it's a terrible idea, like airing dirty laundry; he'll just sweep it under the rug where it will collect dust along with all the other unpleasantries of the academic year. We live here by the WASP code of ethics: what isn't discussed doesn't, in fact, exist. At first things appear to run smoothly this way, but eventually the rug gets lumpy and hard to vacuum until you end up with the same amount of dirt on top as you hid in the first place. I consider this justice. "We will discuss it," he says, "at the next faculty meeting. Let's adjourn then for now. Have a good day, ladies."

I am trying to explain all this to myself in a vocabulary I will understand: gender seems not just a dual system of reproduction, a male/female split, fifty-fifty. It has become a sociological reality with terrible implications.

But consider it biologically: if a body works much in the same manner as a large and complex cell, we consider it as self-sufficient and autonomous. It is self-defined; it has recognizable boundaries. We know that the introduction of a foreign element considered harmful into a cell causes a violent reaction, throws the entire system into disequilibrium. This must be what rape is.

Four extra security men have been hired, said Mr. Riley. Bodyguards, nannies, whole armies of safety patrols. Perhaps next they will erect a barbed-wire fence. But none of this matters anyway. The world is on the other side of the fence, and if we choose to join it, it will be at our own risk. Many women spend their adult lives inside walls, behind fences, under cover. Artificial hence recognizable boundaries, worn like a carapace. When women go anywhere outside the fence unescorted, it's at their own risk.

The buddy system? This is our specialty. In the free hour between study hall and room check, it is usually safest to wink at just a single friend (large groups attract attention), you letting yourself out the front door and her out the back, to meet up again five minutes later down by the canoe shed.

We're low on gin, I say, checking the neat array of bottles under the rotted wood foundation. I pull out two glasses and a candle. She lights up a joint from its flame.

Keep an eye on the time, she says.

Those of us who are forever breaking the rules do so as a matter of honor. And like everything you start out being apprehensive about, do it once and you've mastered it. Like clearing the high-jump bar up another notch, like waxing your legs without tearing off the skin. Besides, we say to one another, knuckling under to authority is the role of the many. If it weren't for the few, what of social change? Some are vocal in assemblies; others speak directly to faculty members of updating rules and regulations; we simply ignore them. We are a necessary presence, an alternate voice, like Radio Free Europe.

"Would you like to come with me on a trip?" asks my grandmother. My grandmother is notorious for taking trips.

I think Angela could use a change of scene, my mother must have said.

Oh really? asked my grandmother, but since nobody knows what's wrong, myself included, that's probably all she said.

"I'd love to," I say. Actually I don't know if I'd love to or not; this is a conditioned response to a generous offer, the kind of phrase that preempts having to think. If I pinch myself, I can feel it. This is reassuring.

I haven't set foot outside my mother's apartment for a month. I haven't been at school. Temporary leave of absence. But I started my leave long before I left; I was AWOL inside.

What do you mean you can't remember February? asked one of my teachers. Why haven't you been in class?

I don't know, I told her. I can't remember anything.

This is serious, she said.

I was thinking the same thing myself, I told her.

What's upsetting you, Angela? she asked.

Everything, I told her, for lack of being able to pinpoint a specific cause worthy of so much grief. I feel like my brain is retreating.

Exactly how does that feel? she asked.

It feels, I replied slowly (describing it to myself / Sleeping Beauty suddenly awakened not to a stranger's kiss but to a hangover, a gray morning, and too many coffee cups stacked in the sink), like I would like to be given a tranquilizer in the infirmary, like I wish to sit quietly somewhere where there isn't anybody else until my mother comes to take me home. Could you call her right now? I asked.

I started crying and I didn't stop until long after we got back to the apartment and I went into my room and closed the door. I opened it a month later to my grandmother's question in the dining room at Easter dinner.

"Some people have all the luck," says my brother. My mother looks at him from across the table.

"You can go another time," says my grandfather. "This trip is just for the girls," he says. "Your grandmother and Angela and Aunt Vera will have ten days of bliss in the sun together. . . ."

What have I gotten myself in for? Still, we in our family do not like to give in to concepts such as "the generation gap." Was there one before they coined the phrase? my mother asks. Certainly not, she says. If we all concentrate on what we have in common rather than on our differences, everything will go fine.

"After the trip," ventures my mother, "maybe you'll feel like going back to school."

"Maybe," I tell her. The dinner talk is about the weather and the turkey: these are things we know we have in common. I don't join in; this is considered uncharacteristic behavior on my part. It is. I've even lost all pleasure in arguing with my brother, though he is carving the turkey like Attila the Hun.

Somewhere inside me things are out of kilter. Is there a time bomb in my brain? A tapeworm in my heart?

On the plane ride, we sit three across.

"Eleven down," says my grandmother, and we successfully fill in the entire puzzle in the airline's magazine. "Here we are, off on a junket," she says.

"To be sure," says Aunt Vera. "The only thing we have to do for ten days is just relax and enjoy ourselves on an island paradise."

This is a wonderful way of looking at life. Can it be true?

"No meals to cook," says my grandmother. "No beds to make." And she sings something from Gilbert and Sullivan in a high wavering voice that lulls me to sleep.

"To the beach," I say to her at ten o'clock the next morning, and we stop to pick up Aunt Vera in her room next door. The three of us trail out the lobby door, down the concrete walkways past the pool, and onto the beach.

"Did you bring the suntan lotion?" my great-aunt asks me. She and my grandmother, sisters for seventy years, wear long matching beach robes and hats to shield them from the sun.

"Don't stay out too long the first day," my grandmother cautions me. I lie on my towel a short distance from them to avoid the shadow of their umbrella. It is very hot. I try not to think anything; this is my new specialty. I am an expert at making my mind a blank, just like the gray plastic tablets you can buy for a quarter at the supermarket, which, when all filled up with writing and scribbles, can be magically erased by the mere lifting of the top sheet. I erase my mind by the lifting of my eyelids when I wake up; I have no past; I can start from scratch any morning of the week.

"Angela, Angela." My grandmother is poking me.

"Hi, Gran."

"I think you've had more than enough sun already," she says.

"I must have dozed off," I tell her.

"You do look a little pink," she says.

"But my skin doesn't feel hot at all." I sit out for another half hour.

Later my skin is the wall of a furnace; my eyes are like puddles drying up in a heat wave. There are red streaks along my chest and up and down my arms and legs like cell bars. They prevent me from leaving the room.

"We need some baking soda," suggests Aunt Vera.

"Baking soda," says my grandmother. "I have some right behind the pancake mix in the top right-hand cabinet in the pantry," she muses.

"I'll try at the desk, Viola," says her more practical sister, but they don't have any.

"Just get me a cold washcloth, please," I tell them and I lay it across my eyes. "You two go to dinner. I'll be all right."

"Oh, we couldn't leave you here alone," says my grandmother, but finally I persuade them, though they long to tend me, their patient, in whom this afternoon they found the first tangible symptoms they could treat.

While they're gone, my skin gives birth to enormous bubbles; all the evils and miseries of the world are rising to its surface in the form of blisters and sores. I can see very indistinctly through my swollen eyes, as indistinctly as this morning when I mistook a snake for the sun. Snakes seek disguises according to our pleasures. Mirages of what we yearn for most. But it's bitten me and kissed fever into my mouth. I try to vomit it back out, but it's endless. I try to vomit out years, screaming in my sweaty bed, but by that time there's nothing left but yellow bile.

You haven't anything to feel bad about, my mother has said. Make up your own rules of right and wrong. It's only when you break *them* that you ought to feel bad.

But it scares me, I told her. What if you make a mistake? And it's tiring, too, to always be reinvestigating systems of behavior, trying out new codes of ethics because you know you can't trust the ones already set up.

Of course it's tiring, she said, but who ever promised that life was an afternoon nap? Every day it's important to continue with renewed energy, to keep resetting up experiments whose recorded results you're not satisfied with. You certainly can't spend the rest of your life in your room.

No, said my mother, it is important, no not even important but essential to keep your hand in in life even though you keep burning it playing with fire. And you'll keep burning it, in some way or other I would imagine, all through your life.

What a thought, I tell her. How do people stand it?

Not everyone, she said, is so fascinated with the flames. Some people keep their hands in their laps some of the time. . . . Was this a reprimand?

After lying in the hotel bed for five days, I feel well enough to get up. The scars, however, didn't go away for a year. And sitting with my hands in my lap is just what I do for the rest of our vacation, holding a rum drink in the dark hotel bar. I've tried them all: the Zombies, the Fog Cutters, the Samoan Oarsmen, the Pineapple Clouds, the Island Punches, the Shark Bites. . . . They all taste the same, but my mother is right. You really can't take someone else's word for it. You have to pursue life with a vengeance.

"We'll be out at the beach, Angela," says my grandmother.

"Can't you find someone to talk to besides those Negroes in the hoochie-coochie band?" says my great-aunt.

They insist that all three of them are named Eddie. They play me Beatles' songs all through the long afternoons with a nice Calypso beat.

"Would you like to go out tonight, Angela?" asks one of the Eddies.

"I'm here with my grandmother and my great-aunt," I tell him.

"Well, we will all go out then," they say.

"They're both married," I tell them. The Eddies find this funny.

On the morning we are to leave I get up very early. I walk far down the beach to a small wharf where I sit and watch the ocean. There is a strong wind and the waves are enormous. On the day of our arrival the water was tranquil, at ebb.

Everything is subject to change: the tides come in and out,

a storm at sea can alter the face of the shore for weeks afterward, cutting it into sharp cliffs. If only we knew what makes waves inside us, exhausted oceanographers working round the clock, daytime and dreamtime, measuring the solid ground left to stand on, the inches reclaimed yearly by the simple erosion of living.

"I think we should just pull the car over to the side of the road and leave it, like everybody else," says Margaret. The dirt road is getting narrower. We've been in bumper-to-bumper traffic for four hours, ever since we exited off the highway.

"It's your parents' car," says Esther. "It's up to you."

"Do you think it's going to overheat?" I ask.

"Well, like, if it hasn't already, it probably won't now," says Penny. This is illogical, but Penny, even when she isn't out of it, has no understanding of anything mechanical. Margaret fixes her in the rearview mirror.

"Penny," she says, "you better leave the heavy-duty thinking to us until you come down a little bit."

"But I don't ever want to come down," she says. "Mescaline is such a gas. . . ."

"Fine, fine," says Esther, "but I think we'd better decide whether or not to leave the car here, OK? The sides of the road may be all blocked with cars farther up. There's a pretty big gap over there and everybody is starting to pull off now. I wonder how much farther it is?"

Cars of every description are parked in the ditches on either side of the road or pulled farther off into the fields: sedans, vans, Volkswagens, trucks, antiques, buses. Many of them are decorated with flowers and astrological signs hand painted in bright colors. Posters are propped in rear windows, banners fly from aerials: "Woodstock or Bust," "We Will Build a New Nation," "Crosby, Stills and Nash," "Get Your Acid Here." Pedestrians are filing past us in steady streams, got up in embroidered jeans, American flag shirts, coonskin caps, paisley shawls with fringe, you name it. Naked babies on top of adult shoulders, like pink balloons on strings.

"It's going to be faster on foot," I say. "Margaret, that field doesn't look too marshy. Let's park over there."

"OK," she says. "I'll put it next to that purple dune buggy with the 'OM' decal so we'll be able to find it again."

"Om," Penny intones. "Don't you like the way that sounds? Interior and mysterious. . . ."

"Oh brother," says Esther. The car stalls to a halt a few feet from our purple landmark.

"Fine," says Margaret, taking the key from the ignition. "I'm so sick of driving I don't care if we have to walk ten miles."

"It can't be that far," says Esther, "but I don't see how we're going to carry all this stuff." Piled up in the back are a tent, a giant cooler, our four knapsacks, blankets, sleeping bags, and an avalanche of groceries.

"Oh shit," I tell them, "we'll probably be ostracized for bringing so many material possessions."

"All right, smartie, what do you suggest?" Esther asks me. At this rate, we may never even get out of the car.

"I think we ought to forget the tent, take a couple of sleeping bags, leave most of the clothes here, and put whatever food we can fit into the knapsacks. All agreed?"

"Fine."

"But what if it rains?" asks Penny, pushing at the bundle of our tent.

"Then we'll just have to get wet," I tell her. "Actually, you know, we've come here to commune with nature not to wrap ourselves up against it. Right, Penny?" Surely this tactic will work.

"If it rains," she agrees, "we'll just get into it. It will keep us cool, it will clean us, it will quench our thirst. . . ."

"That's the spirit," says Margaret. Invite her if you want, I told Margaret, but then you've got to take responsibility for her. I'll try to divert Esther so she doesn't kill her. We are going to have a great time, said Margaret. There will be only one Woodstock.

"Did you lock all the doors?" asks Esther when we've got all our gear assembled.

"But this is Woodstock," says Penny.

"Peace and love, Esther," I tell her. "Here's your knapsack."

Angela, I'm not sure this going to Woodstock is such a good idea, said my mother.

Why not? I asked her.

Well, because anything could happen with all those people: a riot, they might set fire to the woods, if you needed medical assistance or anything. . . .

Mummy, I told her, the *Titanic* sunk, Coconut Grove went up in flames, and it is true that Uncle Freddie once got hit by lightning on the beach. The shrapnel in his leg attracted it. But this doesn't mean that people are supposed to stop taking cruises, going dancing, and eating picnics.

You *have* already sent away for the tickets, she said.

That's right, I told her.

Just be careful then, Angela, she said. And don't take any hard drugs.

"Acid, STP, mescaline, hash, grass, THC, opium," chants a woman we pass on the side of the road that appears to be blocked with cars for as far as we can see. She is carrying a small baby in a harness strapped to her back. She holds hands with a man dressed only in denim shorts and an elaborate tattoo in the design of a Hawaiian shirt. I wonder if they let him into restaurants that way.

"Colombian," he says.

"About how far do you think it is from here?" I ask him.

"I think it's about three miles up the road, according to my directions."

"Directions?"

"Yah," he says, waving a sheet of paper. "They printed them up in the student union at Berkeley. Very accurate," he says. "We've been traveling for about a week."

"Well, I hope you enjoy yourselves."

"Oh we always do," he says, smiling in the baby's face. "Peace."

We can hear the music now. Just a general hum and the occasional whine of an amplifier turned up too high. A boy in a tuxedo passes us. With him is another boy dressed in sandals and a sort of leather jockstrap, a huge head of teased hair, and a beard.

"Hey, girls," he calls over his shoulder, "I got good drugs and I forgot my sleeping bag. Plus," he says, "I know the crew and I can get you backstage."

"Far out," says Penny. "Why not?" He waits for her; she grabs his hand, winking at us. He puts his other hand in the back pocket of her tight jeans, and off they go like skaters.

"Any other takers?" asks his friend in the tuxedo.

"No thanks."

"Well," says Esther, "that's one problem easily solved."

"Do you think she'll be all right?" I ask.

"Sure," says Margaret, "they'll have a wonderful weekend even though she forgot to take along a sleeping bag after all and he probably made it up that he knows somebody on the crew."

"I don't think I understand people at all," I say.

"First of all," says Margaret, "everyone is beautiful. Also interchangeable. Besides, if everyone stays high for the duration of the weekend, they won't find out any of the ways in which they might dislike each other anyway. Got it?"

"Yes," I say, "but, honestly, Margaret, does it work?"

"And should it, more to the point?" adds Esther, who is a romantic.

"A little self-induced happiness never hurt anybody," says Margaret. Esther and I have to agree.

Now we can hear the loudspeaker clearly: "Emily Schwartz, call your mother./ Dean, meet Ronnie at the car so he can give you your insulin./ The next set will be on in twenty minutes./ Watch out for the Black Beauty acid from Oregon. It's bad acid. Don't drop any yourself, and if you know anybody who did, bring him immediately to the first-aid station behind the stage."

The scaffolding looms above the trees like a rocket launcher. If the thousands of people, who suddenly materialize when we crest the final hill, seated and milling around in the natural outdoor stadium that slopes up from the stage, all gave a push, we'd get that rocket to the moon and back.

"Good Lord," says Esther. "I never saw so many people all in one place."

"And it's going to be even more beautiful later on," says a girl walking next to us. "They announced over the loudspeaker that a half million people are expected before tomorrow. Traffic's backed up for twelve hours."

"Do you want to go inside the gates now?" asks Margaret. "Or do you want to explore a little?"

"Let's go inside." We are admitted through a gate in the chain-link fence that encloses the entire grassy hillside. The attendant rips our tickets in half.

"You won't be needing these," he says, dropping the stubs to the ground. "In a few minutes we're just going to open up the gates to everybody, tickets or no."

"That's remarkably uncapitalist of you," says Esther.

"Yes." He smiles. "But the producers have made their money already, and, besides, people have started to break through the fence at the back."

"What about the cops?" asks Margaret.

"They don't care," says the attendant. "But you can't keep out two hundred thousand freaks who want in, anyway." As he talks to us hundreds of people are filing past.

"Listen, friends," says the voice over the mike, "I have some good news. In fifteen minutes we're going to throw all the gates wide open, and anybody who wants to can come into the concert area, with or without tickets." A wild cheer goes up from the crowd. "Take your time and don't push; there'll be plenty of room for everybody. This is the people's festival, and for once rock'n'roll is going to be free like it ought to be." Another roar.

"See," says the attendant, and he pushes his gate all the way open with a clink. "Why wait?"

"Let's find a place to settle," says Esther, and we walk, wending our way between body after body to the back of the bowl, almost to the rim where there's more room. We sit down when we find a clearing big enough for three.

"See that helicopter," says a guy next to us, moving over. "I bet that's Country Joe and the Fish arriving."

"Maybe it's Joan Baez," says his friend. He passes us a joint. "Want a hit?"

"Thanks," says Margaret. "Let's get down to business. Happy graduation," she says to us. We pass a bottle of wine to our companions.

"That's good," says one of them. "At dusk," he says, "they're going to turn the lights on; then we'll have a really good view. Twelve hours of music every day. I don't know if I can handle it."

There are no paths through the thickening crowd; small groups wind their way in and out like a slalom course following someone appointed as trailblazer. A girl steps on the out-stretched hand of one of the pair of boys next to us. He smiles at her.

"I'm awfully sorry," she says.

"I don't mind," he says. She sits down beside him while we all squeeze over. He offers her a toke.

"I've got some good acid," she says.

"Space is the place," says his friend.

"Would you like some wine?" Esther offers her the bottle.

"Rosé," she says. "My favorite. I haven't had rosé since Santa Fe," she remembers. "Hitched all the way and here I am. It only took three rides. Everybody was coming to the same place. . . ."

A husky naked woman with a blanket draped over her shoulders and a dandelion stuck behind her ear is being helped by two young men in jeans and bead necklaces. One under each arm for support.

"She's a little drunk," one of them admits.

"But she wants to go right up to the stage," says the other.

"Tha's right," she beams.

This must be the ultimate happening, a fabulous masquer-ade, a Mardi Gras of hippies. Heroes from our youth pass by me at arm's reach: Captain Hook, Peter Pan, Robin Hood, Daniel Boone, Batman, Billy the Kid. . . . The women are less identifi-able; we had no heroes when we would dress up in odds and ends from the closet, nameless explorers and pioneers in search of ourselves. Here we've returned to fantasyland, all the boys and girls (vicariously through the partners they've chosen) acting out what they really wanted to be when they grew up. No policemen, firemen, lawyers here. Gypsies, nudists, and ragmen. Magicians, (Hell's) angels, and snake charmers.

I'm wearing a sweater, an old pair of jeans, and navy blue sneakers. I don't know what I want to be when I grow up. But this doesn't matter; I won't have to grow up. In fantasyland there is no time.

"How long have we been here?" I ask Margaret, wriggling out of my sleeping bag. It's daylight again and we're still in the same spot where we sat down originally.

"Fifteen or sixteen hours I think," she says, stretching. But nobody anywhere around us seems to have a watch.

"Who cares what time it is, man?" somebody asks.

But I care. I care what time it is. What is wrong with me? I'm a miserable reality addict, and there's no cure for it. If the only time here is suntime and moontime, music time and nonmusic time, then it must be morning (sun/nonmusic time).

"Let's take a look around," I suggest. Outside the gates we head for the portable toilets, but you can smell them before they're in sight.

"Let's go in the woods," says Esther.

Beyond our main metropolis of music (the stage is city hall) stretch vast suburbs of cars and vans and tents and shacks, teepees, hammocks in trees, blankets spread along mossy stream banks. People everywhere. Some, it turns out, have been here for months. Peddlers sell food, drugs, and soft drinks. Drugs are reasonable; food is high. Leather goods, pottery, and T-shirt manufacturing constitute our primary industries.

"Listen everybody. I've got an important announcement to make," says the now-familiar voice of the loudspeaker. "According to news estimates, and they're probably low, man, 'cause it scares 'em to think of us all here together just getting high and happy, but according to the estimates we got over half a million people here and that makes us one of the ten biggest cities in New York State."

Everyone claps and hoots, each feeling somehow responsi-

ble for this self-generative act. We are like a crawling amoeba
that will engulf all of New York if not the entire coastal United
States.

"You know," says Margaret, "I've never seen strangers be
so nice to each other in my life."

"I know," says Esther. "It kind of makes you wonder what
type of place the world would be if people believed in it. . . ."

"We could secede," I suggest.

"And then no one would get drafted and no one would have
to go to work and we wouldn't be alienated by technology," says
Esther.

"What about foreign policy?" I pose. "And, eventually,
we'd run out of food. . . ."

"We could take up farming," says Margaret, gesturing at
the fields all around us.

"That would create problems of ownership, though, and
we'd need a form of government. You see, it would just build up
all over again. There is no escaping modernity. Who would we
elect for President? The person with the best acid?"

"No, that's too tribal," says Esther. "The loudspeaker will
be the President."

"That's good," I agree. "The voice . . ."

"Big Brother with a twist," says Margaret.

"Yes," I say, "the ultimate weapon, the razor blade inside
the shiny Halloween apple: a big brother who's nice, an affable
fellow who reports how happy you are, how high you are, and
how much you like the music twenty-four hours a day."

"Angela, aren't you having a good time?" Esther asks me,
hands on her hips.

"Of course I'm having a good time," I tell her. "But that
doesn't mean you have to suspend all analysis. It's important to
keep a weather eye."

"Speaking of which," says Margaret, "those clouds look
awfully black."

"Poor Penny," says Esther. "Maybe we should hang out
here for a while under some thick-branched trees."

But by the time it starts we've already wandered back to the
treeless bowl. It rains as if it were the Second Flood, a good

chance to drown five hundred thousand ungrateful children in a single downpour, but after a half hour it lets up to a steady drizzle. People take their clothes off and dance in the rain. The grassy bowl has been transformed into slippery pottery; water flows down it in rivulets. A natural slide, people shoot down it for hundreds of yards, coating themselves in the slimy red clay.

"This is what babies must feel like being born," I say, taking a ride myself.

"Isn't this rain ever going to end?" asks Esther.

"I hate to tell you, Esther," says Margaret, "but it looks like the kind of drizzle that lasts for hours."

"So what?" says the girl next to me. "If you've got the sun inside you, it doesn't matter what the weather report is." This is the motto we try to live by through the next twelve hours of rain.

"The only way to get through this is to drop some acid," says Margaret. "Maybe half a tab."

"Just don't freak out," says Esther. "You and eight hundred other people in the first-aid trailer."

"Want the other half?" Margaret asks me. "And I never freak out," she adds. "I'm very relaxed."

"I don't think so," I answer her. "What if, suddenly, I wanted privacy?"

"You wouldn't want privacy. Why this is the perfect place to trip," says Margaret. "We're already tripping anyway, practically. . . . The vibes around here are very outer space, a contact high. . . ." I look at Esther.

"Don't worry," I tell her. "I think this is starting out as a good trip."

"What do you mean?" she says.

"I mean she's starting to get off."

"Yah," says Margaret. "I jumped the gun. I dropped a half about forty-five minutes ago. For this," she says, "we're going to have to go right down to the edge of the stage." The evening set is about to begin. All the lights come up at once. "I can't believe it," says Margaret.

"Excuse us," we keep repeating, threading our way through acres and thousands of people. When we finally arrive within about two hundred feet of the stage, I look up, and it's as if with a quick flick of the wrist we'd turned over a pair of binoculars: now instead of long-distance we're getting close-up.

Now we can see that the loudspeaker voice has a body, that of an ordinary man dressed in jeans and a Woodstock T-shirt.

"Listen," he says when the music stops (a lot of people continue to dance unaccompanied in the rain), "we just found out that the Black Beauty acid isn't bad acid after all. It's been chemically analyzed by one of our doctors here, and it's all right. It won't hurt you. I repeat, it won't hurt you. But a few people have been finding it pretty heavy so if you want to come to the first-aid station and have somebody talk you down, that's OK. The first-aid station behind the stage./ Jeannie Wallace call home. Your father's ill./ The Speed Bus scheduled to leave for Illinois tomorrow is leaving tonight at midnight. Doesn't say why. . . ." He gets handed another bunch of papers by one of the technicians. "Again, the ambulances are having trouble getting through due to the mud and the number of cars left abandoned partially on the road. If you left your car in the road, please move it yourself or we're going to have to tow it away./ And a final thing, one final note for the evening: we really have a city of our own now, as of this evening we have a birthrate of one."

The crowd screams and people rise to their feet again when suddenly Gracie Slick jumps out into the lights in a white, fringed kidskin suit. Band after band, hour after hour. This night will have no end. By the time Janis Joplin is scheduled to sing, nobody is left seated, and I've even forgotten to mind the rain. An occasional ambulance siren sounds.

"That's it," I say to Esther after she leaves the stage.

"What do you mean, that's it?" she says.

"I mean I'm not going to listen to anybody else," I tell her. "She can't even help singing like that. . . ." A voice that makes you cry even in fantasyland where everybody's happy and love is so easy to find. "I'm going to walk around until it's over. I'll meet you at the car around ten in the morning if any of us can find out when that is."

"OK," says Esther, "Margaret and I are going to stick it out."

"Hendrix," says Margaret.

I wander out through the nearest set of gates, through the woods, into fields, some of them pitch dark. There are people almost everywhere I go. People, the perpetrators of almost every known evil, but here in one of the biggest cities in New York State, *there is no crime,* there is no violence, there is no rape. We left our sleeping bags by a particular tree, and when I find my way back to it, they're still there. I sit down and rest my head against the trunk. No one who wasn't here will believe that this existed. But that's OK. It's not statistically possible, my brother will say. He's right; it's not statistically possible. They must have hushed up the less positive details, readers of papers will think. I saw *one* fistfight and it was quickly broken up; the loudspeaker announced that a child was abandoned, but a commune took her in. How many people overdosed? my mother will ask. How many young people will end up burning their brains out on hallucinogens? This part, at least, might be true. I heard the ambulances screaming all night. Though it's unclear to me at this time whether or not it's worth the risk, not being sure of what the odds are. It is more dangerous than crossing the street, probably less so than driving a car at high speeds. It is certainly safer than going to war. War—a more acceptable method of altering your consciousness or extinguishing it.

A man pauses in front of my tree. He holds up a cardboard sign: THE ACID POET.

"You're a bard," I say to him.

"A modern-day troubadour," he says. His clothes are those of a minstrel; another dream come true.

"Taking Trips: a poem," he recites.

"There are several kinds of trips you can take
Vacations in the summer to beach or lake
Trips to the supermarket; trips upstairs,
To Europe to get over our failed love affairs
Trips in rockets to outer space,
To the doctor, the dentist, or any old place

Trips round the world or tripping a wire
Exposing the truth by tripping up a liar
Trips over your own toes, a commonplace kind,
But the best trips of all are those you take in your mind
There's no good trips or bad trips if your acid's effective
Just keep your eyes open and it'll change your perspective."

This is what they are, then, a whole generation trying to look more clearly, to see the world for a more perfect place, to shape it into a respectable image. Maybe I made it up and maybe I didn't: here, for once, for one weekend, realized.

"Did you like it?" he asks.

"Yes," I tell him. "I liked it very much."

"You want to buy some?"

"Sure," I say.

"How many?"

"One."

"One hit?" he asks. "It's good acid, you know."

"One is plenty," I tell him.

"Well, OK," he says, "but you'll kick yourself when you try it."

After he leaves, I think about the casualties, about the people who after too many trips or excursions into a new and more beautiful territory don't come back. Like Icarus who flew too high and melted his wax wings in the radiance of the sun. Like my father who found himself, Icarus fallen, at sea. I put the capsule in my pocket. I have it if I need it.

Chapter VIII

CHILDHOOD

A RE YOU GOING TO MISS ME, NOW THAT I'LL BE living in New York?" I ask my mother. I hand her the map from the seat between us, a tangible reminder of our soon-to-be-realized distance.

"Yes," she says, and she opens it like an accordion player, searching with her fingers for the correct note of our exit ramp. "But that's a mother's job, you know," she continues, "bringing up your children so they'll be self-sufficient and able to live lives of their own. If they can't, then you've been a miserable failure. If they can, then you miss them terribly."

"Kind of a catch-22, isn't it?" I say. I would like to tell her I'll miss her, too, but it is safest to just keep my eyes on the road. I will not cry. "You wouldn't like to come back for a master's degree and be my roommate, would you?"

"It's an idea," she says, laughing, "but then there wouldn't be anybody left to put us through college and we'd both have to drop out."

"And that's not a good move, right?" It's important to get the ground rules set up ahead of time. I glance over at her.

"Right," she says, nodding her head emphatically. "If you don't find out about certain things in college, darling, you may never even know that they exist. Certainly you'll never come across them shopping in the supermarket or going to a cocktail party.

"You know," she continues, pausing for a moment to think, "people's concerns shift rapidly when they have to go out and earn a living. The pursuit of all the unrelated kinds of knowledge slows its pace, often. There are things you should study now or you may go through life never having known them. I'm talking about the classics," she says, "German philosophy, romantic poetry. . . . They won't help you in balancing your checkbook; on the other hand, they are a tribute to the life of the mind, and this can be a great comfort, a balance, when weighed against our

125

daily disappointments, the things that make us think that civilization can't have advanced very far."

"Like murders, wars, famines, and individual catastrophes," I suggest. "Etcetera."

"Precisely," she says, "and this is the exit." I miss it, perhaps on purpose.

An hour later, both of us in tears despite everything, my mother leaves me standing beside my stack of suitcases and boxes at the bottom of a hill near the edge of a parking lot, where a boy dressed all in white busily directs traffic, intermittently blowing the whistle around his neck, gesticulating dramatically to the left or right aisle as new cars pull in.

"He's in theater," says a girl with braids, approaching me, a "Welcoming Committee" button pinned to one of the ribbons. "Oh, ah . . . Angela," she says, glancing down at the stub in her hand then passing it to me, "I almost forgot. When your bags get delivered to your room, just give them this to prove they're yours. Actually, the moving men probably won't even ask for it, but take it anyway; it's got your dorm and room number on it. You're in the big monstrosity," she adds. "Philip Johnson designed it, but it wasn't one of his competition winners. First building up the hill on the right. You can't miss it."

I watch the steady flow of people up the path, carrying boxes, wheeling bicycles, talking. I follow the crowd. *B* floor is written on my stub. This turns out to be *B* for *basement*, and I walk the dingy corridor to its end, along the stained green carpet until I come to the open door of my room.

"Hi," says a girl emerging from the closet. This must be my roommate. "How're you doing?" she asks.

"Quite well," I say. This is my most guarded Boston manner. But I can't help it; it comes over me suddenly, like influenza. Ice water pumping through my veins to anesthetize me to any possible pain of newness. I concentrate on the room, trying to relax. Matching bedspreads and curtains like a motel: royal blue. Two beds, two closets, two bureaus, two desks. Two small windows in the upper quarter of the outside wall. Who is Philip Johnson?

My roommate has stopped unpacking and, lighting a

cigarette, sits down on the edge of one of the beds.

"My name's Winnie," she says.

It is five o'clock in the morning. And now I know the intimate details of every sexual relationship Winnie's ever had. Her current boyfriend belongs to a motorcycle gang called the Howlers. He likes best being blown. Just last week he borrowed a thousand dollars from Winnie to send one of his fellow gang members to Mexico until "the heat is off." This intrigues me in spite of myself; nothing like this ever happened to me. Once a boy touched my breast after a school dance, but I couldn't concentrate.

The rest is less intriguing: I know that her father has worked for the telephone company for nineteen years. Because her mother had the hysterectomy operation last winter, they had to cancel their vacation to Florida. And the tenants who rent their garage apartment do transcendental meditation because it gives them energy and cures depression. When the insufferable grandmother who lives with them dies, her father will be able to retire, though this may mean he will lose his full pension. Once Winnie went on a camping trip to the Adirondacks, but she couldn't sleep at night because she had her period and this attracts bears.

"That's disgusting," I say. Neither of us is sure if there are any bears in the Adirondacks, but there might be.

"Angela, how come you haven't told me anything about yourself?" she asks me just as the glow of morning, a gray lightening, can be discerned through the crack in the curtains.

"Because I'm too tired," I say, pulling the covers up over my head. This is a habit I never learned as a child but later, when I had my first roommate. "Let's go to sleep, Winnie. Orientation starts in four hours."

But what could I tell her anyway? The things I understand I keep to myself, I can't help it. Outside of my mother, I'm not sure I ever had a friend. I sink down into the bed, an unknown future, and the beginning, happily, of something new. Winnie lapses into her asthmatic snoring, rhythmic, sonorous, a pleasant respite from words and the constant going over of lives. Lives that we live hundreds of times in our memories, like a

silent movie for which we must find the dialogue-like reasons.
Orientation—it's a nice idea. A valiant stab at preexperiential
learning. If you believe in the concept.

"It takes a few months to get into the swing of things around
here," our resident adviser tells us at dinner in the fluorescent
aqua and orange cafeteria. In it she looks glamorous and out of
context. She probably frequents nightclubs in New York. After a
week of assigned seating we'll be able to sit wherever we choose,
but it doesn't really bother us now because we don't know
anyone outside these ten people (the inhabitants of B floor),
anyway. And under normal circumstances Gloria would never
even talk to us. Nevertheless, she's the one whose attention
everyone courts. Myself included.

"I chose to come to this college because it has no rules," I
tell her.

"So did everyone else," she says, ending the conversation.
She sticks her spoon into the yogurt she's eating for dinner. I
feel my face heat up red.

"I mean of course some people never change," Gloria
lectures. She lights a cigarette with a silver lighter and pockets it
again. "They're just as straight when they graduate as the day
they arrived." We laugh, but each one of us feels implicated.
Will we be personally resistant to change? Will the eventual
B.A.'s of our diplomas stand for "Barely Altered"?

"You can tell," she continues. "If they don't manifest a
discernible intellectual or psychological upheaval after six months,
then they're a lost cause. No behavior is unacceptable here.
People can develop to their full potentials without fear of ridicule,
a rare thing. And if there is no norm," she asks, "what holds people to the conventions but their own built-in repressions?"

There is nothing more shameful than being repressed.
Nothing more unsettling than the thought of one's own conven-
tionality. The next night at dinner, Sally, Fran, and Lisa switch
to yogurt.

"Angela," says my Greek drama professor one afternoon in
class, "how is it that you know so many of the lines by heart?"

When we discuss character motivation, I illustrate my ideas by citing speeches directly from the text.

"I used to rehearse a lot of these plays with my father," I tell her. She leans toward me across the round mahogany table that reflects the fall sunlight.

"Oh, is your father an actor?" she asks. I consider this.

"I suppose you could say that," I tell her. "An actor of sorts . . . once."

"Really," she says, interested. "Is he doing anything now? Did he ever play Broadway?"

"No, no," I tell her. How will I get myself out of this now? "He used to do mostly . . . dinner theater. He's been out of the country for some time so I don't know exactly what he's doing . . . but I'm quite sure he gave up acting altogether."

"Aeschylus at dinner theater?" she asks, pointing at her open volume.

"Actually, they're starved for culture in the suburbs, you know. Whatever you show them they're happy to see."

"That's very interesting, Angela," she says. "I don't suppose you've ever considered a career in acting?"

"No," I say, "it doesn't really seem to pay off in the long run."

"It most certainly can," says Barry, who'll argue any point. "For a top-notch actor or actress it can be quite lucrative." Also, Barry's mother casts for CBS.

"That's not what I meant," I tell him.

At four, when the class ends, I walk with Melissa, who lives in the room next door to Winnie and me, out the door and onto the flagstone terrace.

"I didn't know your father was an actor," Melissa says.

"He's not," I tell her. Brown and yellow leaves rustle under our feet on the stone staircase.

"Then what was that all about?" she asks, twisting one of the several rings on her fingers, a habit I kid her about.

"I couldn't figure out how to explain it any other way," I tell her. "Then the conversation seemed to get out of control, if you know what I mean." She looks at me, expecting further explanation. I shrug my shoulders. "But what difference does it make, anyway? Everyone sees things differently. There are always several versions of the same story."

"Well, I see what you mean about that," says Melissa. "And, besides, everyone else around here has such fibs to tell that if you gave your father eighteen different professions, no one would raise an eyebrow. I even know a boy who some days talks about his mother's second marriage while others he says she's dead. If he's in a bad mood, he kills her right off. . . . By the way, what *does* your father do?" she asks me.

"He's a seaman," I tell her. "He never comes home."

"Oh," she says, shocked. So am I—that I told her.

None of these people had a childhood, said Melissa that evening. Instead of playing cards, they were inventing systems to beat the blackjack tables in Las Vegas. Instead of watching TV's, they were taking them apart. Instead of writing book reviews in elementary school, they were writing books. A boy in my physics class even built a rocketship when he was thirteen.

Did it get into orbit? I asked her.

Of course not, she said. But it did get as far as the neighbors' garage. These kids are so creative they can hardly get from here to the student union.

Melissa is right. And outside of Winnie and a handful of other students, no one here is conventional; there was no need for worry around the dinner table. Child movie stars, musical prodigies, mystics (tarot), an Olympic swimming star, seasoned psychiatric patients. A myriad of personae, having split their fathers' foreheads full-grown, aged homunculi in their mothers' wombs.

Well, I for one, had a childhood, I told her. Maybe that's why I believe it's important to be able to find your own way almost anywhere.

What was it like? she asked me seriously. Melissa has been studying the violin since she was five.

I guess I'm glad I had one if that's what you mean, I told her. It may not necessarily spark your creativity, but it certainly makes you pay attention to the facts. Those of us with childhoods may not make things happen, but we always remember the things that do. Besides, I said, once you've gotten it over with, you don't have to go through it later on in life when it's less convenient.

To childhood, said Melissa, lighting up another joint, and we proceeded to talk about other things, sitting up in the lounge on our hall until almost dawn.

Like VD or mono, eccentricity seems to make the rounds of our tiny campus. A contagion. An epidemic, uncheckable, tenacious as the army of pinhead-sized parasites that invaded our living quarters right after the Christmas break. But for them, at least, there was a cure:

"I have been informed by the head nurse in the infirmary," says our college president, "that there is an outbreak of crab lice in this dormitory that is entirely out of control." This is one of the benefits of attending a small and exclusive college. Even the president, our star executive fund raiser, takes a personal interest in our welfare.

"Look, almost everybody's had them once in life," he says. "The only thing is they're hard to get rid of in group situations such as this." Group showers, group therapy, group everything . . . in which I never participate. Watching, from outside, the way I always have. Now I go into one of the stalls in the bathroom daily to search my pubic hair. As if, if I found one of the tiny lice, it would mean I belonged to this life. Watching the president laugh. "Remember, you get them not only from . . . ah, intimate contact. You can also get them from sheets and towels and things like that."

"Why shouldn't you take toothpicks into the toilet?" someone yells from the back of the room where we're assembled.

"Because crabs can pole-vault."

"That's pretty funny," replies our president, "but, still, unless we all make a concerted effort . . ."

"Have you got them too?" From the crowd. This is tasteless.

". . . unless a concerted effort is made," he continues,

"there may never be any end to this. I understand that the situation has continued for quite some time. Starting tomorrow morning the infirmary will dispense a body shampoo that kills the lice and their eggs," he says, "but everybody's got to be conscientious about washing sheets and underwear. Either that or we'll have to discontinue our experiment in coed dorms." Everyone boos him. "It's up to you," he says, smiling.

"This is the wildest school I've ever been to," I tell Melissa as we walk down the stairs to the basement.

"Well, you didn't exactly go to Malibu High. You should have been at Music and Art," she says. "If a teacher got too boring, everybody would just get up and leave. . . ."

But it's never boring here, inside the classroom or out. I never know what to expect next. Take the fencer, for instance, who at the end of the hour refused to remove his mask and tunic:

We'll meet again on Thursday, the gym teacher must have said, she usually did, opening the large cupboard under the basketball hoop where the equipment is kept.

I can't wait until Thursday, said the boy, poking her playfully in the abdomen with his rapier, but the tip is off. Two more days would be unendurable, he said.

I knew we should never have begun to admit men, the gym teacher shouted to her assistant. Call the guard.

En garde, said the boy, misunderstanding her, but she reached into the cupboard and, finding a medicine ball, threw it at him. By the time the man from security arrived, he was long gone out the door, parrying with tree branches, practicing his stance in front of defenseless garbage cans.

"Good Lord," I say, looking up from the table to see him prance in through the front door of the dining hall. "What's that person doing?" He fences his way through tables, spearing rolls, slicing the thin air, heading in the direction of the faculty section.

"Is this a happening?" Winnie asks me. But people are getting to their feet now, panic masking faces. A guard runs in through the door.

"Where is he?" he stops to ask. We point to the back of the room.

"He's armed," someone says, and the guard runs back out the door. For reinforcements?

"I can't stand it anymore," shouts the fencer. "Where is he?" As he flails away, people evacuate their lunches, clearing a path for the woodcutter who would do it himself. "There you are, Vance," he shrieks in a high-pitched voice. Our director of student life upends a table full of dishes, barricading himself behind it. I jump up on my chair.

"I told you I hated my roommate," the boy tells him, the rapier within stinging distance, his left arm curved over the shoulder like a scorpion's tail. "I've begged you for a transfer. But you wouldn't listen and now I've got to make you understand. . . ."

"You can have a single," shouts Mr. Vance.

Two faculty members and a dishwasher tackled the boy from behind.

After that they instituted a rooming lottery so the administration could not be held responsible for unfortunate matches. And the admissions committee was advised to screen applicants more carefully in the future for emotional stability. But none of this could keep childhood from surfacing, as if people grew younger here, back to themselves, rather than older and into the world of others.

Visions of preadolescent fear, like the time the Columbia University marching band arrived at our campus on a traveling football pep rally at six in the morning, sounding an initial trumpet note, convincing an entire house of students on acid that Gabriel had blown their destruction, and they waited through what turned out to be a five-hour Apocalypse in the basement. Of fairy tales . . . the fencer, both dueling prince and rescued maiden of his own dilemma. Occasionally even visions of sugarplums, like the round fruit of the sun eclipsed, disappearing one afternoon bite by bite into an open-mouthed moon.

Each week brought its new event. Fulfilling wishes of what

in childhood and dreams is called fantasy.

"What's going on over there?" I ask Winnie, closing the door of the vending-machine room behind us.

"It looks like somebody's jerking off in the coin return of the ice cream machine," she says. She grabs my arm.

"Are you kidding?" But as we go closer, it's true.

"We already called security," says a boy in a lab coat and dark glasses. "I don't think this guy's all there."

"Whatever gets you off," says the girl beside him, counting the change in her hand.

"Well, isn't anyone going to do anything?" I ask. The boy is panting now.

"Listen," says dark glasses, "he's been crashing in the lounge on my hall for a couple of weeks now. He's so spaced out he probably doesn't even know we're here."

"Hello," I shout at the boy hugging the machine. "Hello?"

"So much for getting ice cream out of that one," says Ralph the Marxist, coming up behind us. Dark glasses laughs.

"It's not funny," says Winnie who, thank God after all, had a childhood. "He's sick. . . ."

But by the time the guard arrived almost everybody had lost interest. After that no one could tell us what had happened to the boy. . . .

My mother was right. There are things you learn in college that you might never have known about otherwise. Stories like the events of my first year became the classics. I found out about Hegel and the dialectic in philosophy class. Not all of this a tribute but certainly a testimony to the life of the mind.

As for romantic poetry, a dead giveaway to the life of the heart, it would come later, when it was absolutely unavoidable, when it would become clearer that the only alternatives are embracing machines or caressing the green face of the lawn. After all, I had a childhood too.

Chapter IX

MEN AND WOMEN AT WAR

B UT TRY AS WE MIGHT, THERE WAS NO ELUDING the world of others. The circumstance of birth alone robs us of autonomy, hybrid of our two parents' keen desires, unwitting zygote of human generation. And from there the network extends as if the entire globe were a brain and all the interrelations of people the nerve pathways. The world sends itself messages through us; it thinks its thoughts along the directions our lives take.

The hollow threads that sew families together, umbilical tubes of shared and sensitive information, ensure the flexing of the involuntary muscles of its vital organs. Causing the adrenal glands to secrete a nervous energy, the stomach to rumble and knot, its communal heart to be put through its changing paces. The connections of towns and cities and highways full of people forming countries flex the voluntary muscles, defining the separate appendages and parts of the whole, secreting the wastes of living, allowing the world to talk to itself in many different tongues. People form the circuits for all actions.

But now something has happened to the brain of the world. We have become messengers of violence, transmitting the symptoms of a terrible mental disorder, a global psychopathology. Now the voluntary muscles perform a spastic dance of their own, and the gestures the world makes are the left leg kicking the right; the self-directed karate chop of a military salute; two clenched fists reminding us, like the sun and the moon by which we measure time, that individual lives are too short for us to hesitate in making change.

It is necessary, then, for us to restructure the pathways, extending hands, forming new liaisons, building from existing components the new section of the brain that will be responsible for discovering its own cure. This is the third week of the student strike for peace. No one will go back to classes until the war is over.

"If they drafted women," I tell Mark, "our involvement would grind to a halt; the apparatus of war would seize like an engine. You want to know why?"

"Why?" he asks, but halfheartedly. He pays strictest attention when he's the one who's talking, thoughtful tape recorder for himself. He rolls his extended fingers over the rainbow of markers, shifting slightly its position in the sky of the tabletop. "I think orange will show up well against purple," he says, uncapping one.

"It's because women simply wouldn't go," I continue. "They wouldn't fight. Regardless of personal ideology, political leanings either way. Because we haven't been brainwashed into accepting that kind of self-destruction. Other, more subtle kinds, yes. But the kind that involves tangible, identifiable weapons, no." I look at Mark opposite me at the table, but he won't look up. His brown hair rides his shoulders, dusting the table.

"What if you were a Third World woman?" he asks finally. I reach for the ruler beside him.

"That might be different," I tell him. "I don't know. What if I were the Queen of England, for that matter? Then I could take tea with the poet laureate and bemoan the decline of the empire. . . . No, Mark, I'm merely describing things from my own pitiful American bourgeois sensibility." But even this can't get a rise out of him.

"Some things are worth fighting for," he says.

Since the day we closed down the campus, Mark has suspended, along with any academic involvement, all sense of humor. He will not laugh again until the war is over.

"You may be right," I answer him—because it's also important not to be flippant in thinking through questions that involve persons' lives, "but it often seems that the causes each individual soldier supposes he bears arms for are confused in the end result."

"The individual must be expendable sometimes," he says, "for the greater good. Can I use the black when you're finished with it?"

I end up with what turns out to be a very irregular-looking

peace symbol and hand him the marker. I sit back in my chair. "What's this business about the greater good?" I ask him. "Isn't it for individuals to partake in?"

"Christ, are you reactionary," he groans, at last looking me in the eye. "What an elitist viewpoint." Mark is the master of a potent political vocabulary. Daily he memorizes new words from the primer of protest, as well as their rules of usage:

1. *reactionary*—applied to anyone who doesn't agree with you;

2. *elitist*—applied to anyone who attends this college without scholarship aid or guilt;

3. *revisionist*—applied to anyone who you thought agreed with you but, as it turns out, actually doesn't;

4. *antirevolutionary*—applied to anyone to who any of the above three terms can be applied;

5. *rhetorical*—applied to anyone who is very articulate but doesn't agree with you.

The list continues. As in grammar, the slot into which vocabulary properly fits, agreement is a key concept.

Sticks and stones can break my bones, as can missiles and landmines and machine guns. But words can never hurt me. In this case it's true; the movement will survive its own verbal abuse. But what of the other case? We are all banking on the power of words, reason, to break down the war machine.

"Mark, just hear me out." He's irritated now, attentive. "The best way to stop the war, I repeat, would be to demand that women participate, because they wouldn't. They wouldn't pull pins out of hand grenades; they wouldn't ambush guerrillas; they wouldn't drop napalm from airplanes."

"Too chicken shit," he says nastily.

"*I'm* the one who's reactionary?" I tell him. "You know as well as I do that the government doesn't want women to have a say in how the country is run because, in that case, things would begin to be run quite differently. So they tie one hand behind your back, and when you're in the ring, they dress your wounds and comfort you for not being able to connect. Why it's like having your feet bound and being told after the race what a crummy runner you are. It's . . . "

"Are you quite finished?" Mark asks me.

"Almost. But just think for a minute how you'd feel if you hadn't had a draft card to burn, if you hadn't had to put yourself on the line." This is my trump card, retrieved singed yet still whole from the crossfire of polemics.

"You're goddamned lucky to be a girl," he shouts at me across the three feet of the table, the Rubicon our ideas would pass to convert the other side once and for all. He lights a cigarette, striking vehemently at the matches. "Do you think it was easy doing that?" The smoke pours from his nostrils like the transparency of emotion turned opaque and visible. "What if I hadn't gotten my CO status? My father won't even talk to me now."

"Of course it wasn't easy," I yell back at him. "But what do you think it's like always having everything made easy for you? It's tempting and that's horrifying. You never have to stand up for anything because it's easier to remain seated. Some women even spend the majority of their waking hours in a reclining position. It's a metaphor and it's sickening."

"Metaphors, my ass," he says. "Save it for the classroom."

"You're trained for difficulties," I tell him. "We're not. But I sure as hell wish I didn't have to let life happen in the rotten way it often chooses because I'm not a bona fide participant."

He crushes his cigarette in the ashtray on the table and sighs.

"You and the other women on the steering committee are confusing all the issues," he says. "The most important thing is ending the war; everybody knows that. Other things will come later. That's just the way it has to be. Social change is slow," he adds knowingly. "For the time being everything else must be secondary."

"It's all connected," I tell him, now in an equally calm manner. "I suppose that if you believe in 'the greater good,' of course you'd believe in 'a lesser evil.' I, for one, do not."

"Listen, Angela," he says, "if men refuse to be inducted then the war will have to end. Period. Let's get real."

"Yes," I agree, "let's get real. Like it or not, quite enough men will continue to go. If women . . ."

"That is the height of egotism," he says. This may be true. He shakes his head and continues in silence to letter a poster announcing the big rally scheduled for outside the ITT building in New York City.

When we were children together, my brother Benjie and I indulged different tastes, and our arguments always stemmed from the overwhelming desire to make the other over in one's own image. For a while we toyed with the idea of what it would have been like if we'd been born as twins. In fact, it seems in retrospect that this is exactly what we were trying to make of one another—to engineer a fossil-like print on the other's mind, to train a carbon copy of one's own desires, to convince one's sibling into a sort of transmigration of the soul. Each of us took it as a personal insult when the other differed in any opinion. or course of action. This is the same mistake that married people often make, but we were still in the process of growing up then, and I look back on it now as understandable.

That's why there's chocolate and vanilla, my mother would say to us, trying to find a child's analogy for all the inevitable differences in the world. But this never satisfied us. At the ice cream parlor in town it would take half an hour to order our two cones. We would each sing the praises of our own particular flavor, trying to persuade the other of its merit.

Chocolate is boring, my brother would say. It's the color of mud pies.

But this flavor has nuts, salted almonds, I would answer, which contrast deliciously with the sweetness. Besides, it's crunchy when you chew it.

Behind the glass window of the counter, the big tubs were the repositories for all our personal choices, the mixed ingredients of which, when hardened and solidified like this, would become our adult lives.

You're not supposed to chew ice cream, Benjie said. You're supposed to lick it. It should be smooth and pleasing to the eye, too. Look at the intricate veins of navy blue in the blueberry ripple. It reminds me of ore in the walls of a mine. Maybe I'll be a miner, he said.

I resented his world view, how he could find careers in an ice cream cone. To me it was just food. Were our systems of reference just the shabby results of being brought up male and female? The Betty Crocker/Davy Crockett syndrome of experience? While I dissected and compartmentalized everything I found out about, my brother was forever mixing everything together. I was looking for a niche in which to fit myself, to squeeze in if necessary; he considered the whole world his domain, as if he could span the globe, the way his hand did a basketball.

My desk drawer contained the results of constant inventorying and reordering: small rubber-banded packets, filled envelopes, gold and silver stars in jars, labeled cigar boxes. His was like a big soup, potluck. He sometimes even put his socks there. I found this inexcusable.

One day I snuck into his room and sorted out the offending drawer.

Keep your cotton-pickin' hands off my property, he shouted afterward.

I was only trying to help, I told him.

Want to help? Don't help, he said. And from now on, don't go into my room unless I invite you. Otherwise it's trespassing.

How can you find anything in a drawer that's so cluttered? I asked him.

But he emptied the entire contents onto his bed, breaking down my categories of order with dedication and excitement, like the first scientist to split the atom. And he mixed everything together with his hands as if it were a deck of cards and he hadn't yet learned to shuffle, old and young all at the same time, that was my brother and continues to be. He swept the whole mess then off the edge of the bed into the drawer and fitted it back into the slot in the desk, satisfied.

Now don't fool around with my things ever again, he said.

I did it for your own good, I told him.

I'll decide what's good and what isn't for myself, he replied. It's a free country, you know.

At the time that seemed true, but eventually I had to rid myself of the idea the way I did other misconceptions, pursuing the facts and forcing myself to peruse them, like my face in the mirror. The moon is not made of green cheese, how could it be? Chickens, not Easter rabbits, produce eggs. If there are angels, they certainly do not live on the other side of the clouds but do their work here on Earth instead. Swallowing bubble gum will not stick your insides together. It is very rare for a person to die of the hiccups. You can't catch "cooties" from another person; those with bad personalities are a threat primarily to themselves. As to it being a free country, only through commitment and a sincere eye will this be realized.

When my brother and I were young, we were both, significantly, about the same age. We viewed the events of our childhood each through a single lens of the same pair of glasses. If you combined our two perspectives as vision does, a third dimension would be added: depth. Perhaps this is why we always hankered after the other one so, *because* of our differences as well as in spite of them, searching elsewhere for the other gender buried inside ourselves, trying to unite into clarity.

This is just to say that we had a history together, and it ties us like an invisible linkage between two people who share the same story; who together make up the entire, the truest story, like Siamese twins who share the same kidneys or the same heart.

Now that the operation of growing up has been successful and split us, we try to allow each other the Cyclopean perspective of our separate lives. I don't arrange my brother's drawers anymore. He is content that I will never taste blueberry ripple. So when he joined ROTC in college, what could I do? It's up to him, I said to myself.

This is no surprise. The men in my family have a military history to live up to. Each of the last three generations has grown into manhood and war at the same time. World War I. World War II. Now this one. It's no wonder they've made an equation of the two.

Beyond this, ever since my father left, his son has considered it necessary to follow any unpopular pathway. While other students are bombing ROTC buildings, he sits attentively inside one of their classrooms learning military strategies from a series of circles and arrows drawn in chalk on the blackboards depicting the Battle of the Bulge in which 120,000 German soldiers were killed and only 76,890 GI's.

Following any unpopular pathway, as if to follow in his father's footsteps. ". . . I took the [road] less traveled by," wrote Robert Frost, "and that has made all the difference." But what is this difference? When all is said and done, what can the difference possibly be? I never understood that poem.

If Ben wrote poetry maybe he could finish it for me, with a couplet, with a tag line, "not it." "Not it" is right; he doesn't even read it. Instead he drills up and down the football field on certain afternoons and on weekends. Maybe this is the difference. At least it's our difference.

"I think you should call up Ben and congratulate him," says my mother over the telephone. "He came out first in his class in ROTC." She spells the letters out.

"Over my dead body," I tell her.

"Angela, I am against the war myself," says my mother, "but this is what Ben's chosen to do, and I respect him for making his own decisions."

"He just doesn't want to be made into hamburger meat," I tell her. "An officer is less likely to be slaughtered in combat. Although you're right from the standpoint that if he were really against the war, he wouldn't go. And who does want to get slaughtered?"

"Men have an odd view of war," says my mother.

"Some men," I remind her.

"Well, the men of my generation, particularly," she continues. "They didn't like the idea of fighting, but they considered it an irrefutable fact of life, like shoveling the snow out of the driveway at six in the morning or grabbing a baseball bat and rushing to the front door if they think they hear a burglar."

"When will men ever relax enough to allow themselves to just stay in bed and pull the covers up over their heads?" I ask her. "Good God, once you're trained to be stoic you never unlearn it. Every middle-aged man I know field-strips his cigarettes. They smoke as if they're still in the trenches, holding the cigarette between the thumb and third finger, the lighted end hidden by the palm so the enemy can't see it aglow."

"Angela," says my mother sternly, "they *did* fight against Hitler. They helped save Europe from totalitarianism."

"I know that," I tell her. Nothing is uncomplicated and nothing is singular; everything is its opposite, too. "I guess there was no choice. But this isn't 1945; it's 1970. Don't life and circumstances evolve?"

"Yes," she says. "I certainly hope so. But everyone interprets history differently, which is why you should call up your brother."

"Which is why I can't."

"Just a few words," says my mother. "You can make the call short."

"Words?" I am incredulous. "Words are the personifications of ourselves and our beliefs. It's wrong to use them for any other purpose. Otherwise it's propaganda."

"Angela, you've got a lot to learn," says my mother. "The shortest distance between two points is rarely a straight line."

"Yes, especially when you're dodging bullets," I tell her.

She hangs up on me.

Benjie, the child, imagining himself marching in the ranks of green plastic soldiers he used to set up in rows on the pink basement floor. Ben, the adult, who scared himself with the test results that showed a particularly high aptitude for learning Vietnamese. He used to dress up in splendid uniforms; now they're going to teach him how to kill. I worry about him. He's my brother.

The official strike office has no bare walls. Posters of flying doves, antiwar slogans, and peace signs dress its interior. The bulletin board never sports enough thumbtacks to display advantageously the newspaper clippings and press releases and personal messages people add to it daily. Sometimes two pieces of paper overlap, creating a conglomerate and confusing message: Eileen, tell your/LOCAL DRAFT BOARD TO CLOSE DOWN or COLUMBIA ON STRIKE/to share two-bedroom apartment for the summer.

"I'm sick of answering the goddamned telephone," says Melissa one afternoon, slamming it down at the end of a call, kicking her feet up onto the desktop. This is a symbolic gesture. Its message, at least, is clear.

"For that matter, I'm pretty tired of throwing away all the out-of-date notices on the board," I add. I upend the trash can in front of me, scattering scraps of paper and cigarette butts all over the floor. This overt act surprises even me.

"Hey, what's going on?" says Mark, stopping his yoga exercises. He rises hurriedly to his feet and brushes the ashes from his pants. "Can't you be more careful?" he asks me.

"It's all political housekeeping," says Melissa, gesturing with both hands, a conductor of discord. "And I'm not going to do another thing around here until the shitwork is evenly distributed." We are, I think, striking the strike. "Mark, you can answer the telephone for the rest of the afternoon," she says.

"But I can't," he protests. He hesitates and then points to the big round clock on the wall. "I have a meeting in five minutes. Besides, ask Angela, I do my share of the shitwork. I made posters every day last week." He looks to me for help. This is what my mother calls "barking up the wrong tree."

"Mark," I remind him. "You're a painter. You like making posters."

"I don't see what that has to do with anything," he says.

"I do not plan a career with Bell Telephone, Mark," says Melissa, but he continues to hurriedly throw papers from one of the desks into his briefcase. "I'll go to the meeting for you," she continues. "Then you'll be free to answer the phone."

"But," he says.

"But what?" asks Melissa, walking up to him. Her fists are clenched; will she hit him?

"Well, I don't know . . ." he says, backing up to the desk. "Except that I'm more thoroughly briefed on the events at Columbia than you are. The situation changes there hourly; you have to be on top of what's happening: the arrests, the building takeovers, and so forth." It's true. How will Melissa get around this?

"Of course you know the situation better than I do," she shouts at him. "Whenever they call up, they always ask for you or Billy, and we never find out anything until we attend the meetings, which we usually can't do because we're answering the phone or running some stupid errand. What do you think this is, the ladies' auxiliary?"

"That's ridiculous," says Mark, shrugging as if to get this monkey off his back. "Oh, all right," he says after a considerable silence.

"May I have your report?" asks Melissa. He hands her a notebook from his briefcase. "Wish me luck," she calls, disappearing out the door.

Mark lights up a cigarette and stares at the telephone with hatred. He blows smoke rings, tiny nooses in which to catch Melissa's neck. For once it doesn't ring all afternoon. Clearly, God is a man.

If I had any guts I'd slip out into the corridor and call him from the pay phone. I would disguise my voice and ask him to tell me the entire spring calendar of marches, actions, and rallies. Then I would ask him to repeat it. Instead I go for a walk and ask myself why I can't take things in hand like Melissa.

When she comes into my room to pick me up for dinner, her hair is disheveled and her eyes red. She sits down on the bed and then stretches out while I change my jeans.

"What happened?" I ask her apprehensively.

"I made an ass out of myself."

"Come on," I tell her, "you couldn't have been that bad." She pulls the bedspread over her head and I hear her crying. "That bad?" I ask, sitting down beside her and hugging the blue lump.

"Terrible," she sobs from inside her tent of shame. "I stammered and stuttered, and when people asked me questions, I didn't know any of the answers."

"But, still, what you did had to be done. I admire that,

Melissa." This must be what courage is then: being willing to take a fall, knowing you're going to get it ahead of time and doing what you have to, anyway.

"Want to know something?" she says, her head emerging, wet eyes. "That bastard gave me the wrong notebook. It was all quotations from Nietzsche."

"Melissa, are you serious?" She nods. "Well," I tell her, "this is the last straw. My hopes for the world and all my faith in human nature and its intrinsic goodness are now destroyed. I didn't want to have to write off half of the human race, but that does it. I pledge to you that I will one day marry a man for the sole purpose of ruining his life. Revenge will be had."

"Bravo." Melissa begins to laugh. "I thought I was just going to die," she says. "Not that you're expected to be considerably insightful, though. In these meetings, delivery is what counts. I could have bluffed my way through if I'd had the ah . . . balls. What's the female equivalent of *balls?*" she asks me.

"We don't know yet," I tell her.

"Ready for dinner?" she asks, slowly getting up from the bed. I pick up my jacket from the floor.

"Let's forget dinner," I suggest. "Let's walk down to Ray's and get drunk instead. OK? It's on me."

"I'd be delighted," she says.

That night in bed I sleep with one foot on the floor to keep the room from spinning like all the ideas I have in my head. Airplane bed, my mother calls it. Navigator off his mark. I dream myself standing at the podium of the auditorium in front of a large assembly of students, concisely expressing my political ideas, outlining impassioned and startling strategies for twisting the nation's firing arm. When I am finished, the audience applauds wildly; some of them jump to their feet, marionettes pulled into motion by their heartstrings. Thank heaven human beings were afforded the necessary luxury of sleep and dream, visitations to a netherworld where we imagine ourselves the people we want to be, a testing ground for aspects of our future selves.

But, waking, I feel like a technician without tools, a lawyer without the proper casebooks, a Demosthenes who doesn't know how to rid her mouth of the pebbles. Ladies do not spit, my mother told me.

I'll have to seek the education I need then, attending the night school of my dreams and, following Melissa's lead, the rigorous basic training of the days.

When I joined the guerrilla theater troupe, I bungled my lines, all of them, but I was the best at screaming and falling down dead. A start perhaps?

One war may be slowly ending. But it seems that women will have to learn how to fight after all.

─────── Chapter X ───────
ASKING QUESTIONS

I REREAD THE XEROXED TELEGRAM MY MOTHER
sent me; it is not from her: DEAR ALL/TODAY I TURNED 50/AM
COMING HOME/SHOULD I?/ARRIVING IN NEW YORK NOV 5 8:30 PM/
WARREN. Daddy on paper held up to the light of my desk lamp,
suddenly materialized, the invisible ink of his departure transformed, illuminated into a decipherable message of homecoming.
This can't be fair.

I spent years getting over my father, like a near-fatal illness,
a bitter disappointment, a hurdle whose height you have to grow
into. We all did. All right, said my mother, let's chalk this one up
to experience; and we did. Then we washed down the blackboard
of what we learned from him so clean there wasn't a trace of my
father left. The empty slate of our lives starting over, it was black
as the night sky, but starless, not a dot of white, so that the navigator could never find his was back to us only to leave again.

We forgot that Daddy has an impeccable sense of direction.
I rip up the telegram and throw it in the wastebasket.

Clearly it is dangerous to rediscover a parent. Even
literature teaches us this. Take Oedipus, for example, or
Hamlet. Will I be enlisted in my father's tragic cause?

"Of course you can meet him," says my mother over the
phone later in the evening. "He's your father, after all. I was
only married to him for seventeen years."

"But I don't know if I want to meet him," I tell her. For a
million reasons, but I come up with a tangible excuse. "What if I
didn't recognize him?"

"I think it's more likely," she says, "that he won't recognize
you. You were fourteen when he left, if you remember. You
hardly even had breasts then." This is how my mother outwits
the failing memory of a filled life, by concretizing it through
people's physical attributes. That's when your uncle first began
putting on weight, she might say. Or that was the year your
grandfather had his gallbladder operation.

148

"I remember," I tell her, though my system has more to do with physical absence than its presence.

"It's just that it's such a shock," says my mother. "I mean I assumed that he'd come back to stay eventually, though looking back on it now, after the fact, I don't know why. He could just as easily have chosen to settle in another country." We have come to talk of my father as if he were a character in some novel. We discuss what we consider justified behavior, what is consistent with his motivations. He is the protagonist of a series of volumes: the first ones rich and realistically detailed, written by him; the more recent ones sketchy but imaginative, written by us.

"But I never thought of *when* he'd return," she continues. "It's been six years."

"I don't suppose you have a personal statute of limitations?" I ask her, but she doesn't find this funny.

"I most certainly do not," she says, pausing for emphasis. "But what made him decide after six years as opposed to three or ten, let's say?"

"Now you're expecting Daddy to be predictable?"

"I see your point," she says.

"What exactly does it feel like to you?" I ask her. If she explains herself clearly, perhaps I'll feel it too.

"I don't feel anything," says my mother. This is disappointing, but at least we share our bewilderment. "I feel absolutely numb. Your father is a pro at the sneak attack. He could have wired us weeks ago," she says. "This is not the kind of decision that's made overnight. Instead, he lets us know eight days ahead of time. . . . This is more warning, however, than he gave us when he decided to leave."

"Maybe he wanted to be able to tell himself that we hadn't had enough lead time in case none of us were to show up," I suggest.

"Maybe," she says. A short silence follows. "Though how he has the gall to expect any of us to meet him is beyond me. I, for one, am not." My mother's voice, stretched over two hundred miles of telephone wire, sounds exhausted and thin, as if it were about to break. "Why did that bastard have to choose a port on this side of the Mason-Dixon line, anyway?" she asks.

"What does he think this family is, Plymouth Rock? He ought to go back to Georgia where he belongs, because being southern is a disease whose victims should be quarantined. We should have let them secede when we had the chance," she says.

"He could just be passing through," I remind her, a woman who just for a moment would stop her soul-searching and blame the dissolution of her marriage on American history.

"That's true," says my mother, recovering herself with a sigh. "Angela, we all have our individual feelings on this matter. I am past making accusations against your father. At least I try to be. . . . As one of your two parents, I leave the decision entirely up to you. Go, if you want; I won't feel betrayed."

"Is Ben going?" I ask her.

"He'll be on maneuvers," she says. "Anyway, you have three days in which to decide, you know."

"I know."

"I wonder what he'll do next," she says, as if to herself. "Your father's like a cat he's had so many different lives."

"Does Daddy have any friends?" I ask her.

"I can't speak for this last period," she says, "although, since ships' crews are constantly changing, I imagine friendships or whatever you want to call them last the duration of a single voyage. As to his former friends, there was your Uncle Freddie and myself."

"Oh."

"And, of course, you and Ben."

"Then why did he leave us?"

"Oh Lord," she says. "Hold on while I get a cigarette. . . . Angela?"

"Yes."

"Well, as you know," she begins, "the situation was none too happy as time went on. That was no secret to any of us, how could it be? But it was a marriage not without love.

"If your father and I couldn't agree on most things, it was because of the desperate need we both had to meet the other with our entire selves, to present the full gamut of our concerns. You wouldn't persist in this if you didn't care about someone an awful lot; it's an overwhelming commitment, and beyond that, as it's been borne out, you run a terrible risk." She sighs.

"Then how can two people possibly be compatible?" I ask her.

"More often than not," she answers, "one person gives in by degrees, slowly sliding over into the other's territory of beliefs, and in this way there's a meeting of the minds or mind, if you will. On the other hand, some couples battle through and maintain the fine balance of their differences. Your father and I were caught somewhere in the middle of this siege.

"As to why he finally left, why one *particular* day he suddenly gave up," she says, "that's a question I've asked myself over and over. I still don't know what the answer is; there's probably a different answer for every two people who start out loving each other but find that that isn't always enough. . . ."

I hang up, the weight of this conversation recradled again in its accustomed receiver, silence. But not for long. My father is back, risen from the dead. And I realize that I'll have to go meet him if only to discover the answers to the two questions hidden under my tongue since the day he left. The first is for him. It's the same one my mother asks: Why? The second is for me, and I'll ask myself to answer it when I'll be most truthful, when I've got him face to face.

Instead of going to classes, I spend the next morning calling up the Port Authority, trying to find out where his ship will dock. I keep getting put on hold; then we're disconnected. Why didn't he include this in his telegram? Perhaps he's afraid that one of us will actually meet him, make the successful and dreaded connection finally as I do, after a series of calls, with a clerk who tells me the number of the correct pier. Perhaps he's afraid, as we are, of our questions.

The half-hour train ride is endless. As in the moment before dying, in which everything is remembered, I review our case history with my father, a law court of one sitting in judgment: He used to shave with a safety razor every morning at five thirty before going to work, landscaping the lather and removing it, like the snow he often found in our driveway in winter. He would carve the roast on Sundays, making thin slices the way my mother liked it, to pass around on the platter. Even on Saturdays he mowed the lawn, trimming its shaggy beard, cutting off thin green slices from the roast-shaped hill of the front yard, depending on the significance Saturday had for him in a given week, a day of relative rest or one demanding his attention to numerous household chores.

This being his calendar of events, days of blades, is it any wonder that he could cut himself from us with a single and precise stroke? Human beings are always in training for their futures, though they may not know it at the time.

I chain-smoke, looking out the green-tinted window bottle-like, at the lights of the towns through which we pass. The landscape changes by degrees from trees and expanses of lawn on the banks of highways to factories and warehouses, window-less, floodlit, faded signs painted on their sides: ALLAROUND LIGHTING MAINTENANCE ELECTRICAL SUPPLIES GARCIA'S flats fixed/tires recapped. On to tenement buildings, water towers perched above them on stilts, drab parrots on brick shoulders. The pink neon signatures of bar names. I am passing from home territory into what I imagine to be my father's world: everything unknown.

Most of the seats in the car are vacant; all but a few of its passengers are sitting by themselves, their eyes drawn once in a while from newspapers and books to the dirty windows. Occasionally, when the interior lights flicker and die, our reality shifts from inside the car out onto the sidewalks under street-lights and into apartment buildings whose windows are illumi-nated, small movie screens of changing domestic tableaus. For an instant we are each asleep in our own beds, and the people we see are the characters of our dreams, our other selves.

I light a match in the dark. Waking, my face reflects in the window like that of my shaving father in his morning mirror.

"Grand Central. Grand Central, next," sings the trainman, passing down the aisle as the lights come up. He snatches ticket stubs from behind our heads, last chances disappearing into his coat pocket. Now there is no getting off at the wrong stop, no getting lost upon the way to prevent the arrival.

We enter the tunnel, which makes a crawling snake of the

train, its glowing belly our insular reality, having shed the luminous skin of other people's worlds. Why should I slip back into my father's life, anyway, after scraping it painfully from me on rocks and tree bark?

The train stops; the doors open with a motorized whirring sound. Just after the last person disappears through them, I get up and follow him out onto the concrete walkway, but that's as far as I get. Businessmen, late going home from work, brush past me, geometrical constructs of overcoats, briefcases, ties, and hats. I look for the familiar shape of my father among them. A magnet suspended between the two poles of what I know about him, I can't budge until one of the commuters bumps into me and knocks me in the direction of the open doors of the train. I walk inside and sit down, awaiting the ride back. I don't have to do anything I don't want to do.

". . . board," says the conductor from the entrance. I jump up and slide through the doors just as they're closing.

"Watch it there," he shouts at me through the glass. "Crazy dame." The toe of my left boot is caught. Will the train, the locomotive of my cowardice, drag me all the way home? I yank it free and limp up the ramp out into the downstairs vestibule of the station. People are walking toward the different lighted-up entrances to tracks. The magazine kiosk displays its multicolored tiers of information. A flower vendor sells wilted roses from a cart.

"You got a dime for a phone call?" asks a derelict sitting on the stairs I'm climbing. He's wearing a green army blanket for a coat, tied around his waist with a piece of rope. I pull two dollars out of my pocket and give it to him.

"Have a drink," I say.

I check the time on the clock on the main floor. The facsimile of a Kodak photograph, the huge illuminated advertisement on one of the other walls, shows a family sitting at a picnic table having a cookout. The daughter is passing the ketchup.

I find my way out to the sidewalk where a line of cabs is pulled up to the curb. I climb in the first one.

"Where do you want to go?" asks the driver.

"Downtown," I tell him. "Under the West Side Highway."
"You sure that's where you want to go?"
"No, but we might as well get started."
"Sure thing, lady," he says. He reaches over, lowering the
flag of the meter the way my father used to push down the metal
handle on the grill. He never could get the charcoal lighted
unless he used half a can of gasoline. Once he scorched three of
the rhododendron bushes when he threw in the match .

All right, all right, said my mother. Next time we'll cook
indoors. But once he dug a pit and made a clambake on the
Fourth of July for us and all the neighbors. Nothing got burned
and it was a big success.

But, Daddy, I said, you never even made a clambake
before. How did you know how?

I read up on it, he said, in an old Yankee cookbook at the
library. Angela, it always pays to do a bit of research before you
embark on something.

Well, I've done my homework, all right. I've turned him
inside out like a glove. I've turned him upside down, like a room
in which you've lost something, over on his head. He went
through his days silent as an hourglass. Maybe, in spite of all my
research, that's why I just can't figure out what makes him tick.

The taxi pulls up alongside a pier, to which a ship is made
fast with lines the size of my arm. Metal scaffolding grows out of
the deck, tall iron strands of hair standing on end, multiplying,
casting shadows in the floodlights. Beside it, a warehouse,
missing windowpanes on the topmost floors, is dark except for
the rectangle of an open door facing the street.

"This must be it, miss," says the driver. "You want me to
wait?"

"No thanks." I hand him the money and get out. The slam
of the door is a sharp crack that my feet echo walking along the
pavement to the lighted office. Two men in heavy sweaters and
wool caps are sitting on an old wooden desk next to a file cabinet
and an empty water cooler. The coils of a small electric heater
glow orange.

"Is the crew still on board?" I ask, playing with the buttons
of my coat.

"What do you want to know for?" asks the heavyset one with glasses.

"I came to meet somebody," I tell him.

"I see," he says. The room is cloudy with smoke. I take out a cigarette and he lights it for me with a lighter from the desk top beside him. He uncrosses his legs. "Somebody in particular?" he asks.

"Yes, somebody in particular." I begin to cry. I hate myself for crying, I should have socked him in the jaw. But the man, having clearly got the upper hand, will be nice to me now.

"Come on, honey, we'll find him," he says, getting up from his desk, puffing. "What's his name?" He dispatches the other man to go look. What if he's left? "You just wait right here." But I can't meet my father in front of these people.

"I think I'll go outside," I tell him. He shrugs his shoulders. The only lights out here are from the ship, the dim streetlights, and the cars' headlights as they travel along the elevated highway. Underneath it, trucks are parked, U-Hauls, an occasional car. I wipe my eyes on my sleeve and bite my tongue hard enough to stop the tears. I walk back and forth in front of the pier. The foot I caught in the train door begins to throb. I listen to the gravel crunching underneath my boots against the whine of the cars. The wind from the Hudson blows at my bones, as if like the wino I, too, had no coat. New Jersey sparkles across the river. You can even see the Statue of Liberty. I light up another cigarette. Can people in New Jersey see its glowing tip?

I hear footsteps along the wooden pier, voices. Two men in pea jackets turn the corner out of the gate. What if one of them is my father? But they're speaking Spanish.

"Angela?"

He comes up beside me out of nowhere, as quietly as he left six years ago, and takes my arm, cupping my elbow with his palm, the same way he used to when we went to Boston for the day and had to cross busy streets.

"You shouldn't have been here by yourself," he says. "Let's get a cab." We don't look at each other, crossing under the elevated roadway, passing grayed brick buildings with shipping platforms and all-night garages along a cobblestoned street. He's wearing a trench coat; I feel it brush my knees.

"Is this a downtown avenue?" he asks himself. As he walks out into the empty street to check the direction of approaching traffic, I steal a glance at him. He looks just the same.

"After you," he says, opening the door, his efforts success-ful. But close up his short hair is thinning and gray at the temples. "Luchow's," he says to the driver.

"Luchow's?"

"I went there with your mother once," he says. He looks at me for the first time, the business of being once again the father done. Though he's not wearing a hat, he smells the same way he used to when he'd come through the front door out of the cold, like leather and felt. As if the odor clung to him like a memory.

"That's quite a wild hairdo you have there," he says.

"I decided to let it go natural," I tell him.

"You get your frizz from your mother's side," he says matter-of-factly.

We check our coats.

"I'm sorry, sir," says the maître d', "but gentlemen are requested to wear neckties here." My father reaches down to the floor. He straightens up, tying one of his shoelaces around his collar.

"Will that do?" he asks.

"I suppose so, sir," and we're led to a small table way in the back. My father hasn't changed a bit.

"What do you want?" he asks.

"A Scotch."

"Two double Scotches," he says to the waiter. He lights us two Camels. "Well," he says, looking at me.

I decide that my father should write a travelogue. He says that, although my college, a free-spirited place, has no majors, I should consider a course of study that will lead me to some sort of career. I go to the bathroom three times; he goes twice. This makes five times and this is the same number of trips the waiter has made to our table with new drinks. But now we're ready.

"You were often crabby," I start.

"I couldn't always help myself and sometimes I had headaches," he says. "Do you know that every single year for Christmas you gave me a scarf?"

An oompah band starts to play somewhere in the front of the restaurant.

"You never wanted *anything*," I tell him. "It's lucky you left. I'd run out of colors that would match your gray overcoat."

"I still have them all," he says, "though I mostly traveled in warm climates. Is the dog still alive?" he asks.

"Mummy and I took her to the vet and had her put to sleep last summer. She was going blind and her hind legs gave out so she couldn't walk anymore, just sort of drag herself."

"She was a good dog," says my father. "She barked loudly at strangers and she was gentle with children." The music's coming closer, getting louder. "I always felt you took your mother's part, you know," he says in a raised voice.

"You were right," I answer him. "But you never asked for anyone's support the same way you never asked for anything for Christmas."

"What a kid you were, Angela," says my father leaning over the table. "When I arrived home from work, the second I got the front door open you'd practically push your mother out of the way to give me a rundown on the day's news. Telling me the cesspool overflowed, your mother shrunk one of my good shirts in the clothes dryer, the dog threw up on the living room carpet."

"I felt you should know," I shout at him. The music is deafening. "I wanted you to know everything. I couldn't bear the thought that the tiniest bit of information would escape you. I even wanted to tell you my dreams. . . . So what do you know now that you didn't know then?" I ask him. "What did you find out?"

"Here you are, Angela," says my father, "greeting me at the door again." He smiles, putting his glass down. Four approaching musicians in lederhosen surround our table, serenading us.

"Only this time I'm not telling you anything, am I?" I shout at my father. "I'm asking you questions, instead. What did you find out? Was it worth everything? This time I want *you* to tell *me*. How was your day, Daddy?" I ask him. "How was your six-year day?"

"Oh Angela," he bellows, reaching over the back of his chair, pantomiming shutting a door behind him, "today I did everything." He pauses. The opera of my father's trip: "I read the entire set of the Harvard Classics, the complete Yale Shakespeare, and every *National Geographic* from the first issue. I explored all the major ports of South America, Africa, and India. I drank rum sours, ate curry lunches. I stood watches on deck at night out to sea where sometimes it got so quiet that a man would jump overboard to escape his loneliness."

"What I found out," he continues, "the most important thing, though, was at the end of the day."

"What was that?" I ask him.

"I found that I wanted to come home," he says. He puts his roughened hand over mine on the tablecloth. "And you, Angela?" he shouts. The musicians begin to move away. "How was your day?" My father asking me, for the first time, to tell him what I always told him anyway. The recitation of my day, unaccompanied by music or by my father:

"Me? Oh I spent it growing up. That's what I did all day long; I just got older by the hour," I tell him. "I started out in the morning playing hopscotch and my favorite game, hide-and-seek, in the woods. But since I couldn't find you anywhere, during lunch I helped Mummy move out of the house. And in the afternoon, I moved again, to a boarding school, where I took lessons in amnesia. Before dusk I graduated and went to college. I did a lot of watching today. I watched everything change. Not always for the discernible good or bad, just change, that's all."

"Transformations," says my father. "The funny thing is you have to stay long enough in the same place and you have to be looking for them in order to see them. I didn't know that when I left." He finishes the last of his drink.

"Daddy, what are you going to do now?" I ask him.

"Who knows?" he says. "But I'll think of something. What are you going to do?"

"I didn't mean that," I tell him. "What are you going to do tonight? Tomorrow?"

"I'm going to pick up my bags and go to a hotel," he says. "And tomorrow I'm going to take the train due north and stop off to take a look at our old house."

"What do you want to do that for?" I ask him.

"I don't know," he says. "I just do. Maybe I'll move into your treehouse. Are you hungry?" he asks me.

"No. Are you?"

"No," he says. "I hate German food."

"Anyway," I tell him, "the last train back to Westchester leaves in twenty-five minutes."

The cab pulls up at Grand Central. We walk inside, descending to the lower level by mistake. It's empty. The flower vendor is gone; the kiosk is locked up tight behind a metal gate; the old man in his coat has no doubt transformed it back into a blanket for the night and gone off to some corner to sleep.

Upstairs, my father buys me a ticket.

"Daddy?"

"Yes, Angela?"

"Will everything be all right?" I ask him.

"You mean life?"

"Yes."

"That's a question nobody can answer," he says. "All I know is what I knew before—that the knot in my stomach is the measure of my hopes and fears." We hug and kiss good-bye. "I love you," he says. "And thank you for coming to meet me. I'll call you tomorrow."

"I love you too"—answering, finally, my own question. As for the other one, his, it's probably another of the ones you just can't answer. He stands outside the window, waving, until the train pulls out.

How is it that reversing my father's printed directions to our first home would lead him years later to my mother's doorstep in Boston? Did I mention that he pays her visits now in the apartment she rented two months after we found his note: "En route to Singapore. From there, who knows what? I'm sorry. Warren."?

Sorry . . . said my mother, starting to pack. And my

brother grew as inexorably as the red line he drew through the global seas and oceans, charting my father's slow and steady course for six years, until one day he graduated a semester early from college and entered the army. Shall I tell how I awaited my father in postcards? How he came to us once a month in 3½-by-5½-inch pictures, of the Panama Canal at sunset, a tiny roadside market outside of Valparaiso, Chile? Do I find my father in the red sun receding, in the water that rushes vengefully from the locks into a sealed chamber to raise an entire ship and cargo on its back? Is he the tree that lightning never fells, gnarled and conspicuous, in the center of a planted field? Or the 1942 Ford traveling down the middle of an African byway, like a ship making waves of the dust?

I read our history, as it happened, in my father's telegrams: HAPPY SIXTEENTH BIRTHDAY ANGELA LOVE DADDY/SO THE DIVORCE IS FINAL I LOVE YOU THOUGH YOU DON'T BELIEVE IT WARREN/MERRY CHRISTMAS EVERYBODY FROM COLOMBO CEYLON GUESS WHO/BENJIE CONGRATULATIONS ON YOUR ACCEPTANCE TO COLLEGE LOVE DAD/ANGELA WRITES ME OF YOUR PROMOTION DARLING BECOMING A SENIOR EDITOR AT 44 ISN'T EASY ESPECIALLY FOR A ROOKIE LOVE YR EX/DEAR ALL TODAY I TURNED 50 AM COMING HOME SHOULD I? ARRIVING NEW YORK NOV 5 8:30 PM WARREN

Is this what the Sputnik of my childhood foretold? Did it draw a table in the sky, blueprint and form for the real table below that was built in a Wisconsin factory, shipped east in pieces by train, and reassembled in the dining room of my mother's new home? Because this is where we sit, reunited sometimes, the four of us, on holidays and when we can. My father walks over from his furnished room around the corner, and we like to drink and talk, because, after all, even my mother says so, this is our family. A point where the longitude and latitude of love and birth once met. Our shared predicament.

So be it, we all say. Times change. What's passed has passed. But as for me, I'll take my lovers two at a time in case one of them runs off.

PART TWO

Chapter XI

FIRSTS

I T'S THE FIRST OF APRIL, THE FIRST MONTH OF spring of the first year of the new decade. First base, first born, first aid, first class, first violin, first water, first family, bronzed first baby shoes. How we love firsts. Tonight we will have a dance at the school gym in celebration.

Continuing through the space age, will we measure a milestone every hour, wave flags through holidays of minutes, draw up new desk calendars with a box each for the seconds? Human beings are crazy about starting over. As if we could.

Still and all, if there's one thing we can count on, it's the seasons, natural events beyond our control, that assure us of cyclical beginnings and ends. And it's spring we like the best (no one who's honest says to the contrary); we can't help it because it comes first in the growth of the year, our metaphor for the second chance after the false start. Each year finding ourselves a little further around the track, not running even so in our true stride nor nearly as fast as we had hoped when, suddenly, the voice over the loudspeaker announces to our delight that the starting flag has been waved improperly and that the contestants may reconvene for another go. This is its glory, and even a scrooge gives a sniff in the spring air.

As I walk out of my dormitory, the lilacs near the iron gate are in bloom; occasional stratified snowy clouds mark the sky like the patterned linoleum of a blue kitchen floor. Three gardeners in their shirt sleeves plant red and yellow tulips in the thawed soil of the garden that bounds the rectangle of the main lawn. Students lie in the green grass, half-clothed. Lilac, blue, red, yellow, and green—the merry, bright colors of the Fool's outfit. The April Fool. It is suggested that tonight we go dressed up in costumes, but many of us will be too self-conscious.

Beer cans dot the lawn, cooling in the shadows of stacks of unopened books. Honeysuckle perfumes the air, and bees make beelines above along the trellised walkway that leads to the library, the sun having baked away sufficiently at winter until it has risen and disappeared to far above the treetops. The few dogwoods planted randomly along the outskirts of the campus have passed their blooming, laying white-petaled magic carpets on which to sail anywhere imaginable. But who would go? Fallen yet hopeful, therefore wise and at the same time foolish, we find Eden here in a flower. Spring is the drug of mating, if brief (first man, first woman, first betrayal), the Spanish fly of the seasons.

Still, like my newly returned father, I've maintained a passion for the treatise and phenomenologies. I read, much of the night, until almost dawn, when I switch off the overhead light of my cubicle and slide my legs down into the bed, its iron springs briefly wheezing. Passion spends itself in my head then, too, the also darkened room of a solitary desire.

But which is which? Is all desire the same? Can we imagine the outline of the universe in the contours of a single body? Does the earth's spinning teach us the velocity of the frenzy of love? As consciousness undresses itself, laying bare its exquisite and androgynous form, blood rushes to the walls of the brain until ideas multiply themselves like contractions.

These are equations I make, formulae for the future: Masturbation, like thinking and appreciation, is a solitary and predictable pursuit. Taking someone into your bed, like dialogue and mutuality, is more problematic; you have to relinquish control. This is a terrible state of affairs, but it's part of the life we're born into, inescapable as time and the planet. Because no one is exempt from this lunacy of spring—eradicating the past, looking only to the future, a new beginning—a propensity for pairing in the genes, the desire to cloak our loneliness with another skin. You can't get away from it. Sex, consciousness contorted, the singing heart: where inevitably we act out all our longing, the targets in which the arrows of Eros find their mark, the three-ringed circus of love.

Tonight, uncostumed, we will go as fools anyway, dressed as ourselves. Fools on the first day of April, made sport of, sent bootless on errands. Errands of love.

The very next evening he calls me up.

"I miss you already," he says. "A surprise."

"I miss you, too," I tell him. Also a surprise.

"I worked at home today," he says, "and I didn't take a shower this morning so I could smell your scent all over me while I sat at my desk. I had trouble concentrating."

"Really?" I ask. This is exhilarating and disturbing; I cross my legs on the desk chair. Is life all beds and desks?

"Tomorrow I have to go out of town on business," he says.

"What do you do?" I ask him.

"I sell computer systems," he says, "though I still miss the life of a student."

"Well, take a shower before you go," I insist, "because that's a respectable business, not like rock music or something. And call me when you get back."

"I will. I will," he says. "Listen, I've got your number memorized: 914–337–2109."

"How do I know you're not reading it out of your address book?" I ask him.

"You'll just have to trust me," he says, but this is a little after the fact.

I come from a small town in Bavaria, which I own, he told me the night before. My father was a feudal lord who met with his death while hunting wild boars. Gored through the throat.

My mother was Joan of Arc, I told him. The voices she heard were me, speaking to her from the womb.

We will never be compatible, he said. Anyway, Joan of Arc didn't menstruate so she couldn't have had any children.

How do you know that? I asked him.

Because I was a history major in college.

What if we'd met then? I asked, myself a student of time and circumstances.

You would have been more interested in horses, he said.

I was never interested in horses, I told him.

Why are you shaking? he asked me. We were lying in our clothes, in the halo of a candle's light, on my bed.

Because I'm not used to this, I told him, playing with his beltloops. It makes me nervous.

Then why did you invite me back from the dance, he asked, stammering slightly on the *d*.

It was a premeditated act, I told him, my eyebrows lifting slightly as they often do when I'm being candid in spite of myself. Tonight I would have picked up practically anybody. . . .

Thanks, he said, starting to swing his legs over onto the floor, but I grabbed for them and held him back.

. . . but, I continued, I chose *you*, first, because you're handsome; second, because of the way your two hands felt on my back when we danced; and, third, because of your stutter. . . .

D-do you bring home paraplegics, too? he asked.

I never brought anyone home before in my life, I told him.

Oh, he said.

Men without stutters, I replied, don't let you get a word in edgewise.

Oh is that so? he said, nestling back against the pillows. Perhaps it's just that I'm older than most of the men you know and more subdued.

How old is that? I asked him.

Thirty-two, he said.

That must be it then, I agreed with him, pushing the wave of his blond hair back from his eyes. No more enthusiasm for life . . . past your prime . . . over the hill.

How old are you? he asked me.

Twenty. Enough candles to crowd the cake but not so many that they won't all fit, I said, and I leaned my head against his chest. Beneath the beige wool of his sweater that scratched my ear, his heartbeat was slow and steady. It was an attribute of age I envied then; mine was beating to a cha-cha rhythm.

Is it still ticking? he asked, happily the old man, tenured in the art of love, sliding his hand underneath my shirt and stroking my back.

I think it's good for a few more years, I told him. If you take care of it. You know, I like listening to hearts. . . .

Good, he said. Then it can talk for me and give my
incompetent tongue a rest.

Your tongue talks just fine. What's a few extra syllables? I
told him, kissing him, finding it.

You come right to the point, don't you? he asked me, our
lips parted.

I try to.

Then I will too, he said. Do you want me to leave?

No. Well, yes, in a way I do, I said. Only don't.

Then stop shaking, he said, tracing the circle of my face.

I can't seem to help it, I told him. And I couldn't: like an
irregular heartbeat, a different kind of stutter. The camouflaging
of the targets.

One to grow on, he said, blowing out the candle. We each
took off our own clothes standing in the dark, shedding them
onto the floor. He pulled back the white sheet then, envelope of
a love letter, and we climbed back into the narrow bed. His
breath shifted to my ear, transferring, as if he'd held it burning
inside his mouth, the candle's flame to me. It traveled toward
my brain, like a word spoken, down through the red bloodstream where its echoes fluttered in my groin, fuchsia. I
brushed through the hair on his thighs with my fingertips. He
took my left nipple, erect, in his mouth.

Sing me a song while we're making love, I said, my hands
collaring his neck.

A song?

Any song.

But I can't sing, he said. I never really have.

I never went to bed with anybody before either, I told him.
I hope that doesn't mean I can't.

I grabbed his buttocks and pulled him to me. He began to
hum, so close it might have been me (and did seem to become
me as he entered me), jerkily, slowly, adding an occasional
word. A song I didn't know. Faster and louder, singing like the
Sirens, he was bellowing in my ear, luring me toward a
corporeal shore, the solidity, the inescapability of the flesh. The

pressure of his belly, his arched back. The hair at the nape of my neck, my spastic legs, our bootless feet entwined. Oar skimming water again and again and again until he ceased to stutter just before he came.

How are you? he sang to me finally.

A little sore, I sang back.

It gets better after the first time, he said.

I lit up two cigarettes, duet of glowing tips. He taught me the entire song with all its eight verses, which he'd learned at camp, before we fell asleep.

"Surprise," he says, standing in the doorway to my room, handing me a bottle of wine, his mouth twisted into a grin I had remembered vividly, when I open to the knock a few days later. His eyes meet mine for a curious second.

"Is it really you?" we ask each other, sitting on the bed. He unzips my pants and tastes my cunt.

"It's really you," he says, "and I'm very attracted to you."

"Likewise," I tell him. His hand slips inside the tight crotch of my jeans. I lift myself off the bed so he can pull them down. "This time you don't have to sing," I tell him.

"Good," he says. "Then my mouth will be free for other things." Kissing me.

Who taught you to be so gentle? I write with my fingers on his back afterward.

"What?" he asks, resting his chin on the pillow, concentrating. I write it out again; he guesses word by word. "Gentle?" he asks finally. "Is the last word *gentle*?"

"Yes," I tell him, erasing the smooth skin with my open palm.

"I think it's just part of my personality," he says, turning over on his side, looking up at me, coiling my hair into rings as it brushes his chest. "Look," he says, pulling at a lock of it, holding it to his head. "It matches. How would I look as a girl?" he asks, drawing me to him, arranging the curly ends of my hair around his ears.

"I can't see from this position, you dummy." Upside down,

all I can focus on is the tip of his chin. "Make a beard," I tell him. He does. "You look terrible, like Fu Manchu. You should never grow one."

"Neither should you," he says, helping me upright, tying my hair under my chin in a knot. "A bearded man with tits," he says, cupping my breasts, thumbing the nipples until they're hard.

"Cut it out," I tell him. "You're making me hot."

"What's the matter with that?" he asks, smiling.

"I want to talk to you, Louie," I tell him, climbing onto his body, stretching out, matching him, staring into his face with my elbows propped up on his shoulders. "For all I know you're an escaped con or a Ku Klux Klansman or the heir to a vast textile fortune made off of child labor."

"You've guessed my identity, Angela," he says solemnly. "I'm all of those things." He rolls me over to the side of the bed against the wall, sits up, and puts the sheet over his head. "This is my uniform," he says, "and it was made in my father's factory. I used several sheets just like it, tied to the pried bars of my prison cell, to descend from the window to freedom."

"Louie, you have the mind of an angel," I tell him, lifting up the cloud of our sheet, inside of it holding him as if he were this very moment, palpable and retainable, in which I'm quite sure I'm crazy for him. "It's wasted on computers. How many did you sell on your trip?"

"I'm a champion of the soft sell," he says.

"The gentle sell," I say.

"I sold hundreds . . . thousands," he says. "And how do I love thee? Let me count the hundreds and thousands of ways." He bends over and nibbles my hips, each nipple, my nose, my eyelids, the scar on my left knee from the time I got cut by the ice skate, and every toe. He draws a line with his fingers along my spine, counting the bumps, under the curve of my ass, down along the backs of my two legs, pinching each Achilles' tendon.

"Ouch," I say.

"Aha, I've found your vulnerable spots."

"Two of them," I tell him, "and see that you don't go pinching any of the others."

"I won't. Cross my heart and hope to die," he says.

"Where do you live?" I ask him.

"Seventy-ninth Street," he says, crisscrossing my stomach the way he did his heart. "Now if this line were Seventy-ninth and that were Amsterdam and the natural line of the body that divides us into two distinct and different halves were Columbus, then this would be my apartment building," he says, poking a mole.

"I'm glad I know that," I tell him. "Now I can picture you walking down a real street. . . ." He dances with two fingers along my arm. ". . . grocery shopping, picking up a suit at the cleaner's."

"And I would spend the night," he says, "if I didn't have to do just that tomorrow morning before I go to work. I'll call you tomorrow night or you call me. What's your mother's name?" he asks.

"What do you want to know for?"

"Because I don't know anything about your life either, about the rest of your life, I mean."

"Roslyn, and why do we have so much trouble telling each other things about ourselves? And about our pasts?"

"What's to tell?" he asks.

"Everybody arrives with baggage," I say.

"Well, I started out asking you an easy question," he says, sitting up and putting on his underpants, reaching for his socks. "Ask me one like that."

"All right. I'll start from the present and work back. Do you care about success?"

"No. Do you?"

"Yes."

"And millions of questions are left for next time," he says, standing up, leering at me like Groucho Marx, tipping the ash from an imaginary cigar. He tucks in his shirttails, zips his fly while I move to the edge of the bed. "You can think up some others when you're in bed tonight," he says.

"That's my new specialty," I tell him, reaching out and buckling his belt. "Sometimes I lie awake for hours, and it's your fault, you know." He walks toward the door, putting on his jacket.

"My fault? Why?" he asks, his hand on the knob.

"Because I used to enjoy sleeping alone," I tell him. He blows me a kiss and shuts the door behind him. I watch him walk out of the building and down the driveway from my open window, slowly draw the curtain, and bending down for the half-full bottle of wine on the floor, I take it back to bed with me. I put on my glasses, the ones I got when too much reading started to give me headaches. I pick up *The Rise and Fall of the Roman Empire* from the night table. My mother says she has a friend who reads it every five years just to regain perspective on his life. I hope it works.

When he's out of town, sometimes he calls me long-distance. Last week it occurred to me that we've spent more time together on the telephone than in person. Are we pioneers of the modern age, unwitting researchers in the yet-to-be-discovered science of telemotion?

"Yes," he says, "and I'm sure my company will contribute to funding. In fact, it's paying for this call."

"I'm a business expense," I tell him. "How dingy."

"No dingier than my hotel room," he says, "and out in the sticks there aren't even any decent movies on TV. How are you?"

"Fine, but I flunked another French exam."

"How come?" he asks.

"Because all I do is sunbathe on the roof of the dorm, and on rainy days I drink beer in the snack bar," I tell him. "I've become the worst of hedonists. Besides, I never did understand all those tenses, especially the subjunctive."

"The subjunctive?"

"Well, in English it has a lot to do with if's. It's sort of like our relationship."

"Oh," he says after a moment. "Are we in love with each other?"

"We're not sure; that's the problem. If we are . . . Or if we aren't . . . "

"How do we find out?"

"How should I know?" I ask him, drawing another series of boxes on the desktop, the extending graph of our affair. "I've got nothing to compare it to. Haven't you ever been in love? Or did you keep your heart under wraps all these years? Is that why it's still such a good ticker?"

"I was in love once," he says, "but I'm not sure you always fall the same way. I don't suppose one time is ever like another."

"Sometimes I forget what you look like," I whisper into the phone.

"I have a picture of you in my wallet," he whispers back.

"You do?"

"Yes. Remember when I brought my camera to photograph the dance recital for your friend Ramona? I snuck one of you watching in the audience."

"You didn't have to be so secretive about it. I'm not afraid of having my soul captured like some primitive, you know."

"As a matter of fact," he says, pausing, "I think you are."

"Look who's talking," I tell him.

"Checkmate."

I look down at the playing board of my desktop, hanging up, trying to gauge our relative positions. Whose move next?

His, as it turns out, and he's loaded when he meets me at Grand Central to go to Ramona's twenty-first birthday party.

"What's with you?" I ask him, propping him up as we walk away from the gate, my palm under his elbow.

"I started celebrating early," he says, a grin on his face, which is nevertheless joyless.

"Great. Just great," I tell him, pulling him along. "You know it's at her mother's house, and it would have been nice if you'd *arrived* sober. It's going to be a very straight crowd."

"Wh-what d-do you care what other people think?" he asks me, stopping in the middle of the ramp. A man in a golf cap bumps into me; people elbow past us, a slow stream of congested traffic, annoyed by the roadblock of our argument. I drag him over to the side, against the iron railing. "Stop being so damned hypocritical," he says.

"Why are you picking a fight with me?" I ask him.

"Who wants to go to Sutton Place, anyway?" he replies.

"Yes," I tell him, "we could just spend the rest of our lives in my room. It would be so simple; I could keep putting off my degree, year after year. Then it would never matter what other people think."

"You don't know anything," he says, striding toward the swinging doors. I catch up with him, grabbing his arm, but he shakes it off.

"If I don't know anything about you it's because you don't tell me anything. To hell with what other people think. What do you think?" I shout at him out on the sidewalk as we hail a cab.

"Shut up," he says.

"You don't put on mere clothes when you get up in the morning," I say. "Oh no, it must take you hours to get dressed. You've got to erect the Great Wall of China around yourself before you'll go out." In the lobby, he shoves past the doorman, trying to barge his way into the elevator unannounced.

"That happened," he says as we're ascending, "because this is such a snotty building."

"No," I tell him, "that happened because you wanted it to."

"Of course, Doctor Freud," he says as the doors spring back on a living room tableau of men in pinstripes at a backgammon table and a maid in a black uniform poised with a silver tray of champagne glasses in front of one of the standing trios of women in cocktail dresses. "Oh brother," says Louie, as if blaming the entire class structure on me.

"We don't have to stay forever," I tell him, stepping into the room, "but Ramona would have been hurt if I hadn't come." I would like to find a telephone and call up my mother right now. I am the daughter of a saint. How did she continue to smooth things over for so many years, day after day? "Please be nice to her, Louis, and to me for that matter. What did I do, anyway?"

"Nothing," he says, his body visibly sagging. "I just had a crummy day; that's all." He takes my hand. "We must be ideally suited, more so than we think. You're the only one I wanted to take it out on. I'm sorry," he says, repeating the *s* a hundred, a thousand times.

"Even in a beastly mood," I tell him, surveying the room, "you're probably more fun than they are. Besides," I say, poking his elbow through the hole in his sweater, "dressed like this we'll never be able to make any time with anybody else unless they're keen on slumming."

"You did wash your bluejeans," he says, kissing me.

I discuss the state of the arts with a poet from Boston on the terrace. Louie drinks ginger ale and entertains Ramona's mother. We don't say another word all evening. His sneakers stand out in the room like two grumpy faces. His and mine?

"I'll come for the entire weekend," he says from the pay phone.

"It's not really convenient," I tell him, sitting naked in my desk chair.

"What do you mean it's not convenient, Angela?" he asks. "What kind of a word is that?" I look over at the woman lying in my bed.

"Hold on a sec," I tell him, covering the mouthpiece. "Go into the bathroom," I tell her. "I hate lying with an audience."

"Forget it," she says, lighting a cigarette.

"Well," I say back into the telephone, "I have a lot of work to do; I haven't done any in two weeks, you know that. And . . . I've got to visit my Uncle Jack in Long Island for Saturday night and Sunday."

"Who's your Uncle Jack?" he asks me.

"One of my uncles," I tell him.

"The one with the crazy son," she says from the bed. Is this the first conversation on the party line of my newly complicated circumstances?

"That seems obvious," he says.

"How about Monday night? Can you come then?"

"Sure," he says. "And I'm going to be in town for the entire month."

"That's wonderful," I say.

"See you Monday, kiddo." I hang up the receiver and continue to sit.

"Was that him?" she asks me.

"Yup."

"Come here," she says.

"I don't want to, Jo."

"Oh yes you do."

"You don't pay attention to a thing I say," I tell her. "However, you're right." I sit down on the edge of the bed.

There's a knock on the door. Ramona? Melissa?

"Don't answer it," she whispers in my ear, brushing it with her lips, pushing my shoulders down onto her lap. "Why should we end it just now when we've been happy here for hours?"

"We shouldn't," I tell her, burrowing against her breasts, her long brown hair clothing my back like a woolly shawl. "I wonder what's happening out there," I say, parting the blinds momentarily, but the sunshine is blinding.

"Time is continuing," she says, "but I didn't think so until I heard the knock."

"How many classes have you missed?"

"What day is today?" she asks me.

"It's Friday, I think." Stretching out beside her, getting under the sheet. "I think I'm getting bedsores."

"Don't be silly;" she says, kissing my eyebrows, "that takes weeks. Let's see, if it's Friday, then I missed two classes on Thursday and"—she glances at the clock—"I'm missing one right now." She laughs.

"If you're so smart about everything, tell me why we didn't meet each other before Wednesday night?" I ask her.

"I'm smart enough to know you can't answer questions like that," she says.

"Yes, but . . ."

"Just be quiet," she says. "It isn't necessary to have such speculations, to think through everything until you can pin it down like a butterfly on a mat. Put your net away."

"You're full of good advice," I tell her. She runs her tongue along my neck and down the inside of my arm.

"Just lie back this time," she says, "and let me do the

work . . ." She holds my legs between the vise of hers, rolling on top of me, kissing every lipful of my face.

"You'll cut off the circulation," I tell her, stroking the muscles of her thighs.

"That's from dancing," she says as I trace the hard outline of her leg with my hand.

"Good Lord," I say, prying myself free, jumping up to rummage through my desk drawer.

"What is it?" she asks, getting out of bed too, coming up close beside me and taking my face in her hands. "Is something wrong, sweetheart?"

"No, no," I tell her, lowering her hands, pulling her arms around my waist as I bend over the drawer. "I just remembered. I have a picture of you. At least I think I do, from the dance performance."

We flip through the pile of photos on the desk, our free arms around each other's shoulders. I rest my chin on her head.

"Here you are."

"What a terrible picture," she says.

"I think you look kind of cute," I tell her, taping it onto the wall. "And I thought so at the time, too, though I didn't know who you were."

"Weren't you curious?" she asks. She sits down on the desk chair. I sit on her lap.

"Yes I was curious," I tell her, "but at the time I didn't know what kind of curious that was."

"Life is full of surprises," she says. "Why did you invite me back Wednesday night?"

"Because I couldn't bear to stop talking to you, and in the back of my mind I think I was hoping you'd seduce me," I tell her. "Why did you steal the bottle of Scotch from the party to bring back with us?"

"Because I was hoping that would make it easier."

"When did you first know that you wanted to make love with me?" I ask her.

"Midway through the evening, on the couch, when you tripped over my foot and then kissed it," she says. "When did you know that you wanted to make love with me?"

"Well, finally, when we got back here and you told me to stop moving back and forth from the chair to the bed, that I'd wear out the rug." We both laugh.

"You were making me dizzy," she says.

"You're making me dizzy right now," I tell her.

"Well," she says.

"Well," I say. I count her eyelashes, one by one. She tries both of my rings on every finger. We stand in front of the mirror on the bureau and make each other up.

"We have very different skin tones," she says. "Pink and brown." We go into the bathroom and turn on the shower.

"It's too hot," I tell her.

"It's just perfect," she says. "You're just not used to giving in to your senses." This is true. I lean back against her body.

"Will we feel funny when we rejoin the outside world?" I ask her.

"Life is one big funny feeling," she says. She draws portraits of us on the steamy curtain, surrounded by a big outdoor landscape of hills and trees and cows. We wash each other and sink down to our knees in the emptying water to make love.

"For some reason I never fucked in a bathtub before," she says.

"A first," I tell her.

April is the most unpredictable of months, full of both showers and gentle eddied breezes, women and men.

How fast things change, said my father over the phone, telling me about his new life.

How fast they seem to, I replied, having for a time nearly forgotten his old life.

How are things? my mother wrote me in a long letter.

Hectic, I sent back on a postcard.

Once, due to an oversight on my part, the three of us, Louie, Jo, and I, ended up at a small dinner party together. None of us had a good time. We drank too much, smoked packs of cigarettes (all the same brand—a telltale symbol of our hand in hand in hand under the table), and each left alone.

"Don't you feel well, Angela?" our hostess asked me.

"How's Prince Charming?" Jo asks me on Wednesdays and Fridays and on occasional weekends.

"How's the dyke?" Louis asks me on Tuesdays and Thursdays and on occasional weekends.

Mondays I keep for myself.

Sometimes, then, I read poetry because I grew up with its changing messages on my kitchen wall, drawing strength from it at breakfast to go out and tackle another day. Although it doesn't propose any cures for living, it does stress common symptoms. One poet I read recently speaks of "the April of my time, The sweet of youth." I like to mull this over.

Firsts? Oh no. That was written almost a hundred years ago; you can tell by the two *l*'s in Aprill. It's always the same old errand, though each fool is free to choose his own best route. What's a fool's best route, after all? Some of us even think we can go in two different directions at the same time.

────────── Chapter XII ──────────

RETIREMENT

WELL, IT MUST KEEP YOU BUSY. NO WONDER nobody ever sees you anymore," says Ramona, sitting across from me in the last pink booth of the least-frequented coffee shop in town. She is chewing unbuttered toast. The fan hanging from the center of the ceiling, propeller-like, stirs the air, wafting the smell of eggs frying our way. If it continues, I will surely throw up. "It *is* highly unconventional," she says.

"You're a big help," I tell her, sipping a beer. I mash out a cigarette in the filling ashtray and light another.

"Are you sure you ought to drink breakfast?" she asks, reminding me of her mother. Anybody's mother.

"No, I'm not sure. But I'm not sure of anything right now, which is why I'm drinking breakfast." She reties the ponytail of her straight blond hair.

"It's not that I disapprove," she tells me, opening a packet of sweetener, pouring it sandy into her coffee. "It's just that it's, well . . . unusual."

"Don't you ever read novels?" I ask her, the beer starting to hit me, a more relaxed and cavalier attitude pumping through the veins. Art is my best defense; in it you can find a precedent for anything. "This kind of thing goes on all the time."

"Yes," she says, "and at the end of the book all three parties end up murdering each other in a passionate brawl."

"That's just societally endorsed punishment reflected in culture," I tell her. "In real life you just go on until somebody can't stand it any longer. That's all."

"That's all? It would be terrible if you were the one who cracked, wouldn't it? You're under the greatest pressure as I see it," she says, raising the coffee cup to her lips. "Blow the smoke the other way, will you?" I lean back and exhale toward the ceiling, aiming for the fan. Cracked like shells. Smoky eggs.

"I would just take a train to Long Island and drown myself like Ophelia, only in the Sound," I tell her.

"Ophelia couldn't cope," says Ramona, as if referring to some wretched and sordidly contractable disease. To Ramona this is the worst of afflictions, ever since her father, bowing to business pressures, checked himself into the sanatorium. Upon occasion, enough is enough, I told her then.

"Ramona?" She looks up from her plate. "Sometimes I don't understand your sensibilities at all. Sometimes I'm mystified as to how we ever got to be friends."

"It's simple," she says. "I'm the route you didn't take, that's all. My life could have been your life, too, only it didn't turn out that way. You chose to discard certain things to make room for certain others. I chose to stay with the hand I had."

"You're very smart," I tell her, realizing how right she is, though it may not be a matter of choice. "And that's why you're my friend, too: coming up with ideas like that." I pick up the check. "You finished?"

"Yes," she says. "I never eat the crusts." This must be how the world is divided up then: those of us who are after the whole slice and those of us with limited tastes. It is possible, however, to choke on the crusts.

We walk by the four-story brick apartment building for retired people. Women with broadbrimmed straw hats to shade their faces from the radiant morning sun stroll on the lawn, and men gripping canes, fanning themselves with folded newspapers, sit side by side on two benches in front of a bank of forsythia, yellow medallions for service well done. A few of the retirees are raking, weeding what were once victory gardens in the east corner of the yard. Some of the plots are ripe with flowers, colorful shoots.

"Wait a minute," I tell Ramona, and walking across the springy grass to the nearest bed, I lean over its knee-high stringed boundary and pick an iris. I run back to the sidewalk, fleeing the waving of hoes and arms, and shouts of "Bring that back, young lady" and "Those beatniks from the college. . . ."

"Come on." In midstride I grab Ramona's arm, my stomach

aflutter, and we race down the sidewalk under the trees until we turn the corner onto the street that leads to school.

"Why did you do that?" Ramona asks me, panting as we slow to a walk.

"I don't know. All of a sudden I felt like it."

"My, aren't we spontaneous these days," she says, tugging the strap of her shoulder bag farther up toward her collarbone.

"What exactly do you mean by that, Ramona?"

"Sorry," she says. "That was uncalled for. Only you don't have to be so touchy about everything."

"Well I am touchy," I tell her.

"And doesn't that show you anything about how you feel toward your present situation? About whether it's right for you or not?"

"No," I tell her. "You've been in therapy too long. It only tells me I live in the world."

I leave her behind, taking huge strides, the kind we used to practice when we were kids for the game of Giant Steps, the kind we become less expert at as we grow older. One giant step forward? Two baby steps? Asking permission. May I? Asking more frequently, May I?

"So what are you going to do?" Ramona asks me, catching up.

"Who knows?" I tell her, puffing up the hill. "People don't make decisions. They happen to us—like being hit by a car. When presented with a situation that can have only one outcome, then we act."

"You can censor your experiences."

"I've never been able to," I reply, "and, by the way, for the meantime I would appreciate it if you'd keep all of this confidential."

"Really, Angela, that goes without saying," Ramona says, touching my elbow. "Only. . . ."

"Only what?" I ask her, the pit in my stomach so deep I could dive down into it and never touch bottom.

"Only everybody's starting to talk already, anyway." We stop halfway up beside the chain-link fence of the parking lot.

"What are they saying?" I shouldn't care and I do. Halfway up the hill of my own beliefs I'm sliding, slipping back, losing traction like nerve, mistaking my footing on the sheer path I chose myself. Trying to go forward: big steps, little steps, by leaps or inches. May I? May I? Hobbled, I grab onto the fence.

"Well, you know," she says, averting her eyes, studying the cars in the lot (looking at anything except my face), "but on account of Louie nobody's actually sure."

"You were full of shit before," I say to her. "This makes you uncomfortable just like those people who've got nothing better to gossip about, right?" She doesn't answer. How to go forward? Where to find the energy, the charge, to follow the electric arc that will bridge the gap between the life inside my room and everything that's outside it. Between Ramona and me now, too. Between what things are and what they mean.

"It make things different, doesn't it?" she asks finally. Fuck her and fuck them.

"Everything we do makes things different," I shout at her. "Just look at me, will you?" I grab her shoulders and spin her around. "It's the same face. The same brain. It's me and that's not different. . . . Christ, Ramona, if I can't convince you, how could I ever convince anybody else?" Our faces are a foot apart. "I don't give a shit who *you* sleep with, after all." We continue to look at each other.

"You know what?" she says after an interminable silence.

"What?" I say.

"You're absolutely right." She hugs me; I rest my head on her shoulder, the leather strap cooling my cheek. "I am convinced. . . . It's just that it's hard losing your best friend to the most virulent case of spring fever. . . ."

"Ramona . . ." But she pokes me in the ribs and, as I jump back, swings her pocketbook at my head. I duck it. "Considering the creeps you've been with . . . I wonder who's talking," I muse out loud. "Probably what's-her-name next door. She's always poking her nose out in the morning when I leave for classes, with whomever. Maybe I should up the ante and get her really confused."

"I don't think she'd do that, Angela," Ramona says. "It's just that when the two of you are together you don't really seem to notice that anyone else is there."

"I guess that's true, isn't it?" I say, smiling, trying to hide it. "Well, fuck it. Let them talk."

Make up your own rules as to right and wrong, my mother said. No need for permission, May I? It's when you break your own rules that you ought to feel bad. Would she stand by her philosophy now?

I can't help it. I lose track of things. For instance, just where did Ramona and I part company on our way up the hill? At what gate, what side street did she head off to her room, the dance studio, the biology lab? It must be like sleepwalking, because I come to to find myself passing the president's house, roused by the sound of a lawnmower clipping the grass behind it. Or is it the jet flying overhead, a faulty air-conditioner rumbling? A car without a muffler in the errand-busy traffic? It is not only our own lives that are hard to categorize.

I stopped going to the tennis team practice sessions because I couldn't remember to retrieve the balls I'd missed in the backcourt. I quit the newspaper staff when last week I missed the printer's deadline by six hours, forgetting to deliver the copy, sitting instead in front of the heavy gray typewriter, thinking. Missing things. I'm missing things at quite a rate, including, as I reach into both my pockets, the third room key this month at ten dollars a shot. I'll just have to leave the door unlocked. What gets stolen gets stolen.

"You seem distracted, Angela," says my adviser when I reach the top of the hill for my conference on semester progress. "I understand you've been missing some classes."

"I forget to go, Charlie," I tell him.

"I don't know what it is," he says, leaning back, squeaking the springs of his swivel chair. "The attrition rate in the spring term here is something awful. However," he says, glancing down at his wrist, "you should wear a watch like I do. You find you begin to look at it more and more often, and soon you're on schedule. You can't help it. I took to wearing one in the service."

"What time is it?" I ask him from my sunny perch on the windowsill.

"Quarter to twelve."

"I have to go now," I tell him.

"Come by next week then," he says, opening the door of his office. "And try not to take any incompletes. It'll just ruin your summer. By the way," he adds, "I missed your editorial this week."

"I'm in retirement," I tell him, clutching the iris, running down the stone steps, out of the shadow of the alcove and into the brightness of the driveway. Because this woman is the front-page headlines of my private press; the episodes of her childhood as she tells them to me, wonderful and intriguing, are my lead stories; her habits: the back pages, the small print of my investigations. A reporter on a scoop, I run all the way back to my room.

"Take off your clothes, quickly," she says, throwing open the now-unlocked door, kissing me hurriedly, and then shutting it. "It's too hot out to wear anything. You should try to dance in this weather; it's murder. And I'm a river of sweat," she says, taking me in her arms.

"I like it," I tell her, our sticky embrace.

"Considering the time factor, perhaps I ought to get something with a zipper," she says later, laboriously buttoning up her jumpsuit.

"Look at that iris," I say, pointing to the bureau, the Styrofoam cup I stuck it into.

"It's lovely," she says.

"It's for you," I tell her.

"You shouldn't have," she says.

"I didn't. I stole it from a garden."

"The best things are stolen," she says.

"I know," I say, stealing another kiss, another minute from all the other things she has to do. She shuts the door, leaving behind her the petty thief of flowers and time, a would-be master criminal.

"What do you like most in the world?" she asks me late that night, sitting in the chair opposite the bed.

"Two-hundred-page novels," I tell her, "and the George Washington Bridge, certain bars in the afternoon, and, also, the kind of green vinyl visors that cardsharps wear, jockeys' outfits, and you."

"I like," says Jo, "straight lines, the Chrysler Building, chrome, fins on Cadillacs, brownies from Greenberg's, goldfish in perfectly round bowls, and you."

We put on a record and dance in the dark, smoking shared cigarettes, telling each other stories of real people and made up things, too. Sipping warm screwdrivers because we've run out of ice, stepping every now and then on each other's toes because we're getting a little tipsy, turning the same record over and over and over, humming in each other's ears.

"That's the wrong song," I tell her.

"I never can keep them straight," she says. "They all sound the same to me." Picking one another up off the floor to test our strength, comparing the size of our wrists and waists, measuring with looped fingers and arms, sensitive instruments. For every new thing we find out, thinking up ten more things to discover, looking for the myriad of differences in this extraordinary sameness.

As we continue dancing, entangled, undifferentiated again, my tongue explores her mouth for all the words either of us might ever say, and when I remove it gently from her lips like a stopper, the researcher believing in the possibility of an amazing breakthrough, they rise, gas from a test tube. Our feet have stopped moving, and she must never stop talking: this monologue of odes and incantations; a litany both personal and encompassing what seems like everything thinkable.

"And you know what?" she says finally. "I am also, besides all the other things I just told you about myself, in love with you."

Losing my breath, the wind knocked out of me.

"I adore you," I tell her. Our data, now, for the first time, analyzed.

"You've got to talk to Louie," she says.

"He's coming out tomorrow. I will."

"Look, it's light out," she says, pointing to the gray, hazy outline of the square of the drawn curtain. "What time is it?" I walk over to the clock on the night table and bend down to peer at its face.

"Six fifteen."

"You know," she says, "we're going to be the death of each other."

"Well, then," I reply, "I go willingly to my death"—my arms outstretched, walking an imaginary gangplank. The sleepwalker, entranced, who would sleep forever in the sea.

"Let's go to bed," says Jo. "I've got to be out of here by ten."

"I always had a fun time with you," I say.

"And I always had a f-fun time with you, too," says Louie.

The pine needles are the cushions of our seats. Side by side, our backs supported by the broad tree trunk, we stare into the darkness of the woods like moviegoers in the quick moment before the projector flashes its beam. We will be the star characters. We reach out for each other's hand. It is beginning:

"I noticed you right away at the dance," he says. "You were talking to a girl in a white sweatshirt."

"She's in my French class," I tell him. "However, you didn't come over to talk to me for at least an hour after that."

"I had to get up my nerve," he says. "I had a few beers, took a walk outside. . . ."

"And danced for a while with Celia something-or-other. *I* noticed that."

"She turned out to be sh-shallow," he says. "What attracted me to her was her extremely high heels. The kind my ex-wife used to wear . . ."

"So you were married," I say. "It's funny, your telling me that now at this late date. That's the kind of thing you never would entrust me with before." The tree creaks in the breeze, random notes of the sound track.

"I know," he says, "and you never told me about your father, though you said you would. In fact," he continues, "the day of Ramona's birthday party was the day the divorce became final. . . ."

"No wonder you were so impossible," I say. "As to my father, it is a complicated story, but that's not why I didn't tell you."

"No, we never t-told each other things because we didn't have to and it's easier not t-to. Neither of us ever made the other come clean." Beyond the edge of the woods, approaching on the main street, bright headlight beams illuminate a path that suddenly engulfs us. We look at each other. Each other now. Brief intermission; two red brake lights blinking signal the start of the second half:

"That's why we never fell in love," I suggest.

"I think you're right," he agrees. "I was crazy about fucking you," he says.

"You always gave me the shivers," I tell him.

"But that f-first night I made you stop sh-shaking," he says.

"And I made you stop stuttering, if only for a moment."

"You taught me how to sing," he says. "What a wonderful achievement."

"While you taught me how to make love," I say. "A gentle professor."

"This is not a sad ending, then," he says, getting to his feet and pulling me up. We walk out to the streetlight and along the edge of the pavement, striking little pebbles with our toes, unwittingly, the way one night we struck each other in a room of three hundred people.

"Why don't you stay tonight?" I ask him at the junction of our two streets.

"I don't think so," he says. "I've never liked sleeping with someone for the last time when I knew it was the last time."

"That makes sense, Louie," I tell him.

"You've got my n-number," he says.

"And you've got mine," I tell him.

"Took us a while, didn't it?" he says. We kiss good-bye, and I turn right in the direction of my room as he continues into town, down the hill, toward the train station.

The steady rocking makes our shoulders bump every few seconds. I imagine I can feel her skin through the fabric of our clothes.

"Now we will have a whole weekend to ourselves," says Jo.

"Enough time," I reply, propping my feet up against the green leather back of the seat in front of us, "for a change—with no interruptions, no classes, no dance rehearsals, and no people. Couldn't we just run off somewhere together?"

"That's precisely what we're doing," she says. Outside the train window occasional lighted towns pattern the darkness: the neon of taverns, red and green traffic signals, billboards of vacation homes. The distances between station stops are growing. A dwindling crew of passengers shares our car.

"I meant for good," I tell her.

"You can't do it for good," she says. "Because then the new place becomes home, and you get to know everyone, and the whole syndrome starts all over again. The only surcease from the business of living is the weekend trip." I rest my hand on her knee.

"Jo, will you tell me where we're going now?"

"No," she says. "I want it to be a surprise."

"There are only three stops left," I tell her.

"That's good odds," she says, smiling. "You ought to be able to guess."

"If I guessed it, would you tell me?"

"No."

"Then I'm going to take a nap. It's almost midnight." I lean my head against her shoulder.

I open my eyes. It's the conductor, sweeping up the aisle. Jo is snoring beside me. "Last stop. Exit to the front of the car." I nudge her.

"You snore like a truck driver . . ." I tell her.

"So I'm told," she says, shutting her eyes again.

". . . and unless we were intending to go to the end of the line we've missed our stop."

"This is it," she says, sitting up, reaching down and pulling a sneaker from under the seat. "The very tip of Long Island, the

Atlantic Ocean, the lighthouse George Washington commissioned himself."

"How do you know that?" I ask her, getting up and into the aisle, slinging the knapsack over my shoulder.

"I called up the Chamber of Commerce and they told me," she says. "Our motel is right across the street from the beach."

On the second yank I pull open the heavy door, and we climb down the latticed metal stairs, an elopement of sorts, to the paved walk which we follow to the deserted station.

"We need a cab," she says doubtfully.

"Check the number on the orange sticker in the pay phone around the front," says the man who got off the train with us as he strides by. "Myself, I prefer the night air."

"Marlin Cabins," says Jo inside the booth. "About ten minutes," she tells me, hanging up. We sit down in the driveway.

"It's chilly," I say.

"Sea air. It's only May, remember. And look," she says, "you can see all the stars for once." We lie down, staring straight up.

"There's Orion's belt."

"And that's," she points directly above my left shoulder, "the Big Dipper."

"No," I tell her. "That's the Little Dipper."

"Well, I don't know how you're supposed to tell," she says, lowering her arm again, "unless you can find them both."

"If I didn't see that heaven was up there, I might think that we were in it down here," I tell her.

"A little piece of it fell through space one day and landed right on this spot," she says. "I have it on very good authority."

A car turns into the station lot, pulling up, a beige sedan. The driver rolls down his window. "Marlin Cabins?" he asks.

"Yes." We get up and climb into the back seat.

"You shouldn't lie in driveways," he says. "I could have run you over. Snuff. Out for the weekend, girls?"

"That's right," I say.

"How far to the motel?" Jo asks.

"Coupla miles. It'll take just a minute. No traffic this time of year, not like during the season." He waves at the police cruiser driving by in the other direction. "My brother-in-law," he says. "I haven't gotten a single ticket since he joined the force."

We pass a lake, partially illuminated by a motel on the shore, and continue on for a stretch of highway, through the center of town around a deserted traffic circle.

"You meet all kinds of celebrities here in the summer," says our driver. "Elizabeth Taylor. And Andy Warhol, you know the artist, if you like that sort. Brother, the types I've taken up to this place."

"Really?" I ask. "Does he throw wild parties?"

"*Wild* isn't the word," he says, throwing up his hands. This is disconcerting. "Peculiar, more like it. You know what I mean?"

"Uh huh."

"But Elizabeth Taylor," he says. "She is a lovely person. Very gracious and not tightfisted with the tips, either, like some of them."

We turn suddenly into a gravel driveway, the brakes lurching us to a halt. Little cabins line both sides. A yellow bug light shows the office sign hanging below it halfway up on the right.

"Here's my card," says the driver, leaning over into the back seat. "Give us a call Sunday when you decide what train you want to catch back and just ask for Frank. Have a nice weekend," he says, taking the fare. "Weather's going to be top-notch. Is somebody waiting up for you?" he asks.

"Oh yes," says Jo. "Thanks." We get out.

"Good night now." The slam of the car door, signal of our arrival.

"Is that you, Josephine?" calls a voice.

"You bet," says Jo.

"Where's Napoleon?" he chuckles as Jo walks first through the screen door into the office. He stretches out his hand.

"I left him at home to mind the war," she says.

"Now that's women's liberation for you," he replies.

"And this is Angela," Jo says.

"I'm so glad you could come. I'm Johnnie Martino." He shakes hands with me, too. His wavy hair matches his snowy cardigan sweater. Smile lines draw crescent-shaped wrinkles in his cheeks. "Where's number five?" he asks no one in particular, plucking at the tagged keys hung on a bulletin board of hooks. "The chambermaid doesn't come until June. We're off season now, you know. Well I'll be darned," he says.

I look through the keys myself.

"Here it is, on number seven's hook." I hand it to him.

"That's an odd place for it to be," he says, a conspiratorial grin directed at me. "The girl who comes in to clean twice a week is a nice girl, don't get me wrong, but she's not too . . . you know what I mean . . . bright." Tapping his forehead. "Now that you mention it," he says, "I wonder where number seven is. . . ."

"Maybe it's on the number five hook," Jo suggests.

"No," he says, checking, "but we'll worry about that in the morning. You must be tired; it's after one." He pushes open the office door, and we walk leisurely across the drive up to the front cabin, nearest the road.

"This is my best unit," he says. "You have a view of the ocean in the daytime. Listen, you can hear it." Rhythmic, I'd mistaken the steady sound of the waves for the whizz of cars on the highway. He opens the door with the key.

"It's perfect," says Jo, stepping inside.

"This is the living room," says Johnnie. "Two pull-out beds if you need extra sleeping space. Refrigerator, stove." He looks in the cupboards. "Pots and pans. Plates, silverware. In the other room, a double bed, the bathroom. I guess you're all set," he says. "Come see me tomorrow and we'll have a cup of instant coffee." He puts the key on the counter. "The door locks from the inside. Ten-four." And he's gone.

"I thought we were number five," says Jo.

"Sometimes I think you live in a different time zone from the rest of us," I tell her. "Either that or you have no recognizable frame of reference. That was some special radio sign-off."

"Oh," she says. "Luckily I have you to translate." We sit

down on the couch, and I pull a bottle of wine from the knapsack.

"What a nice man," I say. I spin the arms of the corkscrew.

"When I talked to him over the phone, I knew this was the place for us," she says. "I bet he's nicer even than Elizabeth Taylor." I get two glasses out of the cupboard. "Cheers."

"What good fortune," I say, "a double bed."

"Don't be silly," she says, putting her glass to my lips. "I asked for it."

In the morning she wakes me with the clatter of the raising of the venetian blinds.

"I'm never going back," I tell her, lifting up the sunny covers, though she's already dressed, for her to join me again.

"Good morning," she says. "I love you."

"Unless you are," I add.

"I talked to Johnnie," she says.

"Already? This morning?"

"Over coffee. He says that tonight the moon's going to be full. We have to go down to the beach and see it."

"You must take me in chains then," I tell her. "The full moon affects me. Like my Uncle Freddie who would bar-hop until dawn."

"I thought he always did that," she says.

"Not with the same commitment," I explain.

"So I'm involved with a lunatic. Do you turn into a werewolf?" She strokes my bare stomach.

"Yes. I get hairy all over and kill," I tell her.

"That would be something to put in my diary, anyway."

"You keep a diary?" I ask.

"Of course not," she says. "When would I have time? Under the blankets at night with a flashlight after you've fallen asleep?"

"Then I am your diary," I tell her. "If you ever want to check back on anything, just ask me. I have pages and pages of you."

"We are having sauerbrauten for dinner," says Johnnie.

"Oh no, we really couldn't," I say.

"We're going to walk into town and pick up something," says Jo. Johnnie hands me another beer as I sit on the couch in the tiny office comparing his two reservation books for accuracy. His royal blue sleeping bag hangs over the arm next to me.

"But I've been marinating it for three days," he says. "Besides, it's a recipe with a secret ingredient."

Over the hot plate resting on the half-sized refrigerator in the back room, the three of us crumble gingersnaps into the big pan of gravy.

"How many more?" I ask.

"Six or eight," he says, reaching up to the crowded shelves above. "Jo," he says, "I can't find the flour. Do you see it up here?"

I break each gingersnap in halves with my thumbs. One part goes into my mouth, and the other I crack up into little chunks like tiny dice in my fist. Then I throw them into the bubbling mixture, hoping for good luck, the right combination.

"And here's the recipe book," says Johnnie, fishing it out of the bathroom sink. "Now let's see. Add the flour and the onions, Angela, and let it simmer for twenty minutes." He comes out of the bathroom, pulls three more beers from the refrigerator below, and, edging by me in the narrow corridor to the office, returns to his desk next to which Jo continues to look for number seven on the board. I follow, climbing over the coffee table and back to the couch. "I once had a dinner party for ten in here, he says.

"I can't find the damn key anywhere," says Jo. She climbs over the coffee table, over me, and onto the couch.

"What a crazy business," Johnnie says. "This is what they call retirement?"

"You mean you haven't always done this?" Jo asks him.

"Mother of God, no," he says. "I just took the place over last year. There are lots of things to do in life, and I've done many of them. During Prohibition I ran liquor, I once owned a hardware store, I've been a contracter and a nightclub manager. I even worked for the State Department. But it gets to you, and here I am looking for keys. . . ."

He gets up and goes into the back.

"It's ready," he calls.

Jo and I put the carved meat on the plates with some instant potato dumplings that look like golf balls. Johnnie pours the gravy.

"Have some more, you two," he says, on his second helping. "You'll grow thin as guttersnipes."

"I thought it was the starving Armenians," says Jo.

"I can't fit in another thing," I tell him. "I ate too many gingersnaps."

"Dessert first," he says.

We wash the dishes in the bathroom sink.

"It's too bad you have to go back tomorrow," says Johnnie.

"I know," says Jo.

"But I've got missing keys to look for myself," I tell him, "and I haven't cleaned my room in six weeks. I can't even find my books."

"That's why I have the girl come in," he muses. "Because you know you could stay on a few days. No need to pay. Nobody else is here anyway."

"In fact, he puts Elizabeth Taylor to shame," Jo whispers, taking a dripping plate from my hands. "If only we could," she says to Johnnie, "but I've got an exam."

"Then I'm getting you on the two o'clock train tomorrow. You've got to get a good night's sleep so you'll do well. No flunking in this outfit."

"Yes sir," Jo says, saluting.

"See you tomorrow, Johnnie."

"Ten-four," she says.

"All the good numbers," he tells her. "Like five."

The sand we lie in is cold, but as we pour it down each other's shirts and pants, into ears, through the gaps of toes and fingers, it mixes like a sweetener in our warmth. The stuff of hourglasses, time enough, it should be substituted for sugar in bowls and the granules Ramona and others rip from pink packets into their daily coffee cups.

"Look, the moon's coming out," says Jo, sitting up.
As the night deepens, so does its shade, from a pale lemon
to a tarnished gold.
"I want to take a walk," she says.
"By yourself?"
"Yes. Whistle if you need me."

Diary Entry:

Today when Jo and I walked the full length of the
beach, having passed the strip of motels that lines the
other side of the street, we discovered three houses on
the cliff that rises from the rocky boundary of its width.
One was an intricate geometrical construct, without
windows that we could see except on the sea side. The
second was a ranch house, long and flat like an
abandoned train, behind a scrubby yard with a swing set.
The third was a tiny gray box: cock of a spinning weather
vane in flight over its roof, a set of stairs that descended
from the deck of unfinished wood down to the boulders.

Which is your favorite? I asked Jo.

So we tracked ourselves back and forth below,
carefully studying each one, discussing points of beauty,
practicalities, whims engendered.

This is the nicest, said Jo, sitting on the bottom stair
of the little blockhouse, staring at the green swells. After
all, you don't need much of a house when you've got all
this.

We rolled up our pantlegs and waded out until my
toes froze. She splashed me, soaking me all over, as I ran
in. So I threw a dead fish her way and missed. But my
hands smelled, and when I caught her, I rubbed them all
over her hair.

Shivering, we collected shells and occasional snails,
lucky rocks, you can tell by the white rings around their
middles: our pail the empty shell of a big horseshoe crab.
We watched for bubbles, buried bait, when the waves
retreated. The foam stays for a second longer and then
evaporates, leaving a temporary mark, nevertheless, as
we did with our fingers, writing messages to each other
in the sand which had to get read before the next wave
or be lost.

When we're old and gray, like the color of our
house, I wrote Jo in installments, we will retire there.

You've got a deal, she wrote back. Also a long wait.

But I can wait. There are lots of things to do in life, as
Johnnie said. I know already from my varied career: reporter,
researcher, diarist, thief. I don't want to retire just yet. I like my
work.

High in the sky the moon reflects on the bumpy sea like a
road of light, wide and endless as a highway somewhere in the
West, cut like a straight swath through the prairies, that
continues for as far as the eye can see. Like a bridge. More like a
mirrored pier that extends tonight forever, not joining us to
anything.

"Boo." Jo grabs my shoulders and I jump.

"You scared me, you asshole."

"It was so bright I knew I had to surprise you by sneaking
up from behind. Did you think I was a werewolf?"

"No, just an asshole." She sits down beside me, putting her
arm around my waist.

"Chicken," she says. Cloaked in light, we lie back against
the enormous pillow of the beach.

"The moon," I tell her, "shows only one face to the earth."

"Really?" she says. "How do you know that?"

"I called the Chamber of Commerce," I tell her.

"They know everything," she says.

"Actually," I confess, "it's a common fact. The other side,
the one we never see, is cold and dark. . . ."

". . . and barren," she adds.

"That's right," I tell her. "And this phenomenon of the
moon is called synchronous rotation. Unheard of in any of the
other celestial bodies, it's caused by the overwhelming gravita-
tional force the earth exerts on it."

"This explains what's happening to us," she says. Repeating
it: "Synchronous rotation."

"Something very like it," I say, once again at work, the
after-hours astronomer, moonlighting here in the moonlight.

Chapter XIII

CIRCUS LIFE

THE PROCESSION IS ENDING: STUDENTS IN Bermudas and undershirts, rippling pastel gowns in the shade of parasols, summer-suited and sporting cigars, (one) in tails and hotpants; the professors who would participate in basic black, wearing colorful degrees and honors like gaudy accessories. Barking seals balancing eggs on their noses, skillful jugglers of china plates, dancing bears (true to their kind: dancing the fox-trot), ballerinas on galloping horses' rumps, tumblers coupling to form a human wheel . . .

The very first time I went to the circus, a performer fell in the elephant parade and was lost underfoot, missing rider from a link in the tail to trunk chain. Two attendants in an unscheduled balancing act carried out the body on a stretcher, silver-spangled leotard littered with sawdust. Under the high-ceilinged canvas tent made fast against wind and rain by fraying ropes tied taut to notched wooden stakes hammered deep into the ground (the tenterhooks of the graduates' futures—will life treat them henceforth in the manner of the elephant girl?), the president of the college begins his address.

We get up from our folding chairs near the back.

"This is the boring part," says Melissa. Like the setup between acts. "Let's go call now before the reception."

"Do we have time enough?" asks George.

"We've got enough time to do half the Westchester phone book," Jo says. She points to the open program, and we crowd around. "Look. After this they've got the guest speaker, a woodwind concerto, something called Poetry as Mime, the conferring of degrees one by one, and the passing of the gavel . . . from the outgoing senior class president to the new one."

"What gavel is that?" I ask.

"Would you keep your voices down?" says a mother from the row in front of us. The P.A. system crackles. Up front camera bulbs flash.

196

"I'm not exactly sure," Melissa whispers, "but it's some tradition they decided to resurrect this year; I think they had to buy one."

"Who's the valedictorian?" asks George.

"We don't have them here," I tell him. "Everyone is equal."

"Oh," says George. "I went to Columbia."

We snake along the perimeter of the tent, single file, and parting the flaps near the administration building's front door, we walk up the stone steps, the sound of our feet suddenly muffled in its dark, carpeted main hall. Gladys sits as usual behind the information desk, only today she is wearing an orchid corsage pinned to the blouse, which stretches open between the buttons across her voluminous bust. Gladys's husband died last year (the corsage is a gift from the Administrative Relations Committee), but she communes with his spirit.

"Hi, girls," she says to the four of us. In spite of her past, she will never adjust to coeducation. "Is it over already?" she asks, putting down her teacup.

"No," Jo tells her. "Not nearly. But we have to make a phone call." Gladys counts out change of a dollar from the cigar box in the top right-hand drawer, next to the tin of Band-Aids, a dish of hard candies, Xeroxes of the school calendar, and several Tampax in a jar.

"I think I'll just go take a peek," she says, locking up. "No one will miss me."

We branch off into the corridor behind whose doors typewriters beat out final grades and department memos, arriving at the single pay phone, rectangular glass box enclosing a round metal seat. The kind of box from which the young Houdini might have tried to escape, straitjacketed and bound, while a small audience watched. Unsung sideshow, far from the main tent.

"Who's going first?" George asks. No one answers. I hand cigarettes all around; perhaps we could send smoke signals instead.

"Oh, all right. I will," says Jo, the kind of kid, I imagine, who at the family doctor's volunteered for the first shot while her siblings watched in horror. She refastens the red glitter barrette in her hair, quick swab of the cotton, and dances into the booth, winking. At me.

"Don't take all day," I tell her. She lets the springed door shut in my face and dials. The right combination of digits, as in the case of a safe, will cause the door to pop open again, allowing access out as well as in.

"Hello, Mom?" we hear through the glass. "Yes, I found a place . . . a loft in the city. Of course it has rooms." She gives the address. Repeats it. "That's right, and the people I'm going to be living with are Melissa and George, my friends. Till the end of August. I just wanted to let you know, but graduation is about to start now. . . . I'll call you tomorrow when I find out the number there. OK. Bye-bye." She emerges from the phone booth, a speedy and effortless escape. "Next?"

"It's like the hot seat in here," says Melissa. She pulls off her sweater. Her propped knee eases back for the door to shut.

". . . uh huh," she continues, "and I'm going to be living with two people from school, Jo and Angela. Yes, Jo is a girl. . . ." Her foot taps against the glass, ticking off the seconds until she hangs up. "Georgie?" Record time.

"Just a bunch of friends," he explains earnestly into the mouthpiece. "You know, Mom, some buddies I met in the city. Yes, there's lots of room. What? Forget it," he says, indignant. He sits, hunched over and silent. "OK," he says, finally. "OK OK. I promise. . . . Yes. Same to you." He recradles the receiver and pushes back the door. "She says if we don't clean the broiler we'll get ptomaine, and we have to disinfect the toilet seat."

"I'm sure you'll be very good at both," says Melissa.

"I'll use you as the mop," says George, grabbing her, turning her upside down amidst screams and kicking. Her curly black hair brushes the floor. As one of the secretaries rushes out of the nearest office to see what the commotion is, I slip into the glass case. I like best to perfect my method before performing in public.

"Why, Angela," says my mother. "Hello, darling."

"Hi. Listen, I can't talk because graduation is going on right now, but we did find a place at the last moment."

"Wonderful," she says. "Is the neighborhood safe?"

"Oh yes. Completely." The streetlights on our block don't work. Were they extinguished by rocks?

We will live on the topmost floor of a factory building, over sewing machine assembly tables and labeled bins of button manufacturers: "4 holes/round/1 inch," "2 holes/round/half-inch." We saw them on the tour. As the supervisors lock up, quiet sets in like fog. Pea soup of sound—no chatter of machines, no AM radio refrains, no trucks backfiring or hoopla of noontime in the street. No nothing.

It gets kind of deserted after six, doesn't it? Melissa asked the conga player, soon to be off on his own tour, with whom we signed the sublet agreement for the summer. Will one of us be buttonholed, we wondered, by a robber in the black alley next to our front door? Worker on the night shift?

"Hold on while I get a pencil for the address," says my unsuspecting mother. "I'm going to write it here in my appointment book so I can't lose it. I'll just put it on the front page. . . ."

". . . and I'm going to be living with my good friends, Melissa—you've met her—and George."

"Are they a couple?" she asks me.

"What difference would that make?"

"Well, I just don't want you to feel left out. Excluded," she says. "Three is often a difficult number to handle."

"That I know," I tell her, but I leave it at that. "However," I continue, "I won't feel left out. As women friends, Melissa and I have a very high consciousness."

"Things can't be that different from when I was your age," says my mother. But oh yes they can. "Do you have a summer job yet?" she asks me.

"No. I couldn't look for one while I had exams and papers to finish, and, besides, I have to get off now. . . ."

"All right. All right," she says. "I'm just interested, that's all. Let me know how everything works out . . . when it does."

"OK. Send my love to Daddy."

"I will," she says. "We're going to a movie together Thursday night."

"Oh brother," I say, hanging up.

"Guess who took by far the longest?" says Jo, prying open the door and pulling me out by both hands, the failed Houdini's helper.

"It wasn't my fault," I tell her. "My mother has a master plan all her own."

"Yours and mine both," says George.

"Amen," say the other two.

Everyone had a mother; no one can get over it. As if the umbilical cord, unsevered, were the rope the escape artist must shed to free himself. And pleased at the relative success of today's stunt, we trail out the back door and down the hill in the direction of the dining room to drink champagne in honor of the graduates and each other.

"Why in God's name was gender ever invented?" I ask.

The three of them shake their heads.

"For procreation," Jo adds as an afterthought.

My head is stuffed with cotton batting. My brain lies on it exhausted, a makeshift mattress. Too much champagne. I pick up the single navy blue sock, dizzy as I bend down, from the closet floor and cross the lawn to Jo's room. Inside, her big red trunk in the center of the rug is a quarter full like the heart of a very young person. She is lying on the bed.

"This is yours," I say, dropping the sock into the trunk the way I try to augment the paraphernalia of her own heart as I can.

"One of your sweaters is under the bed," she replies. I lean over, but it is best first to lower my center of gravity. Dropping to my knees and reaching below the springs, I pull it out, covered with dust kittens. I sit on the floor, holding it in my lap, resting the back of my head against her leg. Her hand makes feathers of my hair. I am an Indian chief.

"The guard has been in twice already," she says. "He wants to lock the building. Everyone else is gone. So I told him if he rushed me I would have a nervous breakdown, and he let me have another hour."

If I laugh, my brains will rattle. Instead, a Cheshire cat smile eats up my face, all teeth. I wait for it to subside, for the plastic surgery of reason to recast my features in a recognizable image. There is a deadline, after all; we are under pressure.

"I have the solution to this," I tell her after a pause. "Don't bother to pack neatly; we can just dump it all out on the other end. For the time being throw everything into the trunk, and we'll worry about it later."

"I am never drinking champagne and brandy cocktails again," she says. "I was greedy for the strawberries, only one in each glass. But I must have had a small basketful."

"Have you spoken to Melissa and George?" I ask her.

"Yes," she says. "They'll be by with the car as soon as they finish packing, only George has already thrown up twice. . . . They'll stop at your room first."

"And who arranged that sequence of events?" I twist my neck to look at her; what if it sticks like crossed eyes? The body, as in George's case, in rebellion. She wears the pillow across her face, oversized eyeshades. What she can't see doesn't exist. The mind tricked.

"I did," she says, lifting a corner, peering out at me. "That way I thought you could finish packing and then come over to help me."

"All right." I get to my feet, frowning to mask my own face that would otherwise appear soft with the astonishment at feeling so indispensable. "However, the trunk better be half-filled by the time I get back." An ultimatum. A rigidity of both mien and purpose.

But she carried a pair of shoes, which I'd left one day preferring to go barefoot, back over to my room, one at a time. When she stripped the walls and realized that the posters would be crushed in the trunk, she arrived with them, too, at my door.

What should I do with these? she asked.

Just leave them here, I said, and I put them on the chair. But she decided to take a small rest and sat on them by mistake.

We'll iron them or something, I said, and I crammed the last of my books into an expandable suitcase and set it by the door with the rest of my belongings.

We took the familiar way back to her room for the last time; there would be other rooms and other routes from now on, not straight and direct as this one had been, as the crow flies, but circuitous, probably, and needful of signs in the manner of a more complicated human progress.

Look we've worn a path through the grass, she said. Diagonal of the ease with which we joined ourselves, proof of an often unsolvable problem. But we couldn't be sure if other feet and the spring rains hadn't helped with some of the steps.

We emptied each drawer, the contents of the closet into the trunk; also we threw in the sheets and pillow from the bed, and everything in the bathroom cabinet. I was fastening the clasps when she remembered the hair dryer on a hook behind the shower curtain, but it wouldn't fit. Mind over matter, we rearranged the top layer; matter vs. matter, she climbed on top of it and sat on the mound to try to pack it tighter. Round and fat, the old-fashioned variety, like a small tire, a diminutive flying saucer, the dryer could travel anywhere but into the trunk. Finally she threw it into the wastebasket and again after I'd fished it out.

It isn't working very well anymore, anyway, she said. Words I would remember. I shut the lid, and we heard a car honk outside the open window.

The eerie barking of an invisible dog greets us as we pull up onto the curb of the dark street and get out to unload. Our own assembly line to a new home. We leave the headlights on so we can see what we're doing, but in the same way you can't look into your own face, the direction of vision is off, and we see instead the lump of a man lying in the doorway of the building next door. His home?

I've moved fourteen times since I was fifteen, nine from room to room just at boarding school. This was said to broaden horizons. More to the point, though, I know an elderly woman who was once a union organizer, and she and her five children moved eleven times through four states in 1933 alone. The children, now grown up, often disparage their mother's wander-lust, but none of them complains of having had a boring life. I think of circus people—they say it's in the blood just like politics, but the whole cloth is probably more a matter of training—who've made brief homes in every populous center of the nation. Like everything, this has its good and bad aspects, but children, gallant runaways in the eyes of their own dreams, see circus life as the only adventure. If there are no frontiers any longer, then the exploration, the understanding, is in a certain multiplicity, a collection of the known.

Circus people reckon with the impossible, daily, like brushing teeth. They attempt what others cannot do, transform-ing themselves, sometimes, even into extrahuman forms. Feet to shoulders, tier upon tier, a whole troupe, they stand as pyramids. Balancing on high wires, submerged in aquatic tanks, they take on the lives of birds and fish. Faces in clown makeup, they draw for us different portraits of the soul. At times archetypically human, they perform the tasks of heroes, employ-ing both mythic necessities of force and guile: lifting weights like Atlas, the Titan, who held the heavens on his shoulders; battling as Heracles did with lions; restoring life to bodies sawn in half like Demeter who rescued her daughter Persephone from Hades. Labors of love, for what else could they be?

Homes? They take their homes with them in trunks, setting up in each new place the a prioris of a life, unpacking the impossible, only to pack again what was there before and a few newly gleaned articles. Their babies are born in trunks; this is where illicit love affairs are often consummated; a quality trunk makes as good a bathtub as anything. Events of life. Circus life.

"Where is that dog?" George asks after the third trip up the elevator. He and I have come back for the final load.

We look up and down the street, search fruitlessly for the dog in the dead end of the alley, no place for a dog anyway. Finally I spot him—on the roof of the building across the street, black-coated, blending with the night except for a patch of white he wears on his chest like a bib. Is the dog hungry?

"I hope he doesn't jump," I say. There is no railing.

"A dog wouldn't attempt that," says George. "They have an instinct human beings lack." This lack: a desire for the undoable, the unsurvivable.

"But what if he sees us leave and wants to come after us?" I ask, remembering my own dog who forgot she wasn't human, the way circus people forget they are, and with force of will sprang from the swamp. I push in the knob for the headlights and lock the last door.

"He won't," says George. We drag Jo's trunk into the lobby and slide it inside the elevator. "What's in here?" he asks. "Lead?"

"Just things," I tell him, tugging at the life of yet another performer, who, working daily miracles, has made me happy.

The dog barks all through dinner and into the late night. The four of us cut a deck of cards for the two bedrooms. They win first choice: the double bed with the airconditioner. We are stuck with the bunk beds and the industrial fan. We climb into the upper one, and the noise of air being sucked into the room, loud as a train in a tunnel, blocks out the dog's howls. In the morning, disoriented, I hit my head on the ceiling.

"Are you all right?" Jo asks, rubbing the bump.

"I'm exhausted," I tell her. "I didn't fall asleep until daylight. The goddamned fan wheezed and chugged all night."

"I didn't hear a thing," she says, yawning into a full-bodied stretch. "I slept like a rock."

Every night we go to bed with the fan on. When I think she has fallen asleep, I climb down the wooden ladder, splinters gouging my feet, and push the switch to "off." Then I climb back up, careful not to jostle the platform as I lie down beside her. In July, when the first heat wave settles over the city, our night exercise increases, up and down like a fire brigade with its pole. Jo, battling the blaze, turning the fan to "high" when she awakens in a sweat; Angela, unsuspected arsonist in the ranks, later stilling its circular motion. One night I even moved to the couch in the living room. But that was for a different reason.

Number 905: "Womanpower" is printed in script on the smoked glass door. I knock and enter into a vestibule which reminds me of the waiting room at my dentist's office in Boston: magazines on the coffee table, the obligatory water cooler, a standing coat rack; even the air, inhaled, causes a rush of adrenaline, common side effect of an antiseptic smell. But the woman behind the reception desk is dressed in a tailored brown linen suit rather than the familiar white uniform and peaked cap pinned at a jaunty angle. In fact there is nothing jaunty about her; is this necessary? Yes, she is the job nurse.

"Good morning, young lady," she says, scrutinizing me over her half-glasses, poking a stray wisp of graying hair back into her bun with a pencil. Her jaw set and her eyes flat.

Sometime back in the 1950s she must have one day forgotten how to smile, unlike riding a bike, which, my mother says, you never forget. But I have a past, too, and I can't forget it either: the young lady, young lady, young lady of my boarding school memories, with its litany of responses. The sound of it paralyzes me, like a person hearing her own hypnotic cue. Her voice the same as those of the women I knew then who, like the receptionist sitting before me now, started to dry up from the inside out, lost the flesh early from what I dreamt about as truly cadaverous faces and skeletal frames.

It scared me, because it wasn't dinners they lacked but the other kind of nourishment: the food of the heart. And mine would shrink within me, trying of its own to appear smaller and of less consequence, the way in the presence of poverty we tend to suck in our bellies and pray for a rumble or two.

I'm fifteen again. Back in history. As far back as when the young heart betrays itself, as when the doctrine of free will is only a hope.

"Well?" she asks.

"Yes."

"What's your name then?" But I can't get it out, and I point to the eleven-thirty slot on the open calendar.

"Hmph," she says, pointing to the couch. "There is a client inside with Miss Prince at the moment. Please wait." If I walk very slowly in that direction, not pausing to sit but continue for three more steps, I will be at the door and out before she looks up again. Because, you see, an error has been made. The couch, nevertheless, is a well-camouflaged snare, and I sink down into it.

The fact of the matter is that they are going to pull out all my teeth. Painful extractions one by one without anesthesia. The one at the desk will hold me down while Dr. Prince wields the pliers.

What are your capabilities? she'll ask, yanking at a molar.

Reading, writing, summarizing, organizing. Thinking, I'll add.

Skills! she fumes. Typing?

No.

Shorthand?

No.

Steno?

No.

What are your credentials? she'll continue.

I don't have any, I'll say, and with a sucking sound she'll disimpact the first tooth, jagged and bloody.

College major? she'll ask next.

We don't have any majors at my school, I'll tell her. Triumphantly, she'll file away at my front teeth until she excites the nerves. Uneven, affording a good grip, the teeth are now ready for removal.

Then we have nothing for you, she'll say, in two deft movements denuding my smile. Womanpower.

The door to the inner office opens, and a middle-aged woman comes out first followed by . . . the job nurse? No, twins. She walks over to her sister and rests a hand on her shoulder. The Misses Prince. "Whom have we next?" she asks. The other one nods in my direction.

"This way," says Miss Prince (B), walking erect in the lead. She motions to a straight-backed cane chair directly in front of her desk and shuts the door. This will be conducted in the manner of a prison interview but without the barrier of a mesh screen between us. The kind through which loved ones have kissed, their hungry lips straddling wires. But Miss Prince will not kiss me. Miss Prince isn't hungry. She wants, like a karate expert, to pull my heart, moist and still pumping, from my chest. She wants to make me forget, as if it had a memory, how to smile.

"I see from your letter that you are a generalist," she begins, raising her eyes from a file card on the desk to me.

"What's a generalist?" I ask her. I imagine Alexander the Great in a similar situation. I see that you are a general, he was told. They found him a new army right away. . . .

"It means," she says, "that while you are perhaps capable of fulfilling the responsibilities of, let's say, some junior position, there is no single field for which you are particularly suited."

"I *am* still in college," I remind her.

"Another detriment," she adds, "to obtaining remunerative employment."

"Summer jobs hard to find?" I ask.

"Plums," she says, "already plucked."

I look past her out the window, our first day of sun in the three since we moved into the city. On the sills of the building across the street, fat pigeons hop. Behind them rows of desks make a checkerboard of the office interior.

"Have you got any outdoor work?" I ask her.

"Certainly not," she says. "We cater to only the most exclusive women's colleges in the greater New York area. You can type, of course," she says.

"With two fingers," I tell her.

"Then there's very little . . ." she concludes. She taps the edge of the upright file card against the base of an antique pen and pencil set. We were the generation that vowed never to learn to type so that upon graduation we would not become the "indispensable" secretaries so many of our mothers had. But what else is there? I think of skills.

"I could be a cashier," I suggest.

"We handle only executive work," says Miss Prince. "Well, you tell me; what direction are you leaning in? Managerial? Publishing? A lot of girls go into that. Public relations? Journalism? Why, perhaps even computer science; that's a field rapidly opening up to women."

"I hadn't really thought about it that way," I tell her. What has happened to the revered callings? Missionaries, aviators, astronomers, chefs, tailors, vaudevillians. Either in the blood or in the family. If the jobs we envision and create reflect the age, then we're in a sad time. Or maybe it's me: The portly janitors of our grade school, who ate sandwiches in the toolroom at lunchtime, tacking a detached heel onto a short brown leather lace-up, are now custodial engineers. We have two-hundred-man offices of corporate lawyers where once there was Perry Mason. Can the world have changed so drastically? Can perspective?

"You've got to do your homework first," says Miss Prince, "to use a student's metaphor. Then, only then, can we be of service to you. . . ." She stands up, offering me her claw-like hand.

"Shut up, you old crone," I tell her, turning on my heel, slamming her office door, grimacing at Miss Prince (A), and slamming the outside door, too. This feeling I recognize as elation. Smiling broadly, as if I had suddenly remembered a particularly good joke, I press the elevator button and it lights up red for down.

I buy a paper at the kiosk in the building lobby and walk out into the sunshine to the stone bench, damp from the spraying fountain in the wind, turning to the employment section:

Accountants; bartenders; credit manager. No. Dentist wanted at clinic; doormen; engineers; foundation grants analyst; gal/guy Friday . . . typing, typing, typing. No. Geophysicist. Hosiery sorters. Helicopter mechanic. Idea man/woman in small, midtown ad agency? $15,000 start, at least five years experience. No. Loaders (forklift); massage; messengers; night-watchman; nurses, R.N. Orange Julius—manager. I could wear a paper hat, learn the secret ingredient . . . No, Queens location. Part-time: file clerks, seamstresses (will train). Not enough money, and close work ruins your eyes. Personnel director. Rose grower at nursery? . . . New Jersey. Sales: floorperson, Fuller Brush, medical equipment . . . No, no, no. . . .

"EXCITING OPENING FOR COLLEGE GRADUATE SEVEN SIS-TERS OR SIMILAR CREATIVE TYPE. UP TO $400 WEEKLY FOR AMBITIOUS INDIVIDUAL. PHOTOLETTERING SALES. CHALLENG-

ING." Yesterday I bounced a check to get money for the week; I call the number.

"I'm Gail," replies the tanned blond woman, who's writing on a legal pad, bent over next to the seated receptionist. She puts down the pencil and shakes my hand across the desk. "And some cole slaw," she adds. To me: "Three o'clock and I haven't even had time for lunch. You look like just what I want," she says. "Come into my office." She walks ahead of me through what must be the production area, taking enormous strides for her short legs. "Harry, what about the three-thirty order?" she stops to ask a bluejeaned man sitting in front of one of the humming machines. I catch up.

"Almost done," he says.

"Better be. It's a new account." She opens a door at the back, and we enter a cramped office: chairs, two desks, the file cabinet—all stacked with bills. She clears off one of the chairs. "Sit down," she says, settling on the desk corner in front of me. "So?"

"Well," I start. This is not a strong start; I take a deep breath. "As I told you over the phone, I read your ad and it looked interesting. You know; I didn't want a job that was all typing and sitting in an office, no excitement. So I thought I'd come up and talk to you about just what the job entails." Luckily, I saw a situation like this once on a TV commercial.

"You might fit," she says, cocking her head to the side. "We don't want any shy retiring flowers, to put it mildly. I'm after girls who are personable, attractive, and . . . what's the word? . . . *pushy,* who can get out there and sell. It's a competitive market, you see."

"Clearly," I say. I don't see at all.

"I started out when I was about your age," she says, lighting up a cigarette. She throws the match, without looking, into a wastebasket across the room. "I was with one of our competitors six years, and then I got a partner and started this place. I bought him out. College graduate?" she asks.

"No, not exactly," I tell her. "But I only have a few courses left to go and, frankly, I might not finish." This isn't true, but it is a white lie. Because being honest won't pay the rent. Neither will Jo's $40 a week teaching dance part-time at the Y. Neither will my mother's bank account after the last installment of this year's tuition loan. Neither will my father's unemployment check.

"Well, you don't need to know Plato to sell," she says. "I only had two years myself. I put the college grad bit because I didn't want any naïves, you know what I mean?"

"Sure," I say. "You want somebody walking around with her eyes open."

"That's right," she says, smiling. "You sound like a natural to me. Articulate, the first thing. Poised, only don't chew gum like that on the job." I swallow it. "Use one of those sprays for your breath. . . . And what else?" She looks me over. "You ought to tie your hair back. A hairdresser could do something about that frizz, you know. And no jeans."

"No, no jeans," I say. She hands me a catalogue from the desk beside her. Thumbing through it, I don't see a thing, like an actress on the stage who reads from a blank tablet.

"Those are the typefaces," she says, and handing me a Xeroxed sheet, "these are the prices."

"Competitive?" I ask. A shot in the dark that pierces the bull's-eye with beginner's luck.

"Competitive enough." She nods. "We make it up with service. You're going to have to bust your ass," she says, "but it's worth it. I didn't get where I am at thirty-three by sleeping till noon."

"Certainly not," I say.

"Come in tomorrow," she finishes. "Eight-thirty. I'll tell you your territory and you can meet the other girls. Two months one hundred twenty-five dollars a week base. After that seventy-five plus commission. Within a year, I was averaging three hundred fifty dollars a week. That's something to shoot for."

"You bet," I tell her. Her attitude is infectious; her opinion a new world view. Buy and sell, buy and sell. One of her ancestors must have traded the trinkets for Manhattan. We walk, more like a half-trot, to the elevator.

"You strike me as a sharp kid," she says, "and that can be turned into dollars. A nice one-bedroom, designer clothes, vacations. . . . I just got back from two weeks in Europe yesterday." The bell rings and the doors pop open on our floor. "See you tomorrow, babe," she says, slapping me on the ass as I hurry into the car.

I call Jo from the first phone booth on the street.

"I got a job," I tell her.

"Hurray," she says. I hear applause on the other end. "Doing what?"

"Selling photolettering."

"What's photolettering?" she asks.

"I don't know," I tell her, "but I start tomorrow." And so did everything else.

As Shakespeare said in one of his plays, "When sorrows come, they come not single spies, but in battalions." Shakespeare is always right.

First, it's the job; it's the fact that no matter how much money I try to save I never can seem to make the weekly rent on time (airmail to the conga player); it's that Melissa practices the violin every night for three hours when all I want is quiet; it is also Jo, who one day stopped looking me in the eye and started seeing through me. It is also the fact that I can't quit the job because I can't afford to, that like everyone else's the paycheck is spent before it even gets into the bank, that Melissa has to practice then because she works at Macy's during the day, that I can't force Jo to stop making me feel invisible where before my body had substance and dimensions, defined by her hands. These are the problems and the reasons for them.

This is not to say that the reasons explain the problems, though. Whys have a logic all their own. Why, for example, a forest turns into an army of approaching men. Or why a love affair comes suddenly undone like shoelaces. Even Shakespeare couldn't answer that.

But I don't dwell on the abstract; I can't. Instead I involve with particulars. I practice long hours, like Melissa, getting through days. So I won't lose the knack. Fingering cut-up vegetables, cigarettes, light switches, and house keys like strings.

Every evening when I come home from work, the first back always because the first to leave in the morning, I go into the bathroom and turn on the hot water full blast. Then I pour myself a drink in the kitchen and, returning, sit down on the edge of the tub to soak my feet. My territory is all of Lexington and Third avenues (Eighteenth to Ninety-sixth streets) where each day I claim a few more blocks as my own, farther and farther from the downtown office, paying calls to the hundreds of advertising agencies, magazine headquarters, and publishing houses listed on the wall directories of the office building lobbies.

This is called selling cold, said my father when I called him up. Your Uncle Freddie used to be in that line; I think it's one of the things that pushed him over the brink.

What's the best technique? I asked him, hoping for advice I could apply to other things, too.

You have to really want to make the sale, he said You've got to be willing to try almost anything.

I can do everything but beg, I told him. And that I can't do. I can't physically get it out. The words stick.

I've had the same trouble, said my father. Once I even sold for a year, when you were young, but I came away from it with a poor record. Freddie used to tell me that before he went in to make a sale, he'd remind himself that the other guy was human, too, and took a shit in the morning just like everybody else. I don't know if that will be a help to you. . . .

I'll keep it in mind, I told him.

But I didn't want to imagine the burly, suited men sitting on toilets the way I sit every evening, thinking, with my feet in the steaming water.

At lunch I eat a yogurt on a bench at the edge of the park on Fifth Avenue, and sometimes I cry because I cannot face the afternoon. I use the paper napkin that comes with the yogurt, then, to dry my eyes, and wiping off the spoon I carry with me from the apartment, slip it back into my canvas bag of catalogues. It fell out onto a drawing table once when I was searching for a pen. The man asked me if I sold silverware too. And if I'd go with him after work to a hotel room to get the account. He wasn't the first. Is this what Gail meant by "service"?

When I have covered my entire territory, calling back on possible clients every two weeks to ask for business, then Gail will add to it. Madison Avenue, its desirability clear from the name, is still up for grabs; both Charlotte and Susan, up-and-coming empire builders, have spoken to Gail privately about annexing it. I know. She told me.

Don't you want it? she asked me. Because I'm saving it for you. I know you've got it in you, she says. Push.

Adding to my territory, compounding this problem like all the others, including the main one, that I can't seem to get anywhere with, the same way I haven't made a single sale in two months.

My life is an uphill climb, an ascent to feats I cannot accomplish. Incompetent circus diver, I climb the rickety ladder to the bed only to land the next day feet first in the tub. Aerialist afraid of heights, I take the express elevator sometimes to the fortieth floor or above to show my stuff, too shaky to perform once I get there.

I pause outside of doors, reading the names of offices to be visited that match those I scribbled below on file cards. I don't always open them. Behind each one lurks a different unknown, a possible collapse. One door leads to safety, a surcease, but which one is it? Is it the door to our apartment? No. The side door of the elevator opens directly in, the main entrance remaining shut, but sometimes the mechanism goes awry and the wrong door opens onto a brick wall that is exposed impenetrable, like the one that builds itself daily between Jo and me.

She arrives home around midnight. Melissa and George have gone to bed early. You could hear them fucking if it weren't for the air-conditioner.

"I had a late rehearsal," she says, "and then we stopped off for a few drinks." She sits down next to me on the couch and lays her head on my lap.

"We seem to be on rather different schedules," I suggest.

"Yes," she says. "You're like a dead horse in the evenings."

"I get tired," I tell her.

"It's your head that's tired," she says.

"I know that."

"And this is the way everybody lives their lives: long days of work."

"I don't understand how. Why don't you ever come home early anymore?" I ask her. Why.

"Do we have to talk about this now?" She rubs my leg with her hand.

"You seem to find time enough for everything else," I tell her.

"You're right," she says, sitting up.

"So shoot," I say.

"Well, first, because I've started thinking 'us' instead of 'me.' Even when I'm by myself. You know what I'm saying?" I nod. "And also because it's not working very well anymore, anyway, ever since we moved into this apartment."

"Is everything supposed to work well all the time?" I ask her.

"I don't know," she says. "The whole summer's been like playing house. . . ."

"Who's playing?"

"That's just the problem," she says. "It scares me."

"What scares you?" I ask her, not wanting an answer.

"This," she says, making a gesture that includes both of us. "What am I committing myself to?"

"To me," I tell her. "To the old dead horse." But it doesn't come out funny. "Cold feet?" I ask, my stomach knotting. "Maybe if we had more time together. . . . Or maybe if I moved somewhere else for the rest of the summer. . . ." You've got to be willing to try almost anything, my father said.

"Angela," she says, standing up in front of me, "when I met you I called it quits on everything. Family, friends, other lovers,

all of it . . ."So did I. "What do you want now? Blood?" I recall
the time she painted my face and body with her menstrual
blood: war paint, love paint. It dried and flaked off onto the
sheet, red dust, fallout from the explosion in her heart. Yes. I
want blood, too.

"Just stop pushing. Relax a little," she says, "and maybe
things will improve."

But things didn't improve, and one night the next week she
didn't come home or for the next two days, either. Melissa and
George asked where she was the first morning and, after that,
pretended not to notice, though a circus audience will wait in
line for hours to see just that (something perfected years ago, in
fact, by my father), its favorite, breathtaking feat: the vanishing
act.

The end of August is as sultry and unbearable as her body
beside me at night that sinks into sleep a whole foot away in the
narrow bunk and molds unconsciously to mine as the night ages.
Having given up altogether on turning off the fan, I lie awake
and try not to think, a denial of the future, until the alarm, its
validation, rings. In a week, school will start.

"Are you leaving me?" I ask her one night, holding her in
my arms.

"Yes," she says.

"You're the only person I ever liked more than my
mother," I tell her, only because it's true. We pause in a long
kiss.

"I'm not doing this right," says Jo.

"Who does?" I say.

She starts crying.

"Are you still in love with me?" I ask her.

"I just can't do it," she says, "but . . . yes."

"Then you go to hell," I tell her quietly, "because that's the
only sin there is in the whole fucking world."

On Saturday we pack. All my bags. Jo's trunk. I throw
things into it, some that I gave her, bits of myself.

"Don't worry about sorting out our things now," says Jo.

"You'll only be two houses down the hill." She is about to throw my sneakers into the trunk. I take them from her.

"Actually," I say, "I'm not going back to school this semester."

"What do you mean?" she says, grabbing them back.

"I rented a studio uptown yesterday," I tell her, "after work."

"Don't be ridiculous, Angela," she says.

"It's not ridiculous," I tell her. "I still haven't tackled the Chrysler Building yet." She flips shut the lid of the trunk and sits down on top of it, looking at me. I settle beside her.

I am wondering about circumstances, about the conjunction of two people, like planets, in time and space. Magic, some people have it. Or just an optical illusion. Though either way, it has its special meridians, its own indispensable props.

Who is it, then, that steals the wands? What happened to the top hat? And where did the white rabbit go, wide-èyed and sniffing?

Circumstances. What if one of us had been a different age or the other gender? Or had another name? What if she had chosen a college in the West, or at the time I had had my heart set on children? No one can say, any more than why the magic goes.

We forget the dangers of attempting the impossible: whole families are killed in daredevil high jinks. Young boys shot from cannons miss the net. I am reminded of the fate of the elephant girl.

We brandish saws over boxes, pretending to cut each other in half. Who could have known that sometimes the saw touches flesh and we really do?

─────────Chapter XIV─────────
WEARING MANY HATS

WHEN A WOMAN IS BLUE, MY MOTHER SAYS, her best strategy is to go out and buy a new hat. Either that or scrub the kitchen floor. (It occurs to me that there are two prescriptions for every remediable situation in life: one for the rich and one for the poor.) Lucky for me, as it turns out, my apartment is wall-to-wall linoleum squares, gray and white flecked, which I can swab down any day of the week and do. Balancing the mattress on top of the refrigerator, an aerial crib; stacking the three metal chairs, one inside the other like a nest of blocks, beside the rickety table pushed flush against the windowsill; having wheeled the stuffed reading chair, empty perambulator, into the bathroom: evacuating the nursery where daily I nurse myself. The bathroom floor, it's true, is stained with footprints and littered with hair and dust balls, but I live with this dirt comfortably enough. The kind of washing I do in the other room has got nothing to do with dirt.

I don't use the stuff you can squirt from a plastic bottle like a man urinating, the kind you then spread with a mop, which my mother recommended to my brother stationed in Arizona. Instead, I mix powders and boiling water, my own formula, in a red bucket and apply it with a brush. Squatting, a woman's way.

On warm evenings, as I bend over the ammonia smell, cloudy steam rises and, changing state, liquefies, trickles of water dripping from my forehead down my cheeks, off the tip of the chin, seeking their source. And I remember those diagrams of circular arrows in clean-cut black and white on a page of my grade school science book. Of rain falling, irrigating the soil, then evaporating into the atmosphere, condensing into clouds, only to fall back to Earth as rain again. Each step for a purpose, a marching army of moisture. When I cry I like to think of it in this way, too . . . the tears as soldiers of the water cycle. But that's just the point about washing the floor, because I never think about crying then; at·the time the task is everything.

217

First wondering where to begin. Designing a preliminary floor plan in my head. Next drawing perfect rainbows (promises of a personal dry spell), careful to paint around a path to the door. At a certain moment aware only of physical stimuli: the vapor climbing through the nose to the hemispheres of the brain, the hair wilting into a damp sea grass, the back a bow, your arm the straight arrow, aquiver, when less than halfway through the muscles tire. Containing the animal, vegetable, and mineral of the world inside me so that, crowded and busy, I forget myself altogether. Like a long-distance runner who becomes simply hammering heels, the shoots beneath them, his own wind, no longer a part of the landscape through which he passes but its receptacle. As if tenacity, an elasticity of endurance, enabled one to grow like a balloon, to be filled with the breath of other existences. A kind of pregnancy.

Afterward I sit out in the hall, winded, on the top attic stair in the September Indian-summer heat, my face the rosy color of the bucket beside me: another change of state, from blue to red. But fifteen minutes later the floor is as dry again as the litmus paper of my moods, and I am cooled off, emptied. It is then, sometimes, that I am tempted to drink the cleanser that remains.

"Good morning, Angela," says Gail, glancing up from a newspaper on the receptionist's desk. "You're late."

"I know." I punch in at the time clock on the wall behind her. My father says there's no such thing as a good excuse; I believe this. It's eight-fifty.

"Sit down," she says, tapping on the desk beside her. She folds up the paper, making a place for me, and I deposit my bag between us, turning to meet her eyes while I undo my jacket. "What's going on?" she asks me.

"I guess I'm just not a natural after all," I suggest. The last button won't slide through. "Maybe . . ."

"Two sales," she interrupts in disgust, "amounting to fifty-six dollars and eighty-seven cents." She shakes her head and picks up the container of black coffee beside her, blowing on it. "It's the middle of September, Angela. I've kept you on salary for an extra two months to give you a chance. . . ."

"And surprisingly enough the weather's still good, too. Warm, sunny."

"Fuck the weather," she says. "I'm talking to you about business, *b-u-s-i-n-e-s-s*."

"But it's been a record September," I reply, unable to free myself as well from the jacket of my own concerns. "More days above seventy degrees than any one since 1917, the year of the Bolshevik revolution." I know my facts; I ought to. One of the few calls I make every night is to the Weather Bureau, when I listen to the entire recording, not hanging up after the temperature and forecast like the average layman but expanding my understanding of the patterns that shift inside the natural dome of our New York sky. I note with interest the barometer readings, the relative humidity, the directions and speed of the wind. Though I'm not certain what the "degree day total" is, I've made a chart on graph paper of its weekly variations, hoping to be enlightened by its pictorial progress . . . but who am I kidding? I do it because it's something to do, after the tape of the weather voice has clicked off, when the only topics on the radio talk shows are things like cancer and rape, after midnight or one or two, when I can't sleep. Which is why I'm late this morning, too tired at seven-fifteen to lift the blankets.

"You know, you exasperate me," Gail says. "If I had any brains, I would have fired you at the beginning of this record month."

"Why didn't you?" I ask her halfheartedly, less curious about the changes in my own life than those of the weather. She puts her arm around my shoulders, weightless, a stratus cloud. My body seems to fall asleep during the day the way my mind won't at night.

"Because I like you. You're a good kid," she says. "Only ineffectual, that's all." She chuckles good-naturedly as people often do at dancers with two left feet, singers who reduce a melody to a single note, divers who smack the water in a belly flop. I shrug off her arm.

"You could always work for the charities though," she continues. "Your background is perfect. All you would have to do is smile and say 'please'; the money might as well go to you as to taxes." She pushes at the corners of my mouth with her fingers. I would like to bite them off.

"I was going to suggest that you see my therapist to help build up your confidence, but that wouldn't be necessary for this line of work. What you'd need is charm school instead." She laughs, rocking back and forth on the desk. This rings a distant bell; in fact, it's an idea I'd been crazy to actuate when I was ten—to take courses in stemming the tide of inadequacies that would surely bubble up from deep inside me in adult life: to learn how not to walk, how not to smile (exposing too much of the gums, the brochure said), how not to argue but to demur, how not to be fat, how not to have small eyes. Gail has mastered all these things and more. I bet they can even teach you how not to menstruate. . . . Me, I now live as best I can imperfect. Ineffectual, too, for in this business, as in others with less dignified names, as women it's ourselves we sell.

"That was screamingly funny," I tell Gail, lowering my feet to the floor. "You ought to get a spot on the Ed Sullivan Show."

"Watch it," she says, standing up beside me. "I'm still the boss, you know. Anyway, I was only kidding." The top of her head is level with my chin. She fingers the lapel of my jacket, searching for words between the threads. "But you better hit the road now," she says finally, "because if you don't come up with at least one solid account within the next two weeks I'm going to have to let you go, Angela, no kidding on that score."

"I can understand that," I tell her. And I can, but if there is justice in the universe, one day I will be reincarnated as a dogmatist, deaf to the contingencies of other lives. There won't be a reasonable bone in my body. Each will be forged from a new mold, autonomous of an evolved skeleton: the tangible and inescapable proof of the humanity we share. Or perhaps I will be born a crustacean. Armor on the outside, where it counts.

"You wouldn't be able to live on your base pay, anyway," Gail adds. "And do yourself a favor. Cheer up a little?"

Sitting at my desk in the other room then, I took the letters from all the different-faced alphabets in our catalogue and, rearranging them, wrote out a definition of the world I could approve of. Short of transforming it entirely, nothing would cheer me up, so for that one day that's what I did, hoping to redeem it and the salesman, too, who would sell it a new and fuller meaning.

I covered eight blocks of the sidewalk of my childhood: Step on a crack you'll break your mother's back. Step on a line you'll break your father's spine. A concrete yet mystical map of hurt. Exploring the boundaries of my father's domain. Rivers of my mother.

I paid tribute to science, riding up in elevators, as fearless as the physicists in Einstein's theoretical experiments regarding mass, time, and distance, concepts I have also pondered to the same end: a lack of causality. I encountered nature in a skyscraper, dropping my card with a kind of abandon into the outstretched palms of secretaries, open flowers whose red-tipped petals closed over it again, as if at sunset. Behind the office doors of art directors I regaled each with a new and fanciful pitch in honor of literature, Scheherazade of Third Avenue. It was the best day I had had in a long time.

And my score? Sales entered into the nearly empty, paperbound account book? The usual. Zero. Goose egg. No kidding.

But golden . . . because it didn't matter to me at all that evening, walking across town toward home, streets thick with hurrying people, the sun pink in the west behind a haze of traffic exhaust and mist. Life was not just a series of knocks on doors, petty services exchanged, five o'clock the hour of remission. It had a luminescence, like that September sky aglow at the edges. To my mind other reference points, a complicity, a history. Truly, even a single photographed letter on an other-wise blank page leaves an afterimage in the retina.

Now I come into the office at eight-thirty sharp, slip a card with my name on it into the gray metal box of my timely arrival, only to race out again, not even stopping for the usual coffee with Charlotte and Susan.

"She must have gotten the IBM account," says Susan.

"Either that or she's in love," says Charlotte, but none of this applies. Taking Gail's advice, I am doing myself a favor. The new name on the card I punch (first, middle, and last) is Pedestrian/Tourist/Civilian.

Once outside for the day, I rarely enter any of the buildings as I stroll up and down the two avenues of my territory; peering, through the street reflected, into shops; pausing at steamy vents to sniff the sweet aromas of bakeries; craning my neck to follow upward the stories of deco architecture. I offer my catalogues to bag ladies and small children as portable treasures, primers; while the weather, true to its nightly reports, holds fine except for an occasional very cold day, and on these days I comb the department stores for hats. I feel guilty about this, but I do it anyway. Though sometimes, in a fit of remorse (or is it fear?—picturing Gail's face if she ever found out, which she couldn't, wide as the whole sky, like God's in a dream), I enter the lobby of a building that has been entrusted to *my* care and scan its directory, hoping to read there a reason, an impetus, to then throw myself inside one of the elevators I watch open and close for hours at a time. If I say I have no control over this, it's true. Like a person whose legs boast the muscles intact, each nerve vigilant, everything wrapped into place by a supple and glowing skin, but which nevertheless will not propel the body, I can't walk into those elevators opening and closing on my paralysis. It seems that I am through with this particular kind of experiment.

The matronly and robust woman reflected beside me in the three-way mirror inside Saks Fifth Avenue says that this season's most popular hat is the turban, though over the years the simple kerchief has held its own as America's favorite. I think about this as I try on, systematically, every hat in the store.

I am not driven, but I am thorough, a quality I have never been able to shake the way I did my hips for an entire evening at the first birthday party ever to which boys were invited, where my partner Joey Monroe and I won the Twist marathon. We did not wear ourselves out whenever the Beatles came on the record player; we didn't flirt, not even with each other. Instead, we sipped Cokes for energy and moved our shoulders back and forth in a slow shimmy (you just pretend you're drying your behind with a towel, our parents generation had it . . .) until after three hours and twenty-five minutes the only other participating team had to quit because the girl's father arrived early to pick her up. Hardly a sweet win.

Were any of the boys nice? my mother asked, driving home afterward in the dark bubble of the car.

I don't know, I told her, bursting it. I didn't talk to any of them.

Joey was afraid of girls, and I was thorough, while other couples disappeared from the dance floor as suddenly as the multiple reflections of the saleswoman and me as we walk out of the range of the mirror and over to the table with the charge machines.

"You must like hats," Mrs. Zorb says, thumping down into the opposite chair, leaning happily toward me. I have her card in my pocket: ERICA ZORB, LADIES' MILLINER FOR 17 YEARS. A shared passion? Oh no, I like hats in the same way I liked dancing the Twist one night when I was thirteen.

"Styles come and go," she says, "but all in all, taste stays pretty much the same. I mean look at hemlines . . . up and down, up and down like the stock market, but a skirt just an inch or two below the knee is always appropriate."

I had suspected from Mrs. Zorb just this kind of wisdom. She stood out among the mannequins and other clerks—in a pearl-gray dress; her hair bound up into a neat gray bun pierced by a pencil; "sensible" shoes on her feet that propelled her stocky body in my direction as I emerged from the blouse section. A square-rigger, my father would call her, steering herself easily between banks of hat trees, smiling as she approached to ask, Did I need any help? And yes I did, yes I did. Reaching out one afternoon for her simple wisdom to buoy me up.

"My goodness, I almost forgot the closeouts packed away in the back," she says, abruptly sliding her chair along the carpet and getting up. "You wait right here and I'll just bring them out."

On days like today I wish I were more like Mrs. Zorb, for whom hats are simply hats, or even like women whose taste stays pretty much the same. I imagine myself in situations where kerchiefs are required: at barbecues, in a convertible at the drive-in, lying on a beach of glistening sunbathers, shopping at a mall, picking up the kids after school, over curlers . . . but there is little here I recognize from my life.

What can kerchiefs mean? Are they colorful semaphores, bobby-pinned into the position of an inheritable message of womanhood? Are they uniformic, reassuring in their bounded versatility? A sergeant feels this way about his stripes: with them come certain understood privileges and likewise restrictions.

Other hats, like many of the ones I try on, speak less of an institution and more to the individual. You might even say that in these cases the hat merely induces a particular characteristic in its wearer, an otherwise invisible trait, as one trapped inside a recessive gene. But this is not what I am looking for either; I buy hats of a metamorphic nature, transformational hats, just as a man will grow a mustache or a beard to become a different person entirely, to alter his character.

Mrs. Zorb calls me. "Look what I've got," she says as I look over my shoulder to where she stands next to the mirror, her hand steadying a stack of boxes six feet high. We flip back their covers one by one, digging inside. She fits each hat till it settles just above my ears, and I examine it fullface, both profiles, but the person I see in the mirror is always the same. Finally, I try on one of the boxes, too.

"My Lord," says Mrs. Zorb, laughing, putting her fists to her cheeks. "That might become all the rage. If only it were a few sizes smaller."

"Here," I say, handing it to her, "you try it on."

"That would be silly," she says, but taking it and tying the ribbons expertly beneath her chin. Now her head looks in proportion to her body, and she takes a few steps, pausing to push the box farther back on her forehead. She skips over scattered lids and tissue paper; if she doesn't stop I'll pee in my pants like the time my grandmother put candy wrappers on her ears to act out Uncle Wiggily. But she does, continuing to chuckle as she removes it and, carefully placing a hat inside, relegates it once again to boxhood and us to our task.

"My, wasn't that fun," she says, catching her breath.

"Mrs. Zorb, the Mad Hatter."

"That's just what my husband calls me," she says, nodding her head. "But I tell him," she continues, "sometimes life has to hold off for just a minute. . . ." Bent down over another box, she straightens up with a turban of green feathers. "How do you like this one?" she asks, spreading her fingers inside it, extending her arm.

"Is that the front?" I ask her.

"I don't know." She turns it deftly inside out. "The label's on the seam. We'll have to try it both ways." The crumpled tissue paper falls, an expanding universe, from her hand. She takes the hat by the two earflaps and pulls it down onto my forehead.

"This one is rather way out, isn't it?" says Mrs. Zorb. "Although . . ." She rests her chin in the V of her thumb and forefinger, propping up her elbow with the other palm, scrutinizing the hat. "Although it does something for you," she concludes.

"You'd have to have an occasion to wear it to," I suggest.

We are intent on the mirror. The girl in the mirror. Will she grow larger? Or smaller? Is this the changing hat, the one that opens up another world on the other side of the looking glass?

"Yes, to a play opening or something," Mrs. Zorb agrees. "In fact," she says, "it's the kind of hat you might wear *in* a play. Part of a costume, if you get my meaning . . ." I like this idea. I concentrate on the figure in the mirror. Who might she be? One of the characters from *The Women?* A gun moll? Hedda Gabler? Perhaps a chorus girl . . . Any other identity will do, any other text.

"How much is it?" I venture.

"Let me see," says Mrs. Zorb, peering at the price tag through the bottoms of her bifocals. She clicks her tongue. "Forty-eight dollars. That's highway robbery. . . ." I consider; another few days and I'll be out of a job.

"I'll take it," I tell her.

"You will?" she asks. We are both surprised. "Well, what do you know about that . . . good for you, Angela." She shakes my hand. Business magnates clinching a multimillion-dollar deal could not be more pleased than we are. "And I'm going to cut the price to forty," she says. "After all, it's a closeout."

"Thank you very much," I tell her.

"Don't mention it. I mean that literally," she whispers in my ear.

"Come back and see me," says Mrs. Zorb after writing up the sale and stamping the back of the check. She extends the big shopping bag.

"I will," I tell her, taking it, but I know I won't. Today I spent all the money in my checking account. This is the last hat I can buy.

"I can't remember when I've had such a good time at work," she says.

"Me either," I tell her. I push, waving, through the heavy metal exit door. The railing in one hand, the hat in the other, two at a jump down the stairs.

The bus follows a slalom course from picking me up to the center lane of the avenue and back to the curb again, out and in, and out and in. It would be faster to walk in the rush-hour traffic, and I am sitting in the green plastic seat in hopes of never getting to my destination at all.

It is said that to proceed in one direction but never arrive where you're going is mathematically possible if you pause and then continue half the distance to your finish point, then half again, etc. However, human beings often can't realize the things they know, can't enact them, while prone at the same time to a longing for these abstracts. For example, a person will try to fulfill this particular desire by easing behind the steering wheel of a car after dark with a full pack of cigarettes and a memory mapped with back roads, by buying a whole book of tickets from the attendant when his turn comes up for the roller coaster ride at Coney Island, or by ascending with skis to the very summit of a mountain. A surfer chooses the perfect wave at its crest, dreaming it will curl along the entire coastline of a continent. Children wave tiny hoops of soapsuds, attempting to inflate one bubble that will endure. But time will not be stopped by any of us, and I reach up above my head to tug at the bell wire—like my brother the paratrooper his rip cord prior to landing, with a bump.

It is after closing time: The iron rack in the inner lobby is empty except for a dangling belted trench coat. The box of today, September 30, has been lined in on the wall calendar next to the time clock. The fluorescent lights in the production room ceiling are extinguished, and I walk between the rows of unplugged machines, avoiding their electrical wires in the glow of the pink EXIT sign, up to the closed door of Gail's office. I raise my arm to knock; perhaps I could wait until tomorrow. "Come in," she shouts.

I turn the handle to find her sitting against the gray outline of the window, feet up on the desk, a cigarette in her hand. I cross to the swivel chair. Another cigarette burns in the ashtray on the corner of the desk; I pick it up and puff.

"Christ," says Gail, pointing to it. "I must be losing my mind. My father died of lung cancer, you know," she adds. "Three years ago."

"No, I didn't know," I tell her, "but I read somewhere that a tendency toward cancer skips generations."

"If you read enough, you can come across almost anything," she replies. "My father's partner found his own obituary in the paper one night before dinner."

"What did he do?" I ask her.

"Short of dropping dead on the spot, what could he do? Of course, he called up right away and corrected the error, and you can bet he lost his appetite, too. But cancer's just another word for death," she muses. "These days everybody gets it. It's just a question of sooner or later. You ever been close to anybody who died?"

"Yes."

"It's terrible," she says. "You keep wanting to call up,

somewhere, and correct the error. But you can't; they don't give out that number."

"It doesn't even help sometimes when you've got the number, of people who are still alive I mean."

"Mankind should have called it quits with the Flood," Gail says. Sighing loudly, she takes off her glasses, folding them with one hand and slipping them into her shirt pocket. Her face softens, losing the sharp outline of its bony contours as if I were the one whose vision had been altered.

"My mother hasn't even left the neighborhood since my father died," she says. "I keep trying to get her to go to an island somewhere. Or she could join a women's club or enroll in a yoga class or visit her sister in Chicago. But she sits at home instead, no interest in things." Gail shuts her eyes and massages the bridge of her nose. "I wonder if that could ever happen to me."

"Those susceptibilities probably skip generations, too."

"No," she says. "The great majority of people grow up into being just like their fathers or mothers, whether they like it or not. I've seen it happen everywhere I look."

"Gail's Law," I suggest. "But I can't imagine you ever just sitting at home."

"I guess not," she says, brightening. "Actually I'm like my father—no one could ever get him to sit still—which is why I'm worried about the lung cancer. They say that certain personality types are more prone to particular diseases. . . . So I'm going to get hypnotized into giving up smoking next week; I have an appointment Wednesday after work. You can come, too, if you want," she offers.

"No, I can't," I tell her. This is my chance. "I won't be at work Wednesday. I'm quitting." Now the conversation I dreaded on the bus will begin: the remonstrances, the accusations, the analysis of my failure. Her words will tumble down into the curious pit in my stomach and, backing up, choke me. You're as much a coward as my mother, she'll conclude, and all the words will clamber out again, from my mouth this time, in acquiescence.

"For Christ's sake, you're fired anyway" is what she says

instead, pulling a bottle of bourbon and some plastic cups out of the middle drawer of the file cabinet. "Big deal. You want a drink?"

"A drink," I repeat, trying to keep my head from spinning like the top of the conversation, which is not going to happen, inside it. It is a familiar hum I hear, the result of a forte developed in childhood, pulling strings of dread myself, so as not to be surprised ever again by any unforeseen hand. I set my conical fears in motion and watch them, a time-consuming game in which I follow the erratic configurations their tips draw, a subdermal and intricate tattoo.

"You can still come with me. Hit the light switch," she says. I walk over to the far wall.

I have always been amazed by inventions, by machines whose workings we can't see: telephones, rockets, giant hydraulic presses, TV sets, things that people have imagined out of thin air, constructed, and made work. But everything considered I am more amazed by people: those with schizophrenic personalities, perfect pitch, indivertible opinions, affinities for the lilac or the rose, the endlessness of possibilities both exciting and disheartening. If I studied electricity, I would understand why throwing a switch now causes the fluorescent light fixtures to blink, crackle, and burn, but having studied human beings, I never can predict what properties to expect from the complex and untraceable circuitries inside them.

Gail hands me a drink. "To the future," she says. We bump the plastic glasses together.

"I misjudged you," I tell her simply.

"And, boy, did I misjudge you," she says, smiling, then taking a long swallow. "What's in there?" she asks, pointing at the bag on the floor next to me.

"A hat."

"Let's see it," she says. I push the twine handle down through the slit in the cardboard and open up the round box inside it, pulling out the hat and settling it on my head.

"Good Lord," she says.

"Do you like it?" I ask her.

"I don't know," she says, "but it's quite a hat; I can tell that even without my glasses on."

"That's what I thought."

She lights us both cigarettes and pours some more bourbon into my glass.

"This is like the magic jug that never gets emptied," I tell her, taking it. "I guess that proves that all the fables no one believes anymore are just analogies and in some regard true."

"It doesn't prove that at all," she says.

"Well, it might."

"Yes, it might," she agrees. I put my feet up on the desk, opposite hers. "You can do that now," she says, "now that you're not an employee any longer. . . ."

"And what a relief."

"You really hated it, didn't you?" Gail asks me. "At first, you know, I thought you were just going about it the wrong way."

"There may be more than one way to skin a cat," I tell her, "but you have to have the stomach for it to begin with."

"You want to know a secret?" she says, ignoring me, looking out the window. "Sometimes I do too."

"Do what too?" I ask quietly.

"I hate it too, sometimes." Her face betrays no emotion.

"Then why . . ."

"Because I'm good at it," she says, suddenly pounding her fist on the desk, making my feet jump the way they have for four months in pursuit of orders, for a time of Jo, of myself. Then settling back against the chair again, ". . . because I do it well." I think I can understand not wanting to give that up. "Do you have to go anywhere right away?"

"No."

"Then have another drink," she says, reaching for my glass. "You look like you're out of some fable of your own in that hat, you know." She rests the bottle precariously on a pile of invoices. "You're the only person I ever told that to," she says. "About the business, I mean."

"It does change my perspective on things, sort of like a room that you've always seen in one way until coming in one day you see a different place altogether." Or like her face.

"It changes my perspective, too," she says. "It becomes different when you tell somebody, actually say things out loud. Then they become more like facts."

"I've noticed that." Listening to each other, like the weather voice at night, forecast our expectations, seeking patterns in random events.

"Listen," she says, her speech thick and slow, "my father was in the wholesale fur business, and he never talked about it. He drove into his showroom on Thirty-third Street from New Jersey every morning and back out again. All he ever mentioned was the traffic. He never told us whether he liked what he did or not; in fact, I don't remember my father ever saying a single word about the part of his life that wasn't spent with my mother and me." She crosses her ankles on the desk and uncrosses them again.

"They took two vacations a year: one to Florida like everybody else for a month in the winter and a week around Labor Day to go upstate to a resort. He always wore a duffel coat with a mink collar. When I was in grade school, I was the only girl with a muff. But if you can believe it, and you better because life is full of these tricks, my mother is allergic to animal hides. . . ." She laughs briefly, putting the cup to her lips. "I don't know, maybe she was just allergic to him. Anyway, every year for her birthday he bought her a bottle of Joy, a huge one; at one time it was the most expensive perfume in the world. This was supposed to make up somehow for not having a fur coat. She's still got over a dozen bottles stored away in the linen closet.

"She wore it every day of her married life, but one afternoon sitting out on the lawn—I remember it was about a week after I'd graduated from high school—she hinted to me that she didn't actually like the smell. And she never told him, year after year after year. Can you stand it? Nobody in my family ever said what they liked or didn't like because then they never had to make any decisions, just keep on doing the same things over and over again." Gail rests her head on her lap.

That's one problem we never had:

I hate family life, said my father.

And I hate you, said my mother, though later she changed her mind.

Scoo-be-doo was what my Uncle Freddie said, which we interpreted too late as a love of almost everything but himself. In the same way, we read the dog's barks from deep in the woods as an affirmation of her lot in life.

I love the army, says my distant brother, the dives like orgasms from airplanes. The purest, unpeopled moment.

It seems to me, I say, that the subtext of the topic is invariably and always love.

How we alter each other's perspectives, put on different faces, reverse the room of our lives as if in a looking glass. By speaking to the heart of things, by saying what we mean.

Gail lifts her head. "Still here?" she says. "So I'm going to get hypnotized out of smoking, Angela. They can hypnotize you out of anything these days." This isn't true, and in spite of everything, I'm glad it's not.

"Now take off that ridiculous hat," Gail tells me, securing her glasses back into place. It nests like a green bird in the box.

A woman must wear many hats, my mother told me when I was young. This meant that men didn't have to, though she didn't say so outright. I knew this to be so for empirical reasons.

Every morning my father walked out the door in his gray fedora; for my mother it was different. I am thinking of the time we went to church on a Saturday to pray for my grandfather during his operation, when my brother didn't want to go in because it wasn't Sunday and I was embarrassed to be wearing bluejeans, and because it was the custom in our church for women to cover their heads before entering, my mother pulled a handkerchief out of her pocket and put it on. Do you think God cares about petty details? my mother asked us incredulously. Or the time she went to the cocktail party just before we moved to Boston, a costume party of hats inspired by book titles, when she glued two martini glasses to a skimmer for "Olive or Twist." I loved her that night because it wouldn't be the prettiest hat, it would be the most clever, but when she came home she threw it in the garbage and said, Suburban adults are like these martini glasses. They're shallow and they only come in pairs.

She had a fringed straw beach hat to shade her fair skin, the little strip of mink that matched her stole, the cellophane hood that folded up into a neat packet she carried in her purse when it threatened rain.

A woman must wear many hats, my mother told me. This did not include men; the lives are different. Every morning my father walked out the door in his gray fedora, until one evening he removed it for good and walked out altogether. My mother, on the other hand, stayed and covered her curly hair with whatever she could find. Now I know what she meant.

Hats are a life: We put on our thinking caps. We pass our hats, take off our hats to others for a job well done; we talk through them sometimes or keep things under them. We eat our hats, we doff our hats, arrive sometimes, down on our luck, hat in hand. . . . There is an expression "to throw one's hat into the ring"; to do this means to be considered. I think this is what my mother was talking about, what Gail's mother will not do, what I am trying to want.

It does not matter what the particular hats are or what they connote: My mother was not an overly religious person nor did she drink martinis ever again after my uncle died. The putting on of hats, even the buying of hats, signifies merely the will to action, the intention to be considered, though the consequences are often bitter and it is easier, in the short run, to sit at home. And if a woman must try on and wear a variety of hats like skins before she finds one which reflects the image she longs to find, it is not surprising. I have several stored away in the back of my closet already: a mortarboard, the crash helmet of my love affair, and soon the green plumage of my flight from this now, too.

"Wake up," says Gail, extinguishing the lights behind me. "Let's go get something to eat."

─────────── Chapter XV ───────────

SNAPSHOTS OF THE DIFFERENT WORLDS

A S IN THE CASE OF MY FATHER, IT WILL SEEM necessary to return home (home being wherever my mother is), if only for a visit at Christmastime. And my brother will arrive, too, to make our reunion complete, descending into Logan Airport not in his customary fashion, hanging from the harness of a paratrooper's landing gear, but like a civilian, inside the belly of a plane.

Now the inside of the living room is pink, growing pinker in the glow cast by the setting sun over the Charles River until the wall I face reminds me of my mother's welcoming front door to the house from which we departed, in shifts of one and then three, almost seven years ago. It is the cocktail hour. The gray of my father's hair is spreading up from his temples. My mother holds a newspaper article he clipped for her at arm's length; it's time she got a new prescription in her glasses. Ben's spidery legs are crossed beside mine on the couch, hairy ankles bristling out from under the olive cuffs. The smoke from his diminutive cigar forms a cloud near the ceiling, miniature replica of those I imagine lingering as his diving markers, sounding the sky.

"Hey there, hot stuff," he'll say, poking me with his toe.

"Save it for the babes from the fraternity house," I tell him, eyeing his grimy feet. "Don't they encourage you to wash in the army?"

"You haven't changed a bit." He laughs. "This is from wearing sneakers without socks."

"Then I'll get you a pair for Christmas," I tell him.

"Don't bicker, you two," says my mother. She glances up from the newsprint, still exhibiting the same uncanny ability of young motherhood: focusing a kind of loose attention on her children while engaged in any other task. "Concentrate on what you have in common," she tells us, advice I wish she'd given herself and my father, no third eye overseeing their development, along the bumpy roads and years before the divorce.

They continue discussing the article, a political editorial from the *Globe*, in an at-odds but amicable fashion (the evolution of their relationship), but my brother and I (the evolution of ours) go at it hammer and tongs:

"Don't make me laugh," says Ben. "If we don't have an adequate nuclear defense system, we're at the mercy of the Soviets."

"You sound like somebody's grandfather or a Republican," I tell him, discarding any hopes of achieving our own personal detente.

"I *am* a Republican," he informs me. Even his mother will draw the line at this. "A more responsible position to take," he adds, "than that of your bleeding-heart liberals."

"I can't believe we live on the same planet," I tell my brother, "let alone share the same genes. You haven't learned a thing from living."

"Oh yes he has, Angela," my mother interrupts from across the room, her role as arbiter. "Of course he has. . . . It's just that he's learned something different from what you have."

Does it take forty-six years of living and thinking about that living to figure out something like this? Perhaps the legacy we inherited from my youthful parents, then, is its opposite: the inability to be at ease with another's differences, functioning within the confines of a belief that one can will change in other human beings while, as it has been proven out to all of us, that isn't possible. Sometimes I think that what we *know* doesn't help us one goddamn.

Does it always end in battle or flight? I am referring to years of dinners, to the tiny and defoliated country of Vietnam; or to my father, my uncle, and Jo. Oh it is necessary, it is necessary to find the agreement inside, to seek a reflection in the inside mirror, to build the interior castle of our intentions as I suspected early on when reading about the life of St. Theresa of Ávila, though I do not now view it as a godly act but as a particularly human one instead. There may be other hands willing to help construct just such a castle out of sand on the beach, but it is also another foot that kicks it level again. The poke of my brother's toe—though in the context of more major and unbearable differences, this now seems more like a love tap.

"What does it feel like jumping out of airplanes?" I ask him, in an effort at reconciliation.

"It's wonderful," he replies. "There is no recognizable world. Nothing else exists but you. It's an essential moment."

"A form of meditation," I suggest.

"I don't know anything about that," he says, "but for a time everything is suspended. Everything holds off."

"I bet it's different when you're landing in a war zone," says my father matter-of-factly.

"I bet it is," says Ben, getting up to pour himself another drink. My mother doesn't say anything because her biggest fear is that they'll send him overseas. Womanfear grown out of impotence: fathers, husbands, sons to war. (Which is also why my leave of absence from school didn't faze her finally, seen in perspective.) It may come to that, Ros, said my father the marine. And maybe this is why Ben likes jumping from airplanes—because, for a few brief seconds, he doesn't have to think about the future at all.

"Were you scared the first time?" I ask my brother when he returns from the den.

"I was petrified," he says, sitting down, shaking the couch. "It was even more terrifying than the first time I slept with a woman, though in this activity you're *supposed* to go limp."

"Benjamin," says my mother.

"Oh relax, Ros," my father says. But there is a connection here; maybe it's more like the third or fourth time in someone's embrace, that horrific descent of another essential moment in which we hang from two human arms like straps, fumbling with our hands for a rip cord that may or may not open the folded chute of love.

After dinner we play *Peter and the Wolf* on the stereo, a narrated children's drama in which each character is brought to life by a different instrument and melody. With this record my mother taught us to distinguish the sound of an oboe from that of a clarinet, the French horn from the tuba. My father acts out the part of the wolf, spreading his fingers in front of his own teeth like fangs whenever his alarming theme is played. He jumps out from behind standing lamps, stalks my brother's sneakers.

"Perhaps you should go on the stage for your next career," I tell my father, remembering the first year at college when I made him into an actor because I couldn't think of a label appropriate to his absence. He settles back into the chair underneath the banjo clock. It has to be wound every seven days, twenty-three turns, a number my mother and I found out by trial-and-error months after it ran down one week from the day we found the note. Daddy, the wolf, on the trail of a new and different scent.

"No, no," he says, waving his hands, shunting away this idea of acting. "Besides," he says, "I'm very busy right now; I'm teaching myself German. At first it was going to be Russian, but then you have an entirely different alphabet to contend with and their novels are too long even so."

"Let's play *The Threepenny Opera* then next," I suggest.

"I'll look for it," says my father, going into the den through the open double doors and bending down on one knee to search in the rack underneath the bar. "Ros," he says, "you ought to keep these records in their jackets."

"I'm always copying over lists of things to do," she replies. "The most important things get done and crossed off, and the rest just keep getting transferred. I've been meaning to do the records for months." And while the rest of us sing along in English in the living room, my father sits down on the floor of the den, giving more exact translations of an occasional refrain, patiently matching cover to disc for his ex-wife.

"Phew," he says, joining us again. "That's quite a collection. Listen to what's next," he says to my mother. She smiles as the first few notes sound. My father turns to Ben and me. "That's your mother's favorite song," he says—one record, one fact, in a whole collection they built up together. Something my brother and I couldn't possibly have known. "Benny Goodman. Come on, Ros," says my father, and they dance the two-step.

"Well, here we are, every one of us," says Ben, who's usually uncommunicative when it comes to personal matters. He taps his foot to the swing beat.

This much is clear to me: we are not a family anymore.

Most of the time we exist as four separate lives that grew together into much of what we are in a catastrophic yet catalytic household. So what are we now? Perhaps my mother will find the name for it, accomplished and crossed off finally, on one of her discarded lists. Or my father will come across the word accidentally, in a foreign language, thumbing through his German dictionary. Can it be that we are more of a successful grouping now than we ever were when we took turns every other day combing the dog's curly coat, piling off for vacations to Canada in a four-door station wagon, when we lived together through report cards, dinners, deaths, and tennis matches? Always my father and I pitched against my mother and brother while at bridge we had a duel of the sexes. I don't know, any more than I know which of these childhood alliances is more permanent, in the way that Gail does. I long for the tenderness that is my mother's good advice and her open arms. And I yearn at the same time for my father's outlands.

"Hey there. You," calls the man in the wheelchair as he rolls out the swinging doors of MacGregor's Bar. I look at the other pedestrians passing unconcernedly along the sidewalk with shopping bags and briefcases, pushcarts and baby strollers—things to accomplish; he is talking to me.

"Hello," I say tentatively, walking over to under the awning where he's parked himself, dressed in a navy blue knit cap, a plaid lumberjacket, and a pair of khaki trousers that break and bunch over the tops of his sneakers. You are not supposed to talk to strangers: they may be con artists or rapists or even psychopaths. This particularly applies to men, but here sits a sixty-five-year-old granddaddy with dead legs.

"Would you help me across the street?" he asks. Up close, his gray-blond beard is irregularly trimmed, and the eyes behind the heavy frames of his glasses are watery and half-focused.

"Certainly," I say. Always be kind, my mother repeats, to those less fortunate than you are. I try to do this. On paper and probably in life almost everyone is less fortunate than I am: many have no access to education and knowledge; some, like this man in a wheelchair, must carry parts of their bodies as baggage; still others have lost contact even with themselves. Through this neighborhood of welfare mothers and their broods of children, overladen bag ladies, drug addicts, and winos with no foreseeable future, along the routes of the pensioned and failing elderly, daily I make my way. "Sure," I say.

I bump him down off the curb and push across the two-way traffic of Broadway. He holds his cap to his head, gripping the arm of the chair with his free hand, as we gather speed to beat the blinking, red "DON'T WALK" sign. The wind off the Hudson blows in our faces, gusty and cold.

"Whoa there," he says when I've tipped him up onto the sidewalk on the opposite corner, perilously scraping the back wheels over the rise. "I'm a little under the weather today. Usually I can navigate this just fine." He starts to fumble for the wheels, missing one altogether. "You live around here?" he asks me, rolling his head back, peering at me over his shoulder.

"Yes," I tell him, continuing to push because I'm going in the same direction.

"Make a right here," he says suddenly. "Starboard, starboard." And I do because I'm recently unemployed and I've got time on my hands. "What's your name?" he asks as we descend the slight incline toward the river.

I tell him and he nods. He begins to whistle something familiar; after a few bars I identify it as "We Three Kings." "Isn't it a little bit early for Christmas carols?" I ask, by way of making conversation. "It's nearly two months away. . . ."

"I sing them all year round," he says, shrugging, a whole language in his back. "It cheers me up."

"If it works, I'm all for it," I tell him. "What's your name?"

"You can just call me the Skipper," he says.

"OK." We shake hands awkwardly over the back sling of the chair, a metaphor for first meetings, and I return my grip to the handle so he won't get away from me on the hill.

He pulls abruptly at the break lever. "This is it," he says as I tumble into his back.

Planted on my two feet again, I walk around to face him. "You must be used to driving alone," I say.

"A first mate's got to be quick to jump to commands," replies the Skipper. "Much obliged." He pushes open the front door of the building himself by backing the chair up against it and, making a quick about-face, wheels into the dark lobby and is gone.

Drunk, I say to myself. And crazy.

"You read the recipe out loud," my father will say, poised in front of the counter where the cannisters of ingredients are lined up like tin soldiers awaiting his commands.

"Listen to this part first," I'll tell him, then reading from a dog-eared page of *The Joy of Cooking:* "'About Christmas cookies: Christmas and cookies are inseparable. Stars, angels, bells, trees, Santas, and even pretzels—the pilgrim's token—are memorialized in rich holiday confections. Why not make use of these charming cookie shapes to decorate a small table tree at Christmas? . . .'"

"Let's just get on with the recipe itself," says my father. *"Der kuchen."*

"I was only trying to get us into the spirit," I tell him.

"A table tree," he says in disgust. "What a poor substitute; what a terrible idea. You know," he continues, "that's the one thing I always liked about living in the country. Never raking the leaves or mowing the lawn . . . but each year going off into the woods to search for the perfect Christmas tree—that's what I liked best." Satisfied with this thought, my father takes a sip of his drink and stubs out the cigarette that, unattended, has burned into a gray worm in the ashtray. He looks out the window of my mother's apartment at the city skyline.

"Mummy says the pine sap always got all over the rug," I tell him. "That's why she buys Douglas firs now."

"All we had was pine trees," says my father. "But I prefer pine trees. Maybe Ben and your mother will get one this year. For a change," he adds. We drew straws, and my father and I pulled out of the basket two little strips of paper saying "cookies" while my mother and brother got "go pick out the tree." It is the day before Christmas.

"What did you do with the cookie cutters?" I ask him.

"I don't know," he says, pushing the flour cannister out of the way so he can search behind the lamp. "I thought your mother left them out for us." We look everywhere; we scour the kitchen; we cannot find the cookie cutters. Finally they turn up in the refrigerator. "Oh, that's right," says my father. "They cut much better when they're cold."

We carefully sift the flour and the sugar twice, stirring in the butter and eggs with a wooden spoon. My father is a good cook; he's been known to make waffles from scratch; he can beat the ingredients for fifteen minutes straight without once having to switch hands.

"Get the cutters out of the fridge," he says finally. "We're just about ready. Did you preheat the oven?" he asks me.

"Of course," I tell him. My father's child, my father's apprentice as always, I set out the metal tools of our endeavor.

Having drawn two particular straws and accepted their challenge, my father and I are carving out a world.

First, we form a ball of dough, raw as the planet must have been before there was land or sea, vegetation or animal life, long before there were people to name such distinctions. Then we rest it on the hard surface of the counter, flattening it out just so to match humankind's original conception of the earth. Because my father and I can travel backward through time. The shapes we make are the landmarks of memory; in the strata of the dough resides an arsenal of references.

We cut bells, like the one we used to summon the missing dog when she was caught in the swamp. Communicants, we rang and rang, nevertheless fearful that the sound would not carry beyond our own ears. . . . Santas line up side by side on the baking sheet: a battalion of men bearing not weapons but gifts. When my brother told me that there was no Santa Claus, Fuck you, I told him. But the remark was addressed rather to the world in general. . . . Angels, like the ones my mother and I made in the snow, falling backward into a foot of white, flailing our arms to simulate the wings . . . Trees: the ones my father chopped down for Christmas every year, others that suspended me in the sky on a wooden platform, closer indeed to the stars, like the ones we manufacture now.

"You went a little heavy on the stars," says my mother later, surveying our work. We are almost finished. The kitchen is perfumed with the sweet odor of newly baked cookies and the windows are steamy. My brother pops one in his mouth; the bottomless pit, my mother calls him.

"If I eat a dozen or so right now," he says, "then the numbers should be just about even."

But no pretzels. We didn't have a cutter in that shape. The pilgrims home at last, right here, my father and I are carving out a world we can live in.

But the Skipper isn't crazy at all. When he's not too drunk he's very lucid, and the other times he just drifts quite away.

"Oh, I make all my friends that way," he says. We are sitting in the park, he in his chair, myself on the bench beside, gazing out through the wires of trees, defoliated and sharply etched. The sky is gray and so is the water, white swells curling the flatness. "I just ask them for a little push if I've seen them around and like the cut of their jib, and then we set to talking. It's broadening," he says. "Everyone has a different viewpoint. Girls your age, though, usually pass me by. . . ."

"I was going to be a Girl Scout," I tell him, "but it was a commitment based on someone else's morals—you should have seen all the rules in the handbook—and at the last minute I just couldn't go through with it. Right before the ceremony started I made my mother take me home . . . but I still have a commitment to being helpful."

"Those girls are afraid I might want something," says the Skipper, shaking his head. "And what could I want besides company, an old man like me?"

"How old are you, Skip?" I ask him.

"Sixty-six," he says. "Well, actually, sixty-eight, but I discount the two years I spent in the hospital after the accident."

"When was that?" I ask him. He takes a slug of his beer as if pausing to remember. But I know people his age have years in their heads like clockwork, easy to recall as which hour comes after the next. He squints his eyes.

"Nineteen fifty-eight," he says. "They kept strapping my

legs to those machines and making them run in air. Problem is you can't go anywhere that way. And it proved itself out, too, because then there were the baths—for six months I was wrinkled up like a prune—and the weights and the drugs, and finally the operation, but nothing worked. Have another beer," he says. I bend over and reach into the bag at his feet. "And pull one out for me, too," he adds. It is eleven-thirty in the morning; we've been here since eight (the early hours are the Skipper's best) when I had to hug myself, and jump up and down to keep warm. I pull the blanket that rests partially on the frozen ground up over his knees.

"Tuck it in around the sides," I tell him.

"So what are you going to do for a job now, Angela?" the Skipper asks me.

"I'm not exactly sure," I tell him, "but I still have most of the five hundred dollars my boss gave me when I left. And I hocked a silver and diamond brooch my grandparents gave me when I was born, for a bit of money."

"You shouldn't have done that," says the Skipper.

"Maybe not."

"Help me prop up my legs on the bench there next to you, will you?" he asks. I lift them gingerly from the footrest, one hand under each ankle, to rest on the green slats, straight out.

"I ought to call her up, you know," I tell him. "My boss." But the people I know are as hard for me to reach as the Skipper's ankles are for him. It is not a matter of proximity. The sun glows behind a featherbed of clouds; it won't shine through again today the way I won't pick up my telephone and dial seven consecutive numbers. In the early afternoon, I'll go back to my apartment and read a novel. Its pages are the color of cream.

"Well, you've got to do something," says the Skipper. "You can't just sit around with me like this, day after day."

"I'm a nurse," I tell him, "and this is my job. I take my cases one patient at a time."

"Rubbish," says the Skipper. "Where's your white uniform?"

"I'm plainclothes," I say. "One day I will have accumulated a great deal of money, left to me by private clients who have died, and then you and I will take a trip, good-bye Broadway, and see the world."

"Why wait?" says the Skipper.

"What do you mean?"

"I mean," he says, "that the world is right here. A whole city of lives." He gestures at the people streaming by us on the asphalt path: runners, schoolchildren, families, dogwalkers, bums; at the cars flying past us on singing tires; at the lighted windows of apartment buildings on the Drive. "We're quite a pair," he says, beginning to nod. "Imagine. You won't even walk the three blocks to get on the subway to see what's going on outside of somebody else's front door, and I can't. . . ."

His chin finally rests, at half-mast, on the collar of the gray overcoat in which he wraps himself against the cold every morning. I take another beer out of the bag and sit down again, looking out over the river. I let him sleep.

"Let's take pictures," my mother will say, pulling the Polaroid out of the Chinese chest.

"All right," my father will agree, though years ago he found this kind of thing sentimental. Life is life, he would tell us. Who needs a record? I have it all in here, and he would tap his head emphatically.

"It *is* sentimental," says my mother, poking my complaining brother in the den. "Just put down your book for half an hour."

"And wear your uniform," my father adds.

"Oh, all right," Ben grumbles.

"Angela," my mother turns to me. "Could you put on a dress just for once?"

"No I could not," I tell her.

"Then put on a pair of nice trousers," she says. "Please? And tie your hair back so we can see your face in the prints."

In my room, these are concessions I make. When we are reassembled in the hall, my father is slipping back into his sports jacket. My mother's perfume envelops us all.

"A new scent?" asks my father.

"Yes," says my mother.

"You smell good, but I liked the old one better," he replies.

"They don't make it anymore," she says, in no particular tone.

"Why did you put on perfume?" my brother asks. "It won't show up in the pictures, you know."

"It makes me *feel* more photogenic," my mother tells him. "Ben, you just don't understand women."

Though my father is the most mechanical of all of us, it is known that I take the best snapshots. My subjects do not always come out as they see themselves, but the edges are clear and the settings well chosen. My mother says my pictures tell a story; I like to think of it in this way. When we pose in threesomes for the group shots, everyone takes turns with the camera, but when it comes time for the individual portraits, the job is relegated to me.

I photograph my father in front of the Christmas tree. While it isn't a pine, I find this an appropriate backdrop, the lights plugged in and shining. It glows behind him, a few feet taller and wider, like a persona, an aura. In some of the developed squares it looks as if he's cast an immense shadow. In others, it looks as if my father is on fire.

Next I lead my mother into the dining room and not because this is the world that women for generations have known best but because it was around a table very like this that in my childhood I watched my mother attempt the impossible, night after night. I seat her right in the middle of it, and I pull all the chairs around empty, for once in my mind and as it has come to be. She perches on the bare wood, her legs tucked under her and still smiling: a formidable centerpiece.

When it is time to photograph my brother, I stand him in front of the mantel in his uniform. Today I'm going to shoot my brother not the way I want him to be—but the way he is. I shoot him fullface, in profile, wearing his officer's hat, holding it in his hand, grim-jawed, smiling, at ease. I shoot him the way somebody's going to shoot him in the months ahead, only where they'll use bullets, I use light.

When I peel back the protective covering on these snapshots and they begin to develop, I watch him grow into the adult he is now, filling in the gap of years in which I never knew him—from the time that I was eleven and he was thirteen and he left home for good, really. I study this person I don't know, this person in battle dress. My brother lives in the world of men, and how could he possibly have escaped it? I forgive him for never agreeing with me once.

I made a special trip to the library because I was concerned about the Skipper, and I read there that alcoholics don't dream. The liquor prevents it eventually, and when this happens they start hallucinating, seeing things in their waking hours that shouldn't be there but belong, instead, to dreams. Whenever the Skipper sleeps, I pray he'll start dreaming.

I have dreams and I have them at night. Then I see people I haven't seen in a long time, and things happen—to me. Sometimes I think *I* have my days and nights reversed. If I never even take my phone off the hook while awake, asleep I hear voices that travel along the wires of the brain, making a crackly connection.

My dreams are like snapshots. They document people and places in moments that do not belong to the present, and how could they? My world has a two-block radius, the Skipper my only companion.

This is the dream I had last night: Jo and I were at an airport, where we met a man with a Great Dane. It was clear to all of us in the dream that it was actually Jo's dog, left behind on another continent years ago. But the man insisted it was his dog anyway, had always been, and he began to beat the cowering animal with a leash. We begged him to stop, but, his face set in harshness, he continued. Jo ran off to get help.

I waited for as long as I could, but she didn't come back. It was necessary, then, for me to save the dog by myself. But I didn't know how. I tore the leash out of the man's hands and threw it; when he went to retrieve it, grabbing the dog by the collar, I ran in the opposite direction. I had surprised myself.

The Great Dane grew smaller and smaller, as Jo must have known her, into a puppy, and I picked her up. But by then the airport had changed into a restaurant an acre big, dining room after dining room where seated families, corporate executives and their clients, tables of movie stars, were eating. It was a labyrinth of conversation I would never find my way out of. . . . A waiter appeared and silently pointed to a door which I opened out onto an empty lot where several of my friends were gathered. I gave the puppy to one of them for safekeeping; the man might not recognize her in the arms of a stranger.

But my friend won't run, he won't budge, as if somebody'd nailed his two feet to the ground. I take the dog from the cradle of his hands, wondering where to go next, how to escape the bogus owner who will surely catch us and beat the dog senseless. Once again the waiter appears and points to an alleyway, which as I run down it is transformed into a country trail, wild flowers and tall shady trees lining both sides.

Now the dog changes, too, becomes inanimate, a pottery sphere. As if the trail coming to life, trimmed with living things, must mean the loss of animation in something else. As if there were only so much life to go around. It is up to me to find the dog inside the bloodless globe, and once again I don't know how. But it's Jo's dog and, in the dream, I'm the only one who can possibly do it. Suddenly, it transforms itself again, into a shirt, and shedding my own, I put it on and continue running. At a clearing I disrobe and lay the shirt on the ground. As I stand, half-naked, on the grass before me the dog becomes herself again.

Perhaps this is what the Skipper meant when he said the world is right here, that all is here for us. As in the world of dreams, an airport is an edifice of dining rooms and an empty lot is a vast city. An alleyway becomes a garden trail, a primrose path. And lives are multiple too—the dog to a puppy to a sphere to a shirt I wear, back to a dog again. Is this the kind of world the Skipper lives in by day, wheeling himself along Broadway and into the park overlooking the Hudson? Does he see his boat in a parked car, the garbage scow he commanded every morning out into the river, where one day a bale of waste fell in a terrible accident? Is the forked tree branch of the big elm on Ninety-sixth Street under which we often sit his once nimble legs kicking in the breeze?

The trappings of things are often misleading. The snapshots we view are only as accurate as the conception of the photographer. I am reminded of three things:

1. The children who come up to me outside the department store where I stand every morning now from nine to twelve believe that in my red uniform and white beard I *am* Santa Claus. I'm sure I'm not. Who's right?

2. In the women's bathroom at MacGregor's Bar a black transvestite named Marsha walked up to me at the sink and said this: "In 1942 I was beautiful and I was white and I was a woman." If he believes this, is it true?

3. Though the Skipper has a ruddiness to his cheeks and each day he tackles the world with a good word and a Christmas carol, his insides are very rapidly being eaten up by a cancer that will not allow him to live out the year. If I don't believe this, will it cure him?

Transformations, my father said when he returned from his trip. The funny thing is you have to stay long enough in the same place, and you have to be looking for them in order to see them. He didn't know that when he left, and neither did I.

"It was terrible," my mother will say. "It was the hardest thing I ever had to do in my life." We will be sitting alone in the den on Christmas Eve, long after my father finished off the last of the eggnog and went home to his furnished room, hours after my brother read himself to sleep.

"I don't know about that," I'll tell her. "You've had some other rather difficult things to do over the past few years."

"I should celebrate my birthday on the day your father left," she says wryly. It has not been easy supporting a family all by herself; money is often tight. She wears the same pink-laced bathrobe, now raggedy, that she wore the night we vanquished the bat. "But the day we took the dog to the vet," she says, "stands out to me as one of the absolute worst days I remember."

The ashtrays on the tables are all filled to the brim with butts; scattered drink glasses stand empty on napkins. The room is permeated with an air of latent anxiety, where the field marshals have sat up late planning the next day's strategy, though the early morning hours may see a surprise attack. But by tomorrow, everything will be in order once again. My mother believes, and always has, that there will be no more surprises, and she plans for the future with a belief that all will turn out well. I finally figured it out, said my father recently. About your mother . . . she has no sense of tragedy. My father, a student of the Greeks. . . . This is true and this is a blessing; it is my mother who wipes away our nightmares as best she can, as she used to do, smoothing my brow, when I lay in the big bed between them.

"I remember the moment when you came out of the office carrying her collar and leash." The dog finally gone, missing, never to be returned. "We threw them in the trash can right outside on the street. We didn't want to take them home."

"Was it the right decision?" my mother asks. "If she could have lived for another year, if she could have stumbled through it happy, should we have waited?" The dog was blind and deaf, paralyzed from arthritis: old age.

"I don't know," I tell her. "But I made you make the decision yourself. I wouldn't help; I wouldn't have an opinion. When you took her into the examining room, I just stood outside waiting."

"I made the decision," says my mother. "The vet said it would be a painless shot. I left her there with him."

"I regret that more than anything in my life," I tell her. A horrible, crippling passivity—much worse than the dog's. She shook in the waiting room, panting, her pink tongue dripping saliva onto the floor. She was the worst-behaved of all the dogs there; I think she knew. And I sat down beside her and hugged her to my chest, stroking her tremorous collarbone with my fingers. After my mother grabbed her firmly around the waist and helped her into the office, I was covered with her blond hairs, a visible coat of shame.

He's going to do it this afternoon, my mother said, handing me the empty collar and leash. My mother was weeping and she took me in her arms. Together we walked out to the car, crying puddles, I imagined, onto the sidewalk. I would never say good-bye to the dog; I would never face the last moments, the way my mother had, watching her be led away. The dog—with panic in her eyes. Don't tell me she didn't know; she did. But I didn't have to see anything I didn't want to see, and I didn't have to do anything I didn't know how to do.

"Let's go to bed now, Angela," says my mother, stacking a few ashtrays. Teary and a little drunk, we could go on like this for hours, pinching ourselves with the past. After a time the bruises go away, but often, under the surface, a little pearl of scar tissue remains.

I look at the old banjo clock. In an hour it will be dawn.

"Merry Christmas," I say.

"I have a special request this evening," says the Skipper after I wheel him out of the swinging doors of MacGregor's Bar. "This old salt needs a taste of sea life," he says. "I want to go on the Staten Island ferry."

"Right now?" I ask him. "It's after midnight."

"You're only young once," he says, winking. He pulls a pint of brandy out of his overcoat pocket. "It will be plenty cold, but we have this."

"You're on," I tell him. I hail a Checker, luckily the third cab traveling downtown, and the driver gets out and helps me lift the Skipper and the wheelchair into the back.

"You know, this is the first time I've been out of the neighborhood in two years," says the Skipper as we speed down the West Side Highway. He looks out the window. "It may not be the Mississippi," he says, "but it's the river I know best. Thank God there's enough garbage on the streets that I don't forget my past life altogether." We laugh at this. "Tell me something, Angela," he says.

"What do you mean 'Tell you something'?" I feel shy suddenly in the car with the Skipper. We have never gone somewhere together before.

"Well, I'll tell *you* something," he says, "and then maybe you'll see what I mean. I never once had any plants in my apartment," he begins. "You know why?"

"Why?" I ask him.

"Because I couldn't bear the thought of their being thirsty," he replies. "If I ever forgot to water them, it would haunt me no matter where I went. Whenever I'm near a plant, I check the soil for dryness. It preoccupies me. I can't help it."

"Thank you for telling me that." I rest my hand on the Skipper's knee, but he doesn't notice; he can't feel it. "I never make my resolutions on New Year's Eve," I confess. "I always make them the next morning when I'm hungover and contrite. Then I'm certain to isolate the things I shouldn't do."

"One year when I was young," says the Skipper, "I did everything in threes. I looked in the closet three times before going to bed. I checked the knobs on the gas stove three times during the night. I brushed my teeth a number of strokes that was divisible by three. . . . When I had the accident, it was only on the third try that I was convinced I couldn't get up, that my legs wouldn't hold me."

"My mother told me that my insides would stick together if I swallowed gum," I tell him. "And I believed her. I went around with stomachaches for days. Now my insides are still stuck together, but I don't think it's the gum anymore. . . ."

"Different kind of gum," says the Skipper. "Well, we're almost there. Lucky the next ride we're going to take is so cheap," he says, pushing himself forward from the back of the seat to look at the meter.

"Let me pay, Skip," I tell him when we stop. "You've been buying the drinks all night."

"Nothing doing," he says. "If I'm short, you can pay for the ride back. You got enough money?" he asks.

"Yes."

"Are you absolutely sure?" he asks, looking out the window.

"Positive. What's the big deal?"

"Nothing. Now how about getting me out of here?" he says, putting on a bad mood. The driver helps again, and once inside a big, burly man with a tattoo on his forearm helps me carry the chair up the stairs. There's hardly anyone here but us and what must be the regulars. We wait in the empty hall with some stray workmen and a few sleepy families. The ferry has arrived. I wheel the Skipper along the ramp and onto the boat.

"I want to stay outside," he says.

"It's too cold," I tell him. "But OK."

We sit on the deck and drink brandy in the chill wind. It is unbearably cold, and for the first time in months I am unbearably happy.

"This is the best way in the whole city to spend the night hours," says the Skipper.

"This must be the one answer to every problem," I tell him.

"It is. It is," he says. "And it never stops. You could actually ride on this forever. Only it's no good filled up with people, like in the summer months."

"That's often the case," I say. I look at him; there is a tear on the Skipper's cheek. "Skip, what's wrong?"

"There's something I forgot to tell you in the cab," he says, pointing over at the Statue of Liberty, lighted in the night. "I don't know what it is," he explains. "I'm not patriotic in the usual sense, and my family's been over here almost since the beginning, but it always gets to me. It gives me goose bumps. I even hate the French—I was there in the war—but every time I see that thing it chokes me up. It's just the gesture," he says. "It's just the gesture of holding a torch up like that. The way the whole thing glows in the dark . . ."

We sit in silence for the rest of the ride. As we near Staten Island, the rushing water of our approach sounds loud in my ears. We bump the pilings. I push the Skipper around to what is now the bow of the boat before we head out into the open water again.

"I could probably do this all night," I tell him.

"So could I," he says, "but you've got to be Santa Claus in the morning, and, actually, I have other plans too, though I'll need your help in them."

"What's that?" I ask him.

"Before we reach Manhattan," he says, "I want you to help me over the side." He takes a hit from the brandy bottle and slowly passes it to me.

"You can't possibly mean that, you know you can't," I tell him. "It's a joke, Skip, right?" He turns up the collar of his overcoat. I do not want to be here anymore. Where we are is no longer the answer to all problems; it's the answer to one that I don't want to know about.

"You know I do," he says, "or I wouldn't have said it." He wheels himself around to face me. "Will you do it?" he asks. "In another month or so the pain will start, and then they'll move me to St. Luke's to die."

"Maybe you'll get better," I say.

"I'm not going to get better," he says.

"How can you do this to me?" I ask him. I beat at his hands lying on the armrests.

"You're my best friend," says the Skipper. "I had no one else to ask."

"All right," I tell him. "I'll do it."

The snapshot looks like this: A man whose legs trail limp behind him trying to lift himself over the guardrail, the strain in his arm muscles contorting his face. A gray overcoat slung over the back of a wheelchair behind him. A young woman with her arms about his waist, her head and spine arched against the black backdrop of the sea, as if in the process of a backward somersault, a dive into the metal interior of the ship.

"I'll make you a deal, you captain of garbage," I shout, catapulting him into the chair. "Because I change my mind. Right now. I'll be your first mate from now on . . . a real one . . . and when you go into the hospital I'll visit you every day and read you books and describe to you the weather outside. I'll tell you all my secrets, like in the cab. I'll smuggle you in drinks and I'll sing Christmas carols with you and we'll play chess and checkers, Hearts, Old Maid, Go Fish. . . ." I kneel down beside him in the chair and rest my teary face on his shoulder. "Skip, I don't want you to die," I tell him.

"My God, it must get to you, too," he says, pointing at the Statue of Liberty.

"Shut the fuck up," I tell him. And we both do, for a long time.

"You have a deal," he says, finally. "Only I'm not promising I won't change my mind tomorrow."

"Neither am I," I tell him. We ride back and forth between the two islands for several hours.

Out in the street we can't find a cab. It is four-thirty A.M. I push the Skipper along the sidewalk at a slow and steady pace. There are no people to be seen.

"Where do you think we're most likely to find some transportation," he asks.

"I'd rather walk," I say, and I push him through the deserted streets. We reach Sixth Avenue and I steer out into the center of the street.

"Isn't this dangerous?" asks the Skipper. I let the remark pass.

"There are hardly any cars at this hour," I tell him. "If one comes, it can honk and go around."

In midtown the Christmas lights at the feet of skyscrapers are aglow, tiny lights that bathe our avenue in a white mist. Headlights of a car approach us from the rear; the Skipper's and my silhouette is cast onto the pavement, a daguerreotype. It veers to the side and passes us.

"Step on it," says the Skipper. "We're getting left behind by every other vehicle on the road."

I pull his cap down over his eyes. The lights from another car reflect off the wheelchair, the wheelchair like a diamond. More precious to the Skipper than any brooch, any ring. Without it he would have to drag himself around, like the dog did for months, her dead legs trailing behind. Was this the right decision?

My life has become the love of dogs and old men. Crippled and on leashes, they cannot easily run away. I continue to push, entering Central Park, the captain napping, me at the helm.

Mother, forgive me my apprenticeship. I have taken lessons in drowning, like the men on Daddy's voyages who jumped overboard to escape their loneliness.

I have lowered myself into the cold water like a penitent, countless times, to render myself worthy of vows of my own making. If I rise to the surface again I am innocent of my own accusation. If I sink, I am a witch. But I could as soon sink as sing. Is it the unsounded shout then, the song inside (nothing more than a fretful human bellow) that carries me always to the surface again, ballast for starting over? I cling to myself like a buoy.

I've been set adrift in seas of changes. I have held swelling breasts in my hands, tiny islands by which to chart my course. I dove from a sheer cliff, my body an arc of longing, for pearls, for sunken treasure . . . looking for Daddy, looking for Jo . . . deep into the whirlpools of her eyes, plummeting through her into the belly of the sea where mermaids embrace, the shimmering blue green of their tails entwined like tongues. There I wept my tears into the salt sea, searching for a signpost, where instead an octopus sits, eight tendril arms extended in the possible directions to proceed. You can always chart by the stars, my father said. There are no stars here.

Whirlpools. Like the ones the Skipper would have given birth to as he sank. The Skipper is a witch. Concentric circles of grief, painted targets drawn carefully like maps to scale, drawn with lipstick and rouge and blue shadow, the laying bare and yet the dressing up in plumage, for the piercing, by the longed-for/dreaded arrow, of the heart . . . this heart that scares itself with its own frenzied rumblings, reading itself like a seismograph, that sends itself messages, like a tribal drum, of invasion, panic, and despair. This clenched fist of muscle and blood that is tired and bruised from punching away at the brown, hanging bag of days that never gives and never goes away. I have trained with dedication, mother, jumped the rope of all the moments when I wanted to give it up finally. I have never once suspended my belief that this is a prizefight, though the prize is as invisible as the traces of love in the blood of the heart.

I have traveled in every direction to which the octopus pointed, looking for it. I've kept my eyes wide open when the salt stung them so bitterly I wanted to float blind, blindered. I swim through the filth of ocean liners and barges. Sometimes I bump my head on empty champagne bottles, worn-out hair dryers. I crawl, the antennae of my two arms leading me, through currents of cigarette butts, sequined garters, condoms. I feel old and bald in the skullcap of my bathing gear. Inside, too. Each morning I tear the casings from the hallways in my head, like peeling wallpaper. I do not allow myself the old decorations. . . .

I'm twenty-two years old, Mother, and I keep on swimming. Alternating strokes when I'm winded. The breaststroke. A cupped hand under a weight of womanhood. The crawl, on my hands and knees. The backstroke, defining the spine like a stiff rod of consciousness. The sidestroke, fingering ribs like omens. The dog paddle. The butterfly. Trying to grow wings, the way we wanted to in the snow, to set me free.